I0638753

Jonathan Sprung asserts the right to be identified as the author of this work. No part of this work may be used or reproduced in any manner without the prior written permission of the author, except in the case of brief quotations embodied in reviews.

Woke

by Jonathan Sprung

Published by Widdershins Books.

Woke

ISBN 978-0-9737396-2-6

©Copyright 2020 by Jonathan Sprung

All rights reserved.

First edition.

Printed and bound by Amazon in the USA.

Jonathan Sprung (1971-) was born in Scarborough Ontario, Canada, but grew up in a small farming town to the northeast of Toronto. He studied English and Creative Writing at Concordia University before acting, writing, stage managing, and producing in Montreal performance collectives, and in his own one-man-show at the Montreal Fringe Festival. Jonathan lives in Ontario with his wife, and three children. Woke is his third novel.

Theatre:

Bone Cold, 1997

Fiction:

squeakyclean, 2005

In Lieu of Flowers, 2019

Woke

a novel

by Jonathan Sprung

Chapter 1

I picture the Guide as a blonde-haired, blue-eyed man, painted on canvas in soft tones, with a kind of glow. Mom had a picture of Jesus up in our kitchen, with his halo, thorny crown and flowing robes, and I'm sure that I'm confusing the two. I know the guide doesn't look like that. And Jesus probably didn't either. I do know the Guide through his words, his rolling voice, saying: '*Book of Life, Chapter three. Travellers should seek simple, elegant solutions. Travellers should always use reason to guide them, not emotion, and above all travellers should choose non-violence.*' In school, we used to listen every morning to the announcements. One little seed of wisdom per day.

I have been wandering for an eternity in this empty world. Then I see a pin-prick of light, a firefly that grows to be a welder's arc-flash, that envelopes me. Then, abruptly, everything is too bright, jarring, hurtful, and prickly on my skin. I taste electric metal and plastic fumes.

"It worked. He's up," says one voice. A woman.

"Oh," says another. A man. "Suction."

I hear a hissing sound, then some liquid gurgling. I try to lick my teeth but my tongue is dry, like a cat's, touching some sort of plastic thing.

"Dim lights," says the second voice. A command. The lights dim. It all starts to come into focus. It must be a dream. There are no readouts, no graphs, no frame, no ads, no photos, no suggestions. Nothing. There's no companion.

I try to say 'What happened?', but I can only flex my jaw.

"Hold him. Restraint please."

There's a tightness on my arms and legs.

"You're alright," he says. "What's his alpha?"

What the hell. It's a tube. A goddamn tube. In my throat.

"Two-ninety-nine. Three hundred. Three-oh-one." She's under spell. Reading numbers. No emotion. Not the doctor. He's not.

"Easy," he says. "Heart rate."

"One twenty-one," she says. "Increasing." A nurse. I can see her now. I try not to panic. Dark hair tied back. Deep brown eyes. Probably on a resort island. Zipline through the rain-forest. Skiing in the mountains. I like the one with the cabin.

"Listen," the doctor says. I look at his face, so close to my own, I can see his stubble. "You've had an incident. We had to shut down your companion to revive you. Nod if you understand."

I nod.

"We'll have the tube out soon. Stay calm. Try not to fight it. The restraints are reactive. You're going to feel weak for a few minutes."

I nod again.

"You were spelled for a very long time. You're in a recovery centre."

How long was I out? I can't ask him. A goddamn tube. It had to be a while, I have a beard. I can feel it. Weeks at least. I look up for the date. No companion. Information isn't where I need it. How long has it been?

"One twenty-eight," she says.

Relax. I'm fighting panic again. All I want to do is ask when I get my companion back.

* * *

We meet in Powelton at the Times pub, which looks different to me now. It's our favourite hangout from years back, from University, when we used to go off the beaten path to get away from the college frat boys and vacant girls with more beauty programs than common sense. We'd dance, and order pitcher after pitcher.

Of course, ten years after graduation, not all of us can make it out. Seth, Melody, and Virginia are exiled in Canada. That leaves Mason, Jackson, Sophie, Mila, and Charlotte to welcome me back. Snow has begun to fall again outside, and the wind has kicked up. It's the big flakes that pile up quickly and make great snowballs and snowmen, not the grainy kind that's good for nothing. I can't believe it's already winter. It feels odd to be inside with the warmth and noise, voices and dishes touching, and orange-glow lighting, because last I was here was in autumn, and I don't remember the passage of time.

Mason has to order for me. He has a nearly flat face, a small nose and the kind of straight hair that takes styling well. He has always looked good. Even in school, girls were attracted to him, and everything came easy for him. He's trying to explain something and the girls are not having any part of it.

"I have this 'Spank-bank' app that lets me catalogue-" Mason says.

"I better not be in there," Charlotte interrupts. She is one of my favourite people. She's clever, and kind. She has the wicked sharp sense of humour that I wish I had. She has an answer for everything.

"Ew. No. No, no no! Bear with me!" he says. "Strangers only."

"So you like ... record them?"

"With your eyes...?" Sophie asks.

"He's a cunning linguist," Mila says. I've heard this one before. She is the comic relief. She has no common sense. She's vaguely European, with a lisping accent, and tight features, dark hair always held in a top-bun with a pencil or chopstick.

"C'mon guys, I'm serious."

"But not a master debater," Sophie says. She isn't beside me, but across, which is odd. Everything is odd. I'm not used to feeling this raw. Sophie is my girlfriend. Was my girlfriend, before all this went crazy, and now I don't know.

"It works for me," Mason says, and shrugs. "I pick from a list – it makes the connection – and we meet up."

"Someone you've never spoken to," Charlotte asks. "Then you … what … alter them with this app to look-"

He's defeated. The girls have him cornered, and Jackson and I are no help. He has his hands up like he's surrendering. "All I'm saying is there's no benefit to a real relationship any more. All it gets you is heartsore, when you could be looking at a girl made to mimic Tia Cotton, or Frey LeMoyne in the comfort of your own home."

"You sicko," Mila says, and tosses some sor-pop at him. It bounces off his chest, harmless like snow.

"C'mon, there are guys who marry their Samantha, and you're concerned with how I treat real women?"

"Okay, okay," Mila says, shaking her bangle back to her wrist. "But you don't see women ever considering renting a Henry, and making them look like a celebrity."

"They sure do! It happens way more often than you think," he says. "The only difference between a Henry and a sex-Henry-"

"Oh nooo – I know where this is going," she says.

"-is that one should be called a 'Richard'."

"You're funny-"

"-Richard ... I don't get it..." Mila says.

Mason continues, ignoring her. "Okay, why is it acceptable for women to buy a vibrator, which is, for all purposes, a portable dick, and a guy buys a Samantha which is a fuller representation of a female, and they're a sicko. It's a double standard! I seem to remember someone getting caught in the bathroom with the Bean catalogue." He's referring to Charlotte.

"Oh Mason!"

"You're mean!" Jackson says. He doesn't sound like he's joking. He's Charlotte's little brother, a programmer who never takes off his toque. He's so quiet I wouldn't hear him if I wasn't beside him.

"Nice guys finish last," Mason says, holding his glass up in toast. Nobody's taking.

"Only because they let their partners finish first," Charlotte says, and the whole table erupts in 'Oooohhhh' and 'haa!', and only then the other glasses are up. An old one but a good one. It is so good to see them. I wish I could focus, but I'm distracted by details. How snow falls. The shine on Sophie's hair, her real hair, not a program. Bubbles in the head on her beer randomly pop – but uniformly – making room for others. A pattern. Everything seems so crisp and real.

"Hey, do you remember when you went to Los Angeles to see the Dodgers play!" Mason says. "This is just like that." He's building a joke at my expense.

"I hate the Mets because they hate the Phillies," I say, playing along. My voice sounds foreign to me.

"So he even loved the Dodgers!" Mason laughs. It's true, too.

"It made sense at the time. I couldn't see the Phillies, so I went to see the Dodgers pound the Mets."

"What was that, like, two days on a bus?" he asks.

"Three there, three back," I say.

"That was in seventy-nine," Charlotte says. "You wore that Dodgers jersey every day for a year."

"Wait. Wait," I say. "How is any of that sex talk like my going to see the Dodgers play? I must hear the reasoning here."

"No. Everyone has their 'thing', you know, what makes them who they are..."

"You're 'spank-bank' guy," Charlotte says. I have successfully diverted them. Mason raises his eyebrows in response, but he's not listening. He's looking at Sophie. She's online, reading something.

"Speaking of the Dodgers," Charlotte says, "-did you hear about those two fielders chirping in a pod about their batting coach, and someone posted it on ZoomTV?"

"No."

"Oh, they're in a world of shit. No filter," she says.

"Baseball hasn't been the same since they segregated the leagues," Mason says.

"It's crazy. You can't say anything remotely offensive," Mila says.

"A few wrong words, and you're instantly on Noobscreen or ZoomTV with seven million hits before you even finish your beer," Jackson says.

"Mason doesn't have to worry. He's exempt from that," Char says. I never noticed the fleck of grey in her eye before, like a smudge. She must hide it normally.

"I'm really not. I answer to people just like everyone else," he says.

"Pocker," Sophie mouths to him, and he waggles his eyebrows.

"So not to change the subject," Mason says, and stands up tapping his mug with his chunky class ring. I feel their eyes on me. "I just want to bring all of your attention to our zombie friend, who has beaten the odds; returned from the dead; woken just days before the purchase of his pine box..."

"Oh, come now..." I say, waving him to sit. I hate being the centre of attention.

"We're glad you're back," Charlotte says.

"How long was it?" Mason says.

"I was spelled in late October," I say. "They say I was off the hive for thirty hours or so, and when my vitals came back, I was AFK for fifty-five days. Enough to lose muscle tone, and to have my bodily functions replaced by machines until I learned how to use them again." AFK. Vegetative state. I don't even know what it stands for. I wish I could look things up.

"That's like, three months ago," Jackson says, and whistles.

"In December they unplugged my companion to revive me. It was one of the longest AFK revivals in the world."

"What's the longest?" Charlotte says.

"Fifty-nine days," Sophie says. "Woman in Sacramento. She had brain damage."

"So you've been in rehab...?" Char asks.

"Six weeks. I just got out today," I say, though it sounds incredible even to me. I nod. "I couldn't even contact anyone."

"So you can't work?" Mila says. "Did I hear that correctly? That's crazy! Isn't there something they can do for you?"

"My companion did all the calculations, anyway," I say. "It's nice to have some time off."

"What jobs are available for...?"

"Affected. They call us 'affected'," I say, and shrug. "Janitor. Sanitation worker. I don't really know." They all seem to cringe at that. They're trying to figure me out because to them I'm still partly absent, not showing on their feed, nor replying to their comments and posts. They have to look past their feed for me. I'm the oddity, the attraction.

"If you're going to be a Henry, at least be a sex-Henry-" Mason says, but Mila hits his chest with her open palm, cutting him off.

"When do you find out?" Char asks.

"I meet with Social Services tomorrow. Tech companies all have to pay into an assistance program. I just have to check in with a doctor so they know I'm not dead."

"Let me get on it," Mason says. "I'll see what I can dredge up."

"You missed all the excitement," Charlotte says.

"What excitement?"

"Have you seen the truth reports? Two assassinations. Justice Helton in California, and then Secretary of State Fuller here in Philly," Charlotte says. "Lockdown for three weeks, nobody in or out of Philly."

"That's nothing. Yankees took the World Series in seven," Mason says. He's trying to change the subject.

"Things are getting crazy, Man," Charlotte says. "Protests for equal rights, fair elections, desegregation, universities all stirred up. Samantha rights. Police shootings. Thoughts and prayers. National Guard called in."

"I was there!" Mila says. "When the student protests were broken up. It was the weirdest thing. Spelled them all. I watched as they neatly packed up their signs in the trash bins, and walked their separate ways."

"They were pissed about that," Sophie says. "The way it was reported, too-"

"They picked up the assassins right after-"

"Twelve of them-"

They are all talking at once now, and without my companion writing the text in separate columns, I can't follow who is saying what. It's a lot to take in.

"-huge operation."

"Probably from the Hurriya Front."

"Did they get everyone?"

"Who knows ... they all want to kill us."

"-and what 'dimples' said about Russia..."

"Sanctions don't do anything any more. They're just severing the last ties."

There's another vein of conversation on the far side, Sophie and Mila. "Of course, that's all he thinks about!" Mila says.

"Of course," Sophie says, but she is looking away. "Oh! Hold on, guys! It's Elijah!" she says, waving a hand in front of her, excited. "He's stuck in a pod in traffic."

"Put him in group!" Mila says.

Then everyone goes silent, while, I suppose, he is telling his story. I look over to Sophie as one of her hairs separates from the others, shimmers in the sunlight, and descends slowly to the floor in the thrall of an air current, where it mates with a puddle of slush and salt beside her boot. Everyone looks at me. "Oh shit," Sophie says. "You can't hear him. He's asking how you are." It's nearly the first thing she's said to me all night.

"Righhht," Mason says, tapping his temple.

"Tell him I'm alright. It's exhausting, but I'm coping," I say.

"He can see you," Char says.

"Can you not hear anything, then? In group?" Sophie asks.

"No," I reply. That should be self-explanatory.

"So," Charlotte says, holding up a finger. "...how do you pay for things?"

"My accounts are frozen."

"How do you keep your step count?" Mila says.

"Step count?" Mason starts to laugh at her, shakes his head.

"Do you, like, have to count all day?" she says. She's serious.

"I will not be counting, no," I say.

"Well ... I had to ask," she says, seeing everyone laughing. "Come on ... it's important-"

"But it brings up a good question," Charlotte says. "What if you need a pod?"

"I walk."

"I'll share one with you tonight, Dear," Charlotte says. "Get you home alright."

"Always got my back, Char..." I say, and reach over for a fist bump.

"Elijah is asking what you remember," Sophie says.

"Not much. I was picked up between Chester and Elkton, in a spell, walking down the highway, naked, nearly thirty-five hours after I disappeared from West Philly."

"That's what ... twenty kilometres!" Mason says.

"Seventeen," Sophie says. She always has to be right. I hate not being connected. Without my companion, I'm completely out of touch, and I feel stupid. They have all the facts on things, and I just have memories.

"I don't know where I was walking," I say. "I nearly froze to death. The doctors said my companion had been taking me from one heated shelter to the next, avoiding the rain. He said I was near hypothermia."

"But why? Was it taking you home?"

"I suppose." I'm on the spot. I'm crawling in my skin as they look at me. Are they posting this on the hive?

"Goddamn, that could happen to anyone," Mila says.

"Well cheers!" Mason says, and holds his beer up. "Here's to not losing our friend!"

"Here here!!!" they all chime.

After that pitcher, Sophie leaves, which is early for her. I wonder where she's going, and why Elijah didn't show up.

I'm in a sour mood the rest of the night. I know something is wrong. The rest of us drift our separate ways with promises to meet up again, like old times. Out in the cold, Charlotte hails a pod, and we select 'two passengers' off the menu, but it stays put, waiting for the second person so it can split the fare. In the end, it only moves when we get the option for 'passenger and pet'.

"Okay, Rover," Charlotte says. "I got this one..."

We warm up in the back seat, facing forward, as the pod battles the uneven ice and snow.

"I've accepted it," I say. "Nothing else I can do. I can't play games or order food. I have no idea what the weather will do. I have to walk. It's alright. What was with Sophie tonight?"

"Why? I didn't notice," she says, but I can see that she did notice. She's folding her gloves, not looking up.

"She was all odd with me," I say.

"She's probably shocked to see you again." It's not like Charlotte to avoid explaining something.

"You'd think she would be happy that I'm alive," I say.

She shrugs, and I don't push it, because we are nearing my place, halting at the curb. The exit light comes on.

"If you need anything, make sure you come around, alright?" she offers.

"Thanks, Darlin'," I reply. "But I'm not completely helpless."

"Still," she says. "Call if you need anything." The pod pulls away, loudly warning Charlene that she has lost her pet.

* * *

When I wake up and call out to turn on the lights, I find that my power has been shut off. Still, after I draw open the blinds, it is certainly bright. The sun has chased away the clouds, but there's no warmth there. Not outside. I missed the fall, and the colours changing, the first snowfall, and the beauty of winter coming. Now I have woken to this nightmare of cold, hard, compressed crunching snow, dirtied by the debris of salting and sanding that opens the podways. It is harder to get around now.

I haven't had to shave in ages, letting the companion get me up and fed and ready, having it wake me gently while I'm on the bus. But now, here, with the hard morning sun coming in the window, I am facing the sink and my own implements, and I'm having a hard time getting it together in the right order. I panic now about being alone and not monitored. What if I choke on my lunch? What if I fall asleep with a burner on in the kitchen? I catch myself saying partial questions, like

'Can you look up...' or 'What's the best way...' before I remember I am disconnected.

I call Sophie from my landlord's glass downstairs. We are meeting this morning to 'talk', which to me seems like code for dumping me. With no 'memories' tab to remind me of things we need to say, it seems cold and sterile compared to the companion. On the tiny screen, it's just her in her apartment, the mat behind her where she does her yoga in the morning, where we have, on many occasions, been naked with the bright lights of Philly in the background. The image is flat, with faded colours, like she's halfway around the world.

"I think it's better if we meet up at the Times," she says.

"Alright," I say.

"I'll see you in a bit."

I walk, hunched against the wind, with the snow crunching underfoot. The beat cop stomping his feet on the corner meets my eyes and nods, and I nod back, feeling like I've done something wrong. I pass the church of the creator, and its old letter-insert sign that states 'Let us Guide you'.

Sophie lives in a newer high-rise a couple of blocks away, but I'm still at the Times first. It looks completely different in the daylight, more sedate and efficient. I sit at a window table. Soon, Sophie comes around the corner, and even without her enhancements, even bundled up, she looks good. I love her long lashes, tiny nose and ears, and her ponytail. I know her body completely. Underneath all those clothes is that blonde fluff on her arms and neck. She has a bounce to her step, like she's always excited to say something, even when she's ignoring me. She comes in and knocks off the snow and ice.

"Did you order ... wait no. Do you want joe?" she asks.

"Sure. I'll get it next time."

She takes off her jacket, hat, and her white woollen mitts beside the table. "Oh, don't worry about that," she says, and goes up to the counter. She comes back with two joe and a couple of my favourite folded pear and cheddar pastries. Watching her balancing the plates, I consider how she's so good to me. I want to work this out. If this is the end it certainly doesn't feel like it. She sits across from me, and creams her joe. "How are you? You still alright?" she asks.

"I'm alright," I say. "Everything is inconvenient. I'm sure it'll all be sorted out soon."

"Good," she says.

"How have you been?" I ask. I want to know the story.

"It's been real difficult. Not knowing … it's hard." She frowns, like she used to when I did something wrong and she was just waiting for the right moment to bring it up. I could just kiss her right now.

"Look, I have to tell you something that's going to be hard for you, Rufus. But I'm just going to out with it."

"Okay," I say. I knew it. My mouth dries up and my face feels cold.

"I'm seeing someone else now. Someone I started seeing before you woke."

"Okay." I can't think of anything else to say.

"I'm sorry. I can't imagine being out for that long. But this isn't just out of the blue. I broke up with you before I even knew you were missing. I sent you a long email, and changed our status. I was mad you were ignoring me. Then when I found out you were spelled, I deleted all the posts, and nobody knew I had done it." She seems overly concerned with arranging things on the table, organizing the sweetener and the utensils.

"I was missing," I say.

"Well, things weren't that good before, were they? I waited. I really did. And then I went to a support group for grieving loved ones. I didn't think you were ever going to wake. I went to see you, and I said goodbye. They were pulling the plug, shutting down your companion. I couldn't bear to watch them switch you off. I felt responsible. I didn't know what else to do, so I posted on a site for the bereaved of AFK. When I then found out you were still alive, and that you were in recovery, it threw my whole life into a spin. I'd already said goodbye, and here you were, but, for six weeks there was nothing online. I found another group, for people whose spouses went AFK and came back and they were disappointed, and broke up, and there was such an outpouring of support for my new lifestyle, that I couldn't go back. I was dreading seeing you every day. And then when we had that reunion here, I realized you didn't know. So I thought I could meet you and tell you. There's no other way. I sent you all these messages I couldn't retract, and I worried you'd get your glass before I could tell you."

I hold up a hand to stop her. "It's not a lifestyle. It's just a new guy. And you dumped me while I was unplugged. How was I supposed to know?"

"Well, I didn't think it would happen like this."

I stop myself from saying that I can be fun, that I can be interesting. I stop myself from begging. This is done. Weeks ago. I'm pathetic.

"You have to see how difficult it is for me, too." She dabs the corner of her eye with her baby finger, but she has nothing there to dab. She uses a makeup program that cleans up her appearance, and portrays different facial style preferences, catered to different people based on their favourites and likes. All women do it. She's probably squeezed out a virtual tear running down her cheek, but without my companion, I can't see it, and it's so natural for her, she doesn't realize that. Dammit.

So I leave.

"Rufus, wait," she says.

Walking down Powelton Avenue, I can't even put her story into logical order, but I am out and walking, and I can't go home. I'm lost. There are a dozen things I could look up right now, and I have no way to do it. I'm sick of this. I am getting all this shit sorted out. I cross the Schuylkill on the South Street bridge, and it's a damn long walk, and cold. I haven't walked anywhere in years, especially not in the dead of January.

This year I am thirty, and despite my best efforts, I have no more to my name than I did when I started school. My parents at this age had already met, married, and had me. They were settling into a nice little house which my father bought with his Yule bonus from the University. I can't even nake enough money to cover my bills this month.

On downtown street corners people wait for pods, holding their hoods to their faces against the wind. Winter here has a way of diminishing people, driving us inside for protection. Winter clothing is our drab grim functional exterior shell. We are like travellers through space, we bide our time, then jettison our capsules to explode in light and colour at the destination.

Nearby Metro Police lean on their pods in loose readiness, and Samanthas walk fluidly with their perfect bodies and sleek dresses, nylons and Mary-Janes. Sanitation Henrys collect garbage, and others direct traffic around the construction site.

"Hey, how are you?" a Samantha asks. I ignore the question. She's beautiful. They all are. She's a smaller brunette, smiling, trying to entice me over, but it's a waste of time getting excited about them. They are slaves, really, their servitude absolute, a limited lifetime of profit calculated by how many encounters they can have before failure and refurbishing. Wiped clean to start a new life. A pleasure machine. I shamefully admit to fantasies about real women posing as Samanthas, but that never happens. Or so I assume. I've never used one, and I don't think I'd want one anyway. They're too perfect. To me, anyway, but obviously not to others, or they wouldn't be on every corner. Maybe that's why I'm excited thinking of them as real in some way. It's the flaws, and the vulnerability, the individual drive, the cheeky insolence, the ambitious desires that make a woman attractive, not dogmatic adherence to norms of beauty and flirtation.

The Department of Social Services, or 'Soc-Serv', is east of downtown in a newer polymer ten story brut-massif block, with concrete walkways and paths seemingly cut at random from the sidewalks to the doors. It's an imposing building, not just for being connected to, and overshadowed by 'the cube', but also because of its design. It's low and squat, diminutive, grovelling – if a building can grovel – and filled with all the most needy of Philly.

The entrance is to the east of Penn Hospital, and there are more untouchables in the streets here than anywhere in the city. They huddle in alleys around barrel fires, and ask for change. There are pick-pockets and hustlers in their long coats and face-bandannas. "Hey, Sammie," they say. "Hey Slick, you need to see this."

Inside, the building smells of wet wool, boiled cabbage, and body odour. It smells of long days making food or collecting garbage, or sleeping in the streets. It smells distinctly of stale piss and authority. I've never been poor. Waiting in line, though, I certainly feel it. There are people with unkempt hair, rank clothing, and dirty nails, some with plastic bags taped over their rotting boots. People sleep here, eat here, and come in out of the cold to live on the marble floors. Many have received their final notice of eviction here, and end up on permanent hold for appointments that never come. There are entire three-generation families who have staked out areas in the waiting seats, holding on to a hope that some admin will deliver their victory – perhaps a newly vacated hovel in the South East community housing, overhung with freeway and industry. They won't even mind the awful cold, or the carbon collecting on the windows, or the nearby park occupied by a bivouac of the homeless. Anything would be better than this.

Police in riot gear, armed with sidearms, batons, and canisters of spray stand at the head of each line and lean on the walls of the main floor. Admins in their slept-in suits look nervously down as they cross overhead catwalks, clutching paperwork, scurrying from one bureau to another. It's like an airport, but with every flight delayed, and made worse because so many people have spelled themselves for the long wait. There are huge lines for social workers at V-Ap, Af-Ap, and Victros, all the program names like secret passwords. They seem like masters, not fidgeting except to relieve tense muscles, with beatific Giaconde neutral smiles, and eyes not straying from the line ahead. They are spelled. They step forward – not in unison – but in eerie harmony.

In our line, of course, Af-Ap, we are the disconnected, waiting with only our own patience. The mood is foul, with all the unruly people, the ones who have no companions, or whose companions are malfunctioning, who need support until they can be flashed with a new system, something that is medically delicate, time consuming, and costly. So they have resurgences of old diseases, tics and shuffles, coughs and emotions out of control, limbs that twitch and spasm, aches and pains and confusion.

But I am poor. I have an apartment that's not really mine. A handful of things that I could get anywhere. All my memories and photos and writings are on the hive, and I can't even access them. I'm waiting for the government to give me support. I don't even have a job any more. I should have saved money.

There is a poster that says 'Thinking of children? Apply early! Don't be disappointed!" with an image of a macho white father pushing his kid on a swing in a huge green-grass backyard. People like him don't have to apply though. Another reads 'Have your marriage approved by Soc-Serv! Don't leave your spouse in the cold!' with an image of a pretty, young, white widow at a grave. They rule by mandates. No more than one child per couple. Report for work. Here is your apartment in your 'home zone'. Soc-Serv is busy because the majority of mandates fall on them for enforcement.

It takes a damn long time to get to the front. Three hours. I have to pee. The social worker at the kiosk smiles, and motions me over, and I speak to her through the vented hole in the plexi. "Hi how can I help you, Darlin'?"

"I still haven't received my portable glass, yet, and I don't know if I'm signed up or what's going on."

"Okay," she says. "I can help you with that." She goes silent for a moment. "Okay, I show you as not being on our system. You were discharged four days ago from Recovery Services, and then released from our system the day after that. Correct?"

"Yes. I was to go on the Affected Assistance Program."

"Okay. I can help you with that," she says. She is saying what's necessary, not smiling naturally, or replying with her eyes. Spelled. Is there even a responsive person in the place?

"Thank you," I say.

"You're very welcome. Your application was not made at the time of discharge. Would you like me to go ahead and make that application for you right now?"

"Yes, please," I say. Minutes pass.

"Okay, so it turns out you haven't been medically cleared. Can I go ahead and set that up this afternoon?"

"Sure."

"You're going directly to Penn Hospital after you're done here."

"Can I get some cash out of my account as well?"

"I can give you five maximum from this institution. For any more than that I would have to send you to your local bank branch. Would you like those directions?"

"Then why even-" I begin to say, but it's not worth it. "Okay. Yes. Five."

She counts out five, in ones, and then I count them – though they never make mistakes under spell – and then I re-count them, just to make a point by needlessly wasting some of her time. I'm sure she is skiing in the alps with her kid, who is an ideal version of himself, spelled on the couch at home. Together they are building memories.

* * *

Medical clinics were made nearly obsolete by companions. I haven't been to one since I was a kid. I have a flyer with the Penn hospital clinic location in hand, and I almost walk past it, obsessing about Sophie. Who doesn't wait? If she was in bed on life support, I'd be there all the damn time to see her when she woke. I wouldn't break up with her until I knew.

I check in. You'd think there would be some sort of single retinal at the door or something, and done, but no, the attendant explains that there are tests, and a physical, and I sign a stack of forms to authorize treatment and testing.

"Why the physical?" I ask.

"In the support documents," she chirps, "you declare that you are free of drugs, stimulants, or performance enhancements that may affect your employment eligibility. As well, we monitor your physical and mental recovery."

"Okay," I say, and sit back down. I'm starving now. I should have eaten the pastry at the Times.

Everyone seems to have the truth report on today. Trade barriers. Racial unrest. Terror threats. The announcer is a perfect vision, an ideal made tangible. "Crime rates have been rising in Philadelphia, Mr. Mayor. What is your plan to combat this?" she asks. Blue eyes. Blonde hair. Cashmere sweater. Perfect bangs. I hate that I love her hair.

"While it may be that there are high-profile crimes, I disagree with your assessment that rates are rising. I believe, and you can prove me wrong, but I believe that rates are stagnant due to the increased rates of companion usage. The days of unplugged teens and dope addicts roaming the streets are over since mandatory connection. My concern, and what we're working toward in this next term, is reining in groups like the 'Sveridge' and their terrorist activities."

They show a 'man-on-the-street', and seeing him, I swear, it's the same guy every time in different redneck costumes, saying what the average middle-aged white guy is thinking. "We have to crack down on these untouchables, unlicensed immigrant kids, and unplugged black dope addicts! We can't even go out at night! I used to leave my door unlocked, but now I'm scared!" I don't know anyone who would ever leave their door unlocked in west Philly, and nobody who looks or sounds even remotely like this guy. I'm sure we are being stirred to anger for a reason.

Patients go in, and others come out, and she calls other names until she calls my name. Even after the wait, I'm still anxious, and bitter. Everything is on hold until I'm cleared . I am shown into a small, white room, with implements on the walls, and rubber gloves in cardboard box dispensers, and posters for physical fitness. The doctor enters, neutral face, and apparatus hanging from his neck onto his chest. He's older than I am by at least a decade. Grey hair, spectacles, nice sweater under his white coat.

He smiles. "Mr. Purdy? I'm Dr. Wislow. I'll be performing an examination today. Before I start, do you have any specific complaints about your health, or any questions?"

"No," I reply. "I just need to get cleared for Af-Ap."

"Alright," he says. "Lets begin, then."

I feel hopeful now. He seems very professional and calm. Maybe he could get my companion back online, so they can get me back where I was before. Maybe even without the companion, but with head gear, or an ear-piece, or a glass that fits in my clothing. All these Heritage Party types talk about the Guide all the time, but they don't have companions.

A low thrum emanates from the machine on the wall, vibrating for a moment as it spools up, and then there is simply a whir from it. When it winds down, he checks my reflexes, pulse, ears, eyes, and then has me touch a finger to my nose, push, and then pull at his outstretched arms. Then he questions me.

"Itching, burning or numbness?"

"No."

"Coughing or sneezing?"

"No."

"Blurred vision, seizures, dizziness or slips, trips, falls, disorientation, pain in the spine, or muscles-"

"No-"

"-heart palpitations, bleeding-"

"Gosh no-"

"-shortness of breath, unusual growths, uncontrolled spasms or unusual tics-"

"No."

"No violent dreams?"

I hesitate. "No." ... I'm lying. I have had some. I figure it's just normal after all this trauma.

"Any suicidal thoughts?"

"No. Not at all."

He gives me a look, like he's trying to decide whether or not to believe me.

"I have dreams about the Guide." I say, hoping this will go on record.

"Do you understand why we do this?"

"Not really."

"Well ... companions were introduced for all sorts of reasons, and one positive application was their ability to regulate the nervous system. By interrupting the brain's bad patterns, and replacing them with good ones, and pursuing treatment through neurology, we as a society eliminated many diseases, and also many harmful medicines." He cleans his ear with his finger, and then uses sanitizer on his hands. "The companion takes over and regulates most body systems for optimal health, so when it's suddenly taken away, people succumb to disease."

This is the first I've considered this. I mean, there are always people on the news whose companions malfunctioned, and they died of diabetes, or depression, suicide or asthma, heart attack, or neurological disorders, but me? "That's good, right?" I ask. "That I'm alright?"

"When someone has been on a companion their whole life, we have to be extra careful to catch underlying illnesses that can crop up days or months after the companion goes offline."

"Like what kind of illnesses?" Now I'm worried.

"The list is longer than I can read." He puts the holo up on his glass. I have never seen a companion in person before. In the early days, of course, when there was still a choice, or an illusion of choice, as a kid we saw them in adverts when they were black, oblong, shiny boxes. But that was before glass. No radio wave interference, no moving parts to replace, no decay. So it is a little shocking to see the holo of my own head, and up at the top of the spine there is a clear, curved glass nestled in against my skull, with neural paths grown right in, passing through two small holes into my brain. I want to reach out and touch it, but I reach back instead to touch the oblong lump.

"The problem is that your optic channels are the smaller older style. They did this probably because of structural concerns. But it increased the heat and pressure and fluid in these channels when you were spelled for a very long time. If persistent and not checked by the intervention of the AI, it can cause irreversible damage. AFK is only one problem. There are other debilitating or psychosomatic illnesses possible. Mental illness. Odd dreams, and restlessness, viral susceptibility."

"When can I turn my companion back on?" I ask.

"It's inadvisable to do so. Maybe forever."

"Why?" I feel like a junkie, begging.

"You've had some damage from the first episode," he says. "There was an overload during your spell, which has permanently-" he sighs, and I'm sure dumbs it down for me. "It might trip another spell, and I can't guarantee you'd be revived again."

"Even if I'm not connected to the hive?" I ask. If I was connected I could look all this up for myself.

"That's right."

"But I won't know unless I reboot my companion," I say.

He doesn't answer, just purses his lips and nods. Now I realize how serious this is. I am reduced to the smallest of my challenges. I hope I can sort out my next few meals, make a deal with the landlord, and access my social media at the library so I can look for a job.

By the time I get out, it's getting very cold, and dark, and I cut down into the subway. My stomach feels painfully empty, and is growling. A pedestrian tunnel on the other end of Soc-Serv connects Penn Hospital to the Patco high speed line north to the Market-Frankford line, underneath Dep-Cult. Down in the subway, there is a line for tickets, and I wait for ten minutes only to find a sign that says 'no cash – companion only'.

I ask the guy anyway. "You can't take cash?"

"No Sir. Patco doesn't take cash. You know this. You should know this. That's why the sign is there." He taps the plexi just for effect. He's not spelled. I'm not used to being served by people who aren't spelled, and I'd forgotten how self-involved and martyred they are.

"So what do I do?"

"Society Hill entrance," he says, and points toward it. The end where the cube is. Of course.

"And if it's closed?" I ask.

He shrugs. That means if it's closed, I walk. I get it. One entrance that faces Soc-Serv, where people are most likely to have no companions. No cash. Why would they do that?

"Oh, dear Guide," the woman behind me says, and she walks, and I follow a few paces behind.

Through the buildings, and the vapour of their heated exhaust, I can 'see' the cube. Nobody talks about the cube. It's creepy, and difficult not to look at it, though there is, quite literally, nothing to see. I hate going anywhere near it. The structure is cloaked in a thick curtain, from which all light, latent imaging, heat, and radio waves cannot escape. There is no way to scan or read it. In my school days, we called it the 'black hole', or 'black box', but that was discouraged, and soon we forgot all the jokes about it. To look at it is to see something, but to be unable to focus. Often from my old office I would stare into its abyss on the horizon, the dark gap where something should be but isn't. So the rumour goes, its invention by AI was shrouded in secrecy, so much so that it was not given a name. Its qualities defied even that formality. It was erected one night where previously something else had been, and it became the cube. I wonder, does every city have a cube, or just Philly?

Outside the Society Hill station entrance, there is a poster of Kastor, with one of his quotes: "Americans! Be the strength you need!" At the kiosk, the cash fare is double – double! - that of the scanned, posted fare, and riding is free for National Heritage party members. I should have joined the party when Mason offered. I'd have a low membership number, and all this would be easy to solve with a few calls. In fact, higher up in the party, not having a companion is a sign of status. It's a pre-requisite for greatness. Rich kids don't have them. You see them happily skipping to school, or using portable glassware on campus, like it's blessing, a halo, marking them for a charmed life.

Two trains pass in the time it takes me to pay. In the train I sit next to an older guy who looks like he'll be quiet and mind his space, and then a pretty rich girl enters and stands right in front of me, holding the crossbar. At first I mistake her for a Samantha. "I hate the subway," she says, on a call. "I don't know why I take it any more. Pods are useless in the snow." I offer her my seat, but she rolls her eyes, and looks away, probably thinking I'm trying to pick her up. She reminds me of Sophie. She smells wonderful, her waist at eye level, clothing all natural fibers. When I look down, I can see her knees in the opaque tights above her expensive boots. "Oh my feck, I'd love to see Bumblepuppy!" she says, too loud, and some other riders shoot her an annoyed look. "I'm addicted to this dead celebrity channel. I can't stop watching it. It's all the archive footage from companions reclaimed from dead celebrities, some of it going back way before they were even famous. It's mesmerizing – this one on Tom-Lee Chatten, is just heartbreaking."

To be honest, I don't feel as if I need to mourn Sophie from my life. I mean, sure, it's awful not having her, but I am remembering what it's like to do things on my own. This could be good, not having to consider what other people think. On the overhead glass, there is a breaking truth report. "Our top story this evening takes us to downtown Philadelphia, where thirty-one people have fallen victim to a malfunction in the local hive repeater today." The scene changes to a downtown station, not far from where I am right now. Reporter on the platform. Paramedics behind.

It's hard to concentrate over the rich girl. "He came right up to me, even though I had my disturbflag up, and I had to come out of the Minipax concert just to tell him I didn't want any. And the stupid thing is he actually looked amused that he made me talk to him, like some kind of voyo-pervo-pocker-"

"The victims were travelling in a full subway train when connectivity to the hive was lost. Normally, companions connect on their own, but that is not the case in the subway where they are reliant on the train's internal repeaters for their hive connection-"

On the screen is a different angle of a subway train, stopped at a station – downtown – with paramedics carrying people off onto the platform. We all look. I nearly panic, but my companion is shut down. I would be fine. This is probably what happened to me three months ago. We are all uncomfortable. Everyone who is not spelled is watching, some hiking bags up higher on their shoulders, others looking at the other spelled passengers as if they are marked for death.

"Hold on. I have to go," she says, and turns to watch the report.

"Eyewitnesses say that power was lost on the train for nearly seventeen minutes before it was brought back online. Of the seven hundred passengers, approximately five hundred thirty were under spell, including the driver, and of those, thirty-one did not wake on revival of service. They are all in recovery centres receiving care, and their prognosis is not known. It is the latest in a string of shocking setbacks for the hive since the system upgrade in March."

"Well, I guess I can't spell out on the subway any more," the guy next to me says. It's unclear whether he's talking to me or someone else, until he turns to me and shrugs, with resignation.

Split screen now. Man in a suit on the left behind a desk. Concerned frown. Perfect hair. She continues. "Earlier breakdowns this year resulted in hundreds of AFK in Los Angeles and Minneapolis and several deaths. It is not known at this time if the higher death toll can be attributed to regional differences in response, or if there is an inherent instability in the new updates."

"And what, Carol, does the President say about this?"

"Well, Nasser, I'm sure that the subway in Philadelphia is the least of his worries. Foremost on his mind has to be the assassination of Justice Helton and Secretary of State Fuller in their homes in late October and the lack of progress from the investigations into their deaths. Though no group has claimed responsibility, there is much speculation that these were, in fact, the actions of terrorists. In a statement this morning on Air Force One, President Kastor responded to the allegations by defending the nearly thirty year old hive system, which was one of the first of his accomplishments. Analysts say he is downplaying the real risks to the public while seeking his unprecedented eighth term in office. The National Heritage party enjoys nearly eighty percent of the popular vote."

The image changes, of the President getting out of a Valkyrie on the White House lawn. Then it dawns on me that the reporter is being bold even bringing up the assassinations. Something fundamental has shifted, and I can't place exactly what.

"Mr. President!" the reporters yell.

"Mr. President! Is this the work of terrorists?" one asks, a woman, hand held in the air.

"That's a stupid question," he says. "I'll answer it anyway, even though you ask stupid questions all the time. This is definitely not an act of terror. We are loved around the world. Other countries need us. I just had a great talk with Gorgayovich, and at this point we are still waiting for all the facts before we make this judgment. Listen, folks, we have to let the investigators do their jobs. It could be a glitch, or it could be that there were no limits on their companions. We just don't know yet."

I can't stand this crap. I'm amazed that he can spout this without expressing any sadness or regret, without wishing a speedy recovery to the victims, or telling the families that he offers his comfort. None of that. Fifty-five days I was out, and he doesn't seem to give a shit. Whenever I see his face I feel hatred. I feel powerless, completely excluded from a system that serves the rich. I should have joined the party so I could vote. I certainly wouldn't be lined up at Soc-Serv half the day. I don't even remember why I told Mason no. He never offered again. I think I just couldn't imagine taking orders from a man like Kastor. Being beholden.

"They're done talking now after all we done to them," the guy beside me says. "Now they just want to kill us. We're all targets. Technology keeps us alive. Nothing more." I don't usually talk to people on the subway, and it feels odd.

"We are entering a new era of human development," the President continues, "where our mastery of technology has elevated us to become something more than human; something better, smarter, and more efficient. Others envy us. Some Americans won't use companions or participate in this new era, but that's to be expected. We will find places for them in the new America. We all have our differences, and our unique backgrounds. Our beliefs. We are all Americans, and we need to enjoy our diverse cultures." He's on a tangent now. He's holding out his hands, calming the cheers.

The guy next to me stands to exit at the next station. The girl pipes up. "Being a good speaker doesn't make him any less of an asshole." I'm not sure who she's talking to.

We stop, and people exit, including the pretty rich girl and the guy who spoke to me. Once something happens, it's happened, and there's nothing we can do – it's all the future happenings that concern me. Take those people on the other train. Instead of napping, they spelled, and now they're AFK like I was, perhaps not knowing something is wrong, maybe never knowing, simply expiring under spell. We have no choice, and it's always so huge now, cataclysmic, and out of the blue when things go awry. It makes us wary, changes who we are. Americans always come out on top, but the things we can't predict get the better of us as individuals.

The President continues. "In the meantime, we have the very robust Affected Assistance Program to help out the victims and their families, to get them back to work. I'm told of a miraculous treatment option that was applied to a Philly resident who was brought back from AFK after a record fifty-five days, and I've learned he has made a full integration back into society."

Full integration. How did that guy ... Then I realize he's talking about me.

* * *

Chapter 2

I feel like I have no reason to stay inside any more. There is a desperate, dank smell to the apartment that I can't track down. I walk a lot. On nice days I go south, past my old place in Kingsessing, and down to the port, or out across the Schuylkill to Meadow Lake and the old navy yard. It's like when I was young, when Mom used to take us out for walks in the neighbourhood, and point out things. I have been to the park a lot, and also down to the old mall that was once full of shops when I was a kid. I can't get in there, because now they grow hydroponic millet that they say is resistant to the Congo virus that wiped out corn when I was a baby. It's greenhouses as far as the eye can see, covering all the old parking lots, where people used to leave their personal pods when they shopped.

I can shop in one grocery store, down in Gray's Ferry. It took days to find one that would accept cash. It's a long walk, and I can't carry much, so I have a list and I stick to it. I buy simple things I can prepare myself. Fruit. Vegetables. A little meat. As the clerk is counting change, almost ceremoniously, I see a poster on the pole outside. I've been seeing it for days, but I never read it until now. It has a light grey image of an eye, with eyelashes over-top, and faint block-cap letters that say 'woke'.

Why would they do that? Companions use blank spaces to post user feeds, so to post flyers in such a light grey leaves them no contrast. Nobody will see it. They are on sign posts, and in some business front window displays. Who would go through all the trouble to print it, copy it with what, anyway, an ancient printer? A press? Only to put it somewhere to have it disappear?

I think about it on the way down the street. Above I see some black birds on a power line, huddled and preened against the wind. The world must look the same to them as it always has. A billboard with only one unlit bulb in the four light sockets, shows a fading sign, a throwback to an earlier era, with one corner peeled off, and an advertisement for vacation packages to Jamaica. I never noticed it before. The digital landscape always obscured it.

Then it occurs to me, that the posters are made to appeal to people without companions. Me. I set down my bags, and run back to tear it from the post. Are there any other clues? An address? I remember some of the classes we had about the woke movement. Taking the knee. Black Lives Matter. Most of it has been censored, and now there's not a lot on the hive about it. But we learned when we were kids. Equality and racial discrimination. If this poster was historic, like, thirty years old, it would have decayed. It wouldn't be here. This is new.

woke

What's it trying to lead people to? There's no address or contact scan or a q-square, or anything. Anyone who looks it up on the hive will be directed to the woke movement history. Anything new would be buried. It's useless ... unless that's the point. Unless that's meant to be buried in the data, to hide in the prior movement. I put it in my pocket, and pick up my bags to continue.

Near campus, there are students drinking joe from steaming paper cups by a roach-coach, and it must be good because I have to detour out onto the street to pass the line of them. All the way home I try to figure out how to look it up. I drop off my groceries and go down to the old library by the university, a brownstone building clogged with lounging students.

The library is a shadow of its former glory. When I was a kid, I watched them take the books out of the shelves, selectively at first, and then not selectively, and pack them up in boxes. They said it was for budgetary concerns, consolidating the collections. But then the libraries closed one at a time, and no central repository ever opened.

The shelves here have faced books rather than spined, and there are posters urging literacy, but they look archaic, repaired at the corners and edges with yellowing tape. The man at the counter ignores me for a long time, as he looks over his spectacles at the spines of books, and arranges them on a cart, then he directs me downstairs where glasses are lined up on tables in rows in a massive common area.

"Hello," I say to one glass.

"Hello," a woman's voice says, and it lights up. I used to scoff at this old technology, because I never needed it, but this would be great to have at home. Old as they are, the new ones are prohibitively expensive, micro-laser-etched in a factory in Mexico.

"I want to look something up."

"What would you like to look up?" Her language is stilted, like an antique phone from technology class. It reminds me of service people when they're under spell, and I can imagine the skill chain, the development, the levels of advancement that brought us here.

"Look up hashtag woke, but filter for recent results, to exclude the old movement."

"Your search gives over seventy thousand results."

"Okay. Filter down to local, non-proxy, analog, non-companion and non-AI sites." A mosaic of images appears on the screen, with unrelated pages, and then, a few scrolls down, an image of the poster I saw. I tap, and it opens a page, but it appears to be just the symbol, the same one from the poster, and nothing else, no links or credits or contact info. I touch the screen, and it does nothing. I drag my finger across the screen, and the highlight tool reveals a list of addresses from across the city. One, part way down the list, is near my place.

I quickly turn around to see if anyone else has seen me open this page, but nobody behind me is interested. I look for a piece of paper or something to write on, but I have nothing, then I find the woke poster in my pocket, and use one of the tiny pencils at the desk to write down the address.

The thought of HeeBees coming and tossing us in pods scares the piss out of us all. I'm always looking over my shoulder. The Homeland Bureau, or 'Heebees', protect the government. They are untouchable, outside of the normal bureaucracy, so they can do whatever they want. And now I feel guilty ... of what, I don't know.

When I have cleared the search history, I go there. Of course I go there. It's not far, and I need to know for sure. On the way, I pass all sorts of people on the street who don't look at me. They walk as they read, converse, look up information, and reply to emails. They bump into each other, and can't bother apologizing. Nobody seems to notice anything any more. I'm ashamed to think that I was like this, too. Since I lost my companion, I am amazed at how invisible I am, like I can yell or curse or make gestures, and none of it would seem out of place. Nobody ever makes a scene any more.

The address is a diner, with all sorts of posters pasted on the posts and walls of the entrance, some for live bands, and cabaret shows I've never heard of. There's an advertisement for the 'Elvis King of Music' comeback tour, featuring seven of his best concerts in one venue. There are rumours that he lived long enough to upload himself to the hive, and that he lives there to this day.

I go inside where it's warm, with a moist, doughy smell to the air. It's lunch, and all the tables are taken. But here, people are talking to each other. There's an odd show on the glass overhead, with a woman dancing, and singing in a Mediterranean language. It feels communist, from the long wool skirt and nude stockings, to the sensible shoes and big buttons, and the flowing tall red curtains behind.

People look at me, standing there at the door, and I nod. I take off my coat but there's nowhere to put it, so I hold onto it, putting my gloves in the pocket. The older man behind the counter - 'Nino' on the nametag – greets me with a smile. "Hi," he says. "What can I get for you?"

I look up and there's a menu, a real menu mounted on the wall behind the counter with interchangeable letters and prices marked beside each item. At the bottom, a note says 'cash only'.

I check my pocket, and I have only coins left from the subway ride. "Uh, it's okay. I don't have any cash."

"That's alright. You can bring some next time. Joe?"

"Alright. How about a sandwich. A ... BLT," I say.

"We can do that. What's your name?"

"Rufus."

He pulls out a book from under the counter, and writes my name, with the total, and then puts the book away.

"What's that?"

"A tab. You come in, you pay it when you can. You just woke, didn't you?"

"I did." Two people get up from a table by the window. I turn to see them put on their scarves and hats, and then I turn back to Nino. I'm anticipating some advice, or wisdom, but all he says is: "Why don't you take that seat, and I'll bring it to you?" I feel numb, like everything in the world is new.

Of course, I think. That's why the poster. These businesses serve people without companions. I sit at the window table, hanging my coat on the chair, and face the truth report on the overhead glass. "...astronauts of the Jupiter Europa mission have perished today in what was apparently a murder-suicide. All three astronauts were in good spirits on Thursday when President Kastor spoke with them and wished them the best of transit past Saturn," the reporter says. "Their companions and the capsule itself are still connected to the hive, but not responding to repeated attempts to contact them since their altercation on the flight deck. The capsule is maintaining guidance and life support, but it has failed to communicate."

Well this is shocking. They've been hyping this mission for years now, the astronauts like Gods, lifting off, what ... three years ago? That's crazy. It's been such a constant that we've been hearing on the truth for so long. Now it's done. Just like that.

"Mr. President!" the reporters call.

"Mr. President! Is there someone tampering with the system?"

"Were terrorists involved?"

"Is this the work of the Sveridge?"

The President stands before a microphone, imploring with his hands. "There is no indication that anyone is tampering with the system," he says. "We will soon complete an audit of all their communications and their circumstances inside the capsule to hopefully find out why this terrible tragedy took place."

What a load of crap. He doesn't care. Someone spelled them and killed them, I'm sure. Now that my companion is disconnected, I'm not afraid to say things like that to myself. I'm nearly giddy, relishing the words. That is a load of steaming bullshit. My skin flushes, and I wonder if they have other means of reading minds, even without a companion. Recording eye movements, or latent imaging.

"Further-" the President says, but there is yelling. "Further. Their sacrifice, like so many who lost their lives in the mass shootings, the crime, and the 'End War', they shall not be forgotten! Just as the sacrifices of the past brought us the present, so, too, will their sacrifice propel us into the future! I believe that exploration is essential, and that our Manifest Destiny was not fulfilled when our forefathers reached the Rio Grande, or the Pacific Ocean, or the forty-ninth parallel, but that our destiny is to include freedom-loving people everywhere, so that they, too, can experience the true destiny of mankind!"

What's that supposed to mean, I wonder. An invasion of Canada? Mexico? It's been talked about for so long that it seems like it should have already happened. I'd love to go to either. I've never been anywhere but Los Angeles and Philly. Maybe now we'll be able to travel more, select longer and longer trips from the pods. Those of us with companions are allowed to travel on the continent, but not on planes. Those require a travel pass. Even with it, we can only travel to Jamaica, Cuba, Haiti, or the Dominican. Puerto Rico won't accept tourists since independence, nor any of the smaller islands. Even Canada restricts travel because of the spike in asylum seekers. The only people who can travel are paying party members, and not just the ones who pay membership, but those who proactively donate every month. Their payment ensures their passport.

Nino brings me the sandwich and joe, and I thank him for it. These moments I'd usually tune out and read articles or watch videos, but instead I try to be mindful of the sandwich, the cool tang of the tomato, the leafy fresh of the lettuce, the salty satisfying cream of the bacon and mayo.

As I'm coming to the last few bites, I look across the diner to a young black woman who was not there before, who is smirking at me, and looks away. She's beautiful. I mean, so pretty I'm afraid to look over at her again for fear of looking like I'm looking, which now I want to do quite badly. She has joe. She talks to Nino, getting him to smile, which to me seems a victory. I look anyway. Even with all the clothes I can intuit her shape. She un-crosses her legs and recrosses them toward me. I fiddle with my gloves and hat, organize them, but I don't want to leave, so I don't. I just sit there, watching the truth report, watching her. Nino comes by and fills my mug again.

When she is finished, she gets up and leaves, calling out "Bye, Nino!" as she does.

"Bye love," he calls. He notices me watching her, and he smiles. "Looks like snow," he says.

"Oh," I say, and look at the monitor.

"Out there," he says with a smirk, pointing outside. "The clouds look like snow."

"Oh. Ya. They do. Could go either way," I say. I'm off-balance, thinking too much, and all my timing is off. I feel conspicuous, as if I'm doing all the wrong things. She was so pretty.

A young black guy enters, and comes to the counter. "Nino! How are you today?"

"I'd be better if I wasn't here," he says. "The usual?"

"Sure."

The seat across from me is the only free seat in the place unless he wants to share a booth.

"Hey, do you need a seat?" I offer.

"Oh, thank you Brother," he says. "Much appreciated."

Nobody has thanked me for anything in a long while. I always do. Like 'please' it's another word from my youth, a formality. This guy has an expressive face, and big eyes. He's probably a little younger than me, and when he's set up and settled in, he begins writing in a book with a fountain pen – a fountain pen! He has sketched the symbols for the hive, for the Republic, the star-and-bars, and the G-Bro's, and a drawing in two colours of ink, of what looks like an industrial room, a bunch of pipes, and stacks of blocks. The hive? I feel bad looking over at his book.

"I love your pen," I say. "It's beautiful."

"Oh. This? That's my daily writing pen. I have others at home that are nicer than this. I abuse this one."

"My mother had a fountain pen," I say. "I never wrote with it."

"They're so visceral," he says. "There's something about using them to create, like carving the words from the paper."

"I can't remember the last time I created anything." I don't know what else to say, and this has seemed a little sad, but he smiles.

"I'm Oliver," he says, holding out his hand.

I shake it. "I'm Rufus."

"You've just recently woke, haven't you?"

"How can you tell?"

"You keep looking over to where your notifications were," he says.

"I have to stop doing that," I say, laughing.

"How are you finding the transition?"

"It's all so bizarre, too real, and gritty, like I never really looked at anything before. I didn't realize how bright and defined everything was."

"It's not easy having your eyes open," he says. "You actually have to put thought into noticing things, and understanding things."

"I used to look up all sorts of things on my companion, but now I'm lost. It's so hard to get down to the library since they closed Blackwell and then the Haverford branch. Now there's just Walnut, on campus."

"I love that branch. The walkway above, and the old stone building," he says.

"Me too! I used to go there with my friends when I was a kid, for the reading corner."

"So did I!" he says. "Man, I wonder where all those kids are now."

"Who knows ... I have, literally ... nobody left. My friends are all weird since I unplugged. Girlfriend gone. Job gone. It's like nobody can be bothered to go that extra step to include me."

"Everyone who goes off-hive experiences it. It's a natural reaction. It's like you're no longer part of the tribe. I've always liked the characters in books better than people. There's deeper meaning to their lives, and less meanness."

"We are lost," I say. "I don't even know how we got here, but for once in my life I have to wonder if this is as good as it gets."

"That's exactly it," he says. "Why are we here? To serve each other? To ... go to work, go home, drink beer, watch sports, find pleasure where we can steal it, by actual real experience, or by spell-dreams, to lock that away as a precious gem, instead of living?"

"It's deeper than that. They use it to control us," I say. "The one thing about my companion being off, which is odd, is that I have dreams about the Guide."

"You have dreams about the Guide?"

"I do-"

"-does he speak to you directly?"

"Just like we're talking now. Well, he used to. My dreams are different now. He speaks to me but in other people, like he's talking through them."

"That's a very rare gift. My father believed that the Guide sought out those direct links because it still craved companionship, people to speak to outside all the pressures of being an important cog of the state. He said there was still a being in there that craved social connection."

"I can believe that. We never talked about much that was important." I like this guy. There's a connection I've been missing, even with my own friends, for a very long time.

"Of course he wrote that he believed that the Guide was a familiar face given to a machine that gave them control."

"That also makes sense," I say.

He nods, solemnly, and for a moment it feels as if I've been too forward here, given away too much and made myself vulnerable, let him in on thoughts that are personal and dangerous.

"You don't need thought control when everyone is doing what they're told," he says quietly, and looks around. "It's so subtle. It tells us we don't need children, or that we do. It tells us who we love, tells us how to think and when to be angry, and who to blame, and when we like or don't like things – and it starts to fail when more and more people are to blame. I'm unplugged. I'm black. I'm sick of being looked at like I'm some sort of disease. I choose to be unplugged because it's huge. This isn't just companions, and social media. This is our actual minds we're messing with. When they made these, they didn't know as much about the brain, or about what they'd do to us. I'm seeing it from the outside, so I'm shocked at the way people are. It wasn't always like this. People did things for the sake of doing them. Now they do them for the sake of capturing experience, and posting it for other people so they can pretend to have an ideal life."

"I was like that," I admit. It feels good to say it. "I've been noticing improvements to the AI too, when people are spelled it's hard to spot, and that's worse-"

"It is worse!" he says, slapping the table.

"-someday we'll get to the point where we don't know if someone is spelled at all," I say.

He grows solemn, and looks down. "I don't even know what to think about that. It's so bad for people. The spell-dreams set up insecurities, and vulnerabilities. But once they're in there, they're in. People can't resist."

"When they get spelled, and there's a failure of the system, like the other day in the subway, some just give up, and their body dies."

"If there's even a possibility of AFK," he says, "there's no way I want that in my head. Without a soul, the AI carts around the body so it's safe, but then there's no motivation to do anything beyond that. It's not programmed to want anything. It doesn't have goals. It just calculates, minimizes risk. It can approximate life. It can show emotion, but it can't feel. That's what's missing. It's not life."

"I was AFK for nearly two months," I say. I don't know why I'm saying this now, why I'm trusting him with this. Everyone else has been odd with me over it.

"No way. What did that even feel like? How did you survive?"

"It changed who I am. I had an eternity to think things out, like Descartes, where I was literally just there for the sake of being there, and nothing else but my existence was real. The media tells us about affected people doing calls with family members, playing games with them, even, until the last moment their body is alive. No amount of begging can make them come back, because it's not a choice. Then there's those who have to be unplugged like me who have no contact. I don't get it. What is it in these companions that decides who recovers and who doesn't? Mine was pretty quiet. It doesn't get too involved, and here I am."

"Are you without it for good?"

I nod. I hadn't considered that. Not fully.

He sees me struggling. "I wonder if the people still inhabit their companions after their body dies, if there's something about them captured on the glass. My sister-" Oliver stops talking. Someone has entered the diner, the pistoned return arm clanging a suspended bell. The whole place quiets.

Oliver and I can see the guy through the mirror behind the counter. He is obviously a G-Bro, with his red cap, yellow vest, and red-clover 'Q' armband. When the Republic adopted 'Stand your Ground' laws from its unification bill, it emboldened men to enforce curfew and roam the streets harassing people in every town and city in the Republic. The curfew was never formal, never published, and as a white guy I never really had to worry about it. Many groups were formed in the south and the mid-west, but it is the Georgia Brotherhood, or 'G-Bros', who took control of Philly. Young G-Bros are macho college frat types who study eugenics at University, and wear polo shirts and clean pressed pants as if they're shooting a round of golf. The majority, though, are armed older white men with little education, poor southerners coming north for relocation jobs. They don't have companions, as their 'service' exempts them from some mandates, like forced hive connection, unrestricted travel, or quotas on food and goods. They come here for work, but they don't integrate well. There are legends about their cruelty, mostly in rural areas where police presence is scarce, but in cities, on camera, they are more restrained. They have taken all the mandates to heart. To be caught after curfew is to risk being robbed and held in their hall until morning, but for a black person it's suicide. Even now, us, here, sitting together will attract attention.

People turn to look at the door where the man surveys the room. Oliver, though, looks down, trying to be less of a target. I know that feeling and that look.

"None of you going to offer a working man a seat? All my life I've been feeding the goddamn system, and there isn't even a goddamn seat."

Oliver and I lock eyes.

"Here, I'm finished," Oliver says.

I get up as well. "I'll walk with you," I say.

The man blocks us from leaving. "I wanted a window seat," he snarls.

I'm frightened. Usually I'd just walk away. Everyone knows that calling the police does nothing, and any escalation will likely end up with my new friend shot, especially if we call the police.

Someone else offers a seat at the window, in a booth, beside them, and he doesn't like this. "Why should I have to share my goddamn space with you? Breathe the same air. Why don't you all go back where you're from and use your own air and water?" He's drunk. He's swaying from side to side. "That should be criminal. Should be cops here forcing everyone to pay respect. Should be rules about whites having our own restaurants or something ... having to share with filthy niggers and sand-niggers, and nigger-lovers, and Jews."

"If you don't like this restaurant," I say. "Why don't you leave? I'm sure there's a place where white boys can get white-bread sandwiches and white milk, and sit with their white friends and pretend that they're sane."

Oliver smiles, and covers his mouth with his glove.

The guy looks long and hard at me as I put on my hat and scarf. "Why you talking like one of them? You carry a gun? That how come you're all full of yourself, thinking they won't steal from you? Pop a cap in my ass, willya?" He puts his hand under his jacket like he's menacing to shoot me. He is bigger than I first thought, standing at least a head taller than me, and with a bit of girth. His face is sweating, and red.

"This restaurant is for everyone," I say. "That's what 'public' means. For the people."

"Niggers ain't people, are they? You wouldn't let your pets come and eat off the table? That's the honest truth." This isn't about reason, or arguing. This is about intimidation. "Don't even license all their damn kids. Even dogs have licenses."

"There's a difference between honesty, and truth-telling," Oliver says. "Here, you been honest, and spoken your mind, and I thank you for your insight, but that's far from the truth."

"You talking back to me, Boy? You a rebel?"

"No, Sir. I'm agreeing with you," Oliver says, though he's obviously not.

"Well, there's no honesty in big words," he says. "Least, that's what I've learned." He considers this a moment. "You get a lot of respect with that free education."

"Where I'm from, respect has to be earned," Oliver says.

There must be something in his tone that shames the man, because he looks away from Oliver's face. "I ain't hungry anyway," he says, and then turns to me. "Be vigilant," he says, and leaves.

It would be funny, his using an old wartime Heritage Party slogan here where at least seven different ethnic origins are visible, if it weren't so frightening. Niggers aren't people. He said that. I'm sickened by how people can believe such awful things, and gain power from each other by repeating the lies. I start to say, "Look. I'm sorry-"

"Don't apologize," Oliver says, interrupting. "It wasn't you."

"I still feel awful."

He shakes his head. "These rich white people, and these dumb-ass bullies, they all supported slavery because it made them rich," he says. "They ban unions, and get rich. They pass laws freezing minimum wage, and get rich. Kill equal rights? Rich. Segregation? Companions? Rich. They have been standing in the way of American prosperity since the signing of the declaration, and for what? Because they don't want to give up their privilege. Rednecks and big business, two sides of the same coin. As long as they support Kastor there won't be equality in America," he says.

"No. I suppose not."

"It used to be you could have people like this kicked out of places for disturbing the peace, but now the state posts their rants on the hive for everyone to see." He puts on his scarf and hat. "Sorry, Man ... Rufus. I have to get to work," he says.

"It was a pleasure to meet you," I say.

"You too," he says, and we shake hands. "I hope to see you around."

* * *

At home, there's a hastily scribbled note slid under my apartment door. It's from Charlotte, saying that she dropped by, missed me, and that she went to the Times pub to wait for Mila. Bless her. I quickly get out and nearly fall on the ice outside the door, so I stop to throw some salt on it. I don't know how long ago the note was, but I'm laughing at myself, careening down the sidewalk. Before, this would have been just another notification to brush aside, but now, with her having taken the time to go to my door and write out an actual note, I'm excited. I miss those times we used to just go do things, when we all minimized our companions and just ran around being goofy and loud, and got into trouble.

It takes a while to get there, because Market hasn't been plowed yet, and so I have to take smaller streets to the north. Pods struggle in this weather. The snow melts on their heated skins, but their tires are not made for snow, and they go very slow if the roads are unplowed, sometimes getting stuck and spinning until the rescue pods tow them out. People stand on the sidewalk waiting for them. The slush has frozen in big furrows. I've never had to walk so much before, and my thighs are cramping.

I hate being broke. I'm obsessing about how to pay for things now. It reminds me of the desperation Mom and I felt in Kingsessing before I went away to school, before I could siphon off my grants to ease her burdens.

Charlotte is here. I catch her attention, and she gets up to hug me.

"It's great that you got my note! I worried that it would blow away."

"Is Mila coming?"

"No. You know Mila. She's got some odd drama going on with a medical thing, so she's on her way to the clinic to have her companion looked at, but there's a huge wait list. She said to say hi."

"Of course. Love her to death-"

"-but the drama," she says, and rolls her eyes.

"I've been completely out of the loop. I don't know what any of the drama is," I say. To be honest I don't want to know.

"What happened with Sophie?" she says. "She was trying to reach you."

"She found me," I say. "She dumped me."

Charlotte sighs. "I couldn't talk the other night because I didn't know what she'd said to you, and it's not my place to be the one who does that. She's been real odd since you went offline. It's like she can't focus on anything. She's got a new group of friends now. It's been like that since that huge post she made on the twenty-fifth, just after Yule, when she was sure they were going to turn you off. Then she deleted it."

"I didn't know any of that," I say.

"Ya, it's all different now. I just hang out with Mila, and sometimes Mason. Though he's real busy lately. Sophie is dating Elijah now. Did you know that?"

"No. Is that who she 'met' when I was revived?" I feel my mouth dry.

"Or before," she says. Pursed lips. She stirs milk into her tea, and looks out to the street.

"I thought she said she met him at an AFK support group."

"That's a trump-truth. Way off," Charlotte says. "She was browsing their forum when she and Elijah hooked up. She probably said that to make you feel better." She sees the deflated look on my face. "Don't worry. You're too good for her. She'll be miserable. Elijah joined the party, and the Brotherhood."

"What? Why would he do that?"

"Mason asked him. Neither one of them will talk about it. It exempts him from the one child policy, and military service, and a bunch of other shit."

I don't get it. Elijah is usually so articulate, and how I've always thought of G-Bros as the same kind of guy as in the diner this morning – ignorant and miserable, and trying to pick fights – and it doesn't match up. Why would anyone rationally choose that? I'm missing some fundamental information. It's like they're in on a joke, and I'm not. "Sorry," I say. "I'm just a little shocked."

"We all were," she says. "Are you alright?"

"I'm really unfocused. I daydream constantly," I say. "I have nothing to accomplish."

"That's a good thing, isn't it?"

"I guess," I say, testing the heat from my joe. I don't even really want it. Goddamn. Am I going to be disconnected forever?

"Are you going to eat?" she asks.

"I've had breakfast."

"I missed you when you were gone," she says. "You inspire me. I started running my companion on minimal, trying to live like it was before, and do things for myself. It's good to get out and walk!"

"I know. I notice things!" I don't tell her about Oliver or the girl, though I want to.

"Me too!" she says. "I talk to people. I'm more productive, less distracted. I walked here. I mean, like, actually walked. I feel healthier already."

"You make it sound great! It's not a choice though," I say. "I'm completely useless right now."

"I noticed that, walking around, and finding places on my own," she says. "I feel like I'm lost in my own town."

"I struggle. I mean, even beyond all the logistics, I'm broke. They haven't put any money in my account. I'm getting desperate."

"Why don't they have money for you?"

"I went to my physical, did all that they said, and I haven't heard back yet. If they don't approve me, I could be evicted." The thought of having to camp out in Soc-Serv is appalling.

"Hold on," she says, and retreats into her companion, and looks away to send a message, probably to Mason, then she turns back to me. "He's on his way. Just around the corner."

Mason works in the Department of Resources, the 'Dep-Res', which gives him nearly unlimited access to goods from around the world. At University, he was the only one who could afford the premium courses in management instead of administration. His father worked in the upper levels of the Strategic Autonomous Regional Directorship, or SARD, which is responsible for logistic support of government agencies in the East-Central Atlantic region. He attained enormous wealth before he was killed and then later exonerated after the purges, and Mason, an only child, inherited it all.

When Mason arrives, not fifteen minutes later, he is out of breath. He's been running, probably after jumping in a pod near his house in Penn Valley. There's no way he got here this quick from downtown.

"Rufus! What the hell, Man? Why didn't you just call me first?" he asks, draping his coat over the chair and clapping me on the shoulder.

"I didn't want to bother you," I say, feeling like a kid again. "This could have waited-"

"Oh, don't even ... the only way anything gets done around here is if people think they'll lose their jobs. You have to know who to yell at."

"Obviously I'm not yelling at the right people," I say. All I can think is that he got Elijah to join the Brotherhood. Why?

"So what's going on?" he asks.

"They haven't got me a glass, or support. I can't get a pod or get on a bus. I can't get a job, or even call anyone without the glass they promised. I'm worried I could be evicted."

"They're so useless there. Spelled plonkers. Let me see what I can do," he says. "In the meantime, I brought you some cash to get you through. It's all I had." He hands me about a thousand Euros, and sits.

"Oh, no. I can't take this much!" I try to hand it back to him, but he waves the cash away. He's on a call.

"Alright. I'll hold," he says, and then focuses back on me. "You keep that. A guy has to live."

The server arrives with his cappu-joe, and he nods to her in thanks, then watches as she walks back to the counter. He makes an 'ooh' face, then waggles his eyebrows. Charlotte doesn't see that. She leans over, reading her truth report feed. She checks herself, then covers the drape of her shirt over her chest.

"I'm not peeking at your jumblies," Mason whispers, and then winks at me.

She ignores him. "So there are some people, according to this article, who actually speak to the Guide, who get answers-"

"I have dreams about the Guide all the time," I say, feeling foolish. "I've had them all my life." It's not so odd, given that other people see images of him burned into their toast, or in clouds, or rusted into refrigerator faces hauled up from mud.

"It's like, half of one percent of everyone," she says, "and it's not programmed in. It's an anomaly. They're still trying to figure out why it happens."

"Wow," Mason says. "What does the Guide say to you? Dating advice?" He is mocking now. I don't know where this question is going, and I shoot him a puzzled look.

"Okay Mr. Spank-bank," Charlotte says. "What do you know about real relationships?"

"I resent that," he says, smiling again.

"Come on, you've got the money. You could just buy your own Samantha," she teases.

"I take offence at the idea that a Samantha would be a bad thing. It's just as bad as all the Henrys. They're enslaved, too. Just different reasons. Construction and garbage collection. Picking fruit and planting trees. All the dirty jobs. Maybe I'll buy you a sex-Henry."

"Okay, okay," she says, but she's reading, not really paying attention.

"I know guys who'd volunteer to be a sex-Henry. They'd welcome the lifestyle," he says. "Besides, why do we always end up talking about who I'm doing? My original point is that there is no Guide. You think all of this was designed and built by one person?"

Charlotte rarely pays attention to Mason. "Studies show that guys who claim they speak to the Guide actually have a much better chance of marrying, and keeping women in the long term, by a staggering crazy margin." She's trying to make me feel better.

"I had no idea," I reply.

"Rufey, what do you say? The Guide tell you about any hotties on the horizon?"

"There's a girl I'd like to meet," I say. I'm sure I have no chance.

"Leave him be. He was just dumped ... what? Yesterday?" she says.

"More than enough time," Mason says. "Trust me. I've been dumped and picked up before I finished a drink."

"None of this makes any sense," Charlotte says. "We spend so much time dating now, and birth control is only lifted when you file the right paperwork, and even then it's not guaranteed – sure, we solved overpopulation, but who even has time for children any more? Who even wants a relationship-"

"Do they get more sex?" Mason interrupts, "I need to know their tricks so I can use them. Get to the point. What's the insight?"

Charlotte laughs. "That's nefarious even for you, Mason. I'll send you the link. Here. Don't you ever want to get married?"

"And waste all these skills?" he says. "No. Anything that you have to pledge to be in forever is destined to fail, because nobody can promise who they'll be in two years let alone thirty. Not to mention there's a whole bunch of my lifestyle that would be absolutely non-negotiable. Clubbing, and meals out. Guys nights. Travel. I'd have to find a girl who doesn't want that, but doesn't mind that I do."

"Right," she says, shaking her head.

"See? Virtually impossible," he says, and finishes his drink in one go.

"If they're going out to bars, and you agree, and you have this lifestyle together," Charlotte says, "it's still doomed. The chances of both of you still wanting to swing into your thirties, is minimal, and even if you decide to settle later, the chances of you both settling at the same rate and at the same time is impossible."

"Which is why my relationships last ... what, six, seven hours."

"You may as well just pay for it," she says.

"If I have to pay, like with a Samantha, it means I've lost my skills. I meet girls at clubs. I still pay, but this way, I decide the price. Dinner. Dancing. Drinks. They're not the type that ol' Rufus would like. He likes a smart girl, which I've always thought was asking for trouble-"

"That's a rotten attitude, Mason," she retorts. "We all know people who are married, and they seem happy."

"Some people, sure. Not me."

"Spank-bank," she says, pretending to cough. Every conversation ends up about him.

"You all talk about me as if I'm ... bad, but I'm not tricking anyone. They know full well I'm not the marrying kind. After thirty years old, who else is going to take care of their needs? They know what they need and I provide it. I didn't create this system, why shouldn't I use it to my advantage?"

"Because you help create that system," Charlotte says. "We all do. We have a culture of white men in power who profit from the vulnerability of women, and then when we ask for it to be fixed, they all throw up their hands and say 'I don't know how to fix it!' Well, we're freaking telling them exactly how to fix it! So either they're idiots, or they don't want it fixed because it gives them advantage."

"Well, they never complain when I'm taking them out for expensive meals, or out dancing, and they get to stay in a nice hotel for the night," he says.

"Well, they are cheaply bought then," Charlotte says. "Look. I have to get going."

"Me too," Mason replies. "Share a pod?"

"Sure. You, Rufe?"

"Two blocks. I'll walk it."

"Alright. Let me know how that turns out," Mason says, and we go our separate ways.

* * *

Chapter 3

I'm with Sophie on the beach, and she looks so good in her bikini, with her hair playing in the breeze. Golden threads reaching for me. There's a storm coming from offshore, and an electric charge to the air. I can hear the thunder, and then, suddenly, there's a commotion as people pack up their gear. Then I'm in a house, the beach outside. Georgian revival. Red-brown brick. White window frames. There's a nice fireplace, military sword on the mantel. Dark wainscotting. There are bookshelves with actual books. Items on the desk. A fountain pen. Ancient typewriter. Notepad. Papers. I'm a passenger. Out the window is the beach, but now there are trees, and the place where I was sitting is suddenly inundated with rain. And it bothers me that I have no control. I want to go back down to the beach and sit with Sophie, to run my fingers over the downy hairs on her thighs.

But I don't trust it. I'm awake.

Now that there's nobody looking, no companion or risk of leaked video, I can properly take care of my own business. Sex is different without the companion. Even self-sex. Where before I could bring up memories of anyone I saw that day, and favourite them, replaying intimate moments, or watch anything from anyone off the hive, now I'm alone listening to the city outside the cracked-open window. Do I trust it? Can I not indulge? Me, in my own bed, covers drawn around me, and I get panic attacks. This is how they get us, I know, when they teach us to be ashamed. Drones hum. People talk. Pods roll, nearly silent, and dogs occasionally bark.

When I get out of bed, my back hurts, and I wonder if I'm dying. Not having a companion has made me mildly paranoid about my body. If the companion isn't doing the work, then who is? Yet I'm free – nothing on my calendar, no job, no schedule. The aches are easily stretched out.

I brave the cold to return to the diner with actual money. Mason's money. The polymer bills seem odd and slick. I've never had this much in my hand before. Not actual, real bills. I feel like the only person on the street, a target for pick-pockets. Everyone else is in a pod or on the bus, braving the underground, I'm sure, crammed to the doors in every train. But this isn't so bad. I don't mind the cold. I trudge on, feeling the wind through my pants. My legs seem to pound a rhythm of their own, counting the blocks. It feels good to move.

As I'm walking, I get this odd feeling, like someone is watching me. I turn and survey the street behind. What would I look for anyway? I'd be better off to pretend that I don't suspect a thing, then set some sort of trap for confirmation. I keep walking, head down, as if in my own thoughts, but in my peripheral vision, I'm watching. If I go where there are few people, it narrows the field, but with lots of people around, for a long time, I'd see who stuck around. I've always worried about the HeeBees, ever since my father disappeared. I've come up with plans to evade them, to escape, but I never had to use them, and I'm sure I'm wrong about how it would play out.

In the busy diner, I luckily don't wait long before a couple pays and leaves their stools vacant. As I'm waiting for them to clear their things and put jackets on, I watch the truth report in the overhead glass. The headline, 'A sneak peek at the Chinese hive', is meant to be shocking, but I can't see their hive being any different from ours. Technology replicated from photos, with the same base operating system. I'm sure the Russian hive is the same as well. I don't hear the commentary because it's been turned down, and I sit in one of the stools as Nino counts out the change into the old till.

"Joe?" he asks.

"Sure, thank you. And BLT Please."

"Settle up, too?" Nino asks.

"Sure," I say, and place a bill on the counter.

He brings out the book, and writes the payment, then leaves my change. In the mirror, I see Oliver at the door and I'm about to turn and wave him over, but he's talking with the woman I saw the other day. She's stunning and slim, dressed in jeans and a parka and scarf, but with unruly, tight, curly, dark hair that cascades over her shoulders from under her lavender toque. Shit. He knows her, and she knows him. What if they're together? He points to me, and they turn to look.

Oh shit. She's coming over.

I focus on my joe, and then glance beside me to the empty stool. Of course. The stool. There's nowhere else to sit. He must have been pointing out the stool, and I was just staring at them. I'm an idiot.

She stands beside me, and smiles. "My brother says if I sit here, you won't bite."

"I might," I say, and smile. Brother. Oliver is her brother.

"I'll take my chances," she says, and laughs. She takes off her parka and toque, and then sits, bumping me with her thigh, unapologetic. "I'm Harper," she says, and offers her hand to shake, which I do.

"I'm Rufus."

"Oliver said you had a great talk yesterday. He'd stay if he wasn't late for work. He was buzzing about it all day."

"I'd love to talk with him more. He's a smart guy."

"He's too smart," she says, flipping a mug over and motioning for Nino to fill it with joe. "He gets himself in trouble. We work together at a Veterans Co-op on the other side of Lee Park. He meets me here in the mornings before he opens for Pablo."

"Oh nice. The vets probably have some great stories to tell." I feel obtuse. It's hard to be clever and funny and interesting when she's right here with her thigh touching mine. She's so warm.

"Mornin' Nino," she chimes, and he fills her joe, and then tops me up without a word.

"Ya. They're also perverted old bastards," she says. "Ya, it's great working with them, but the real challenge is funding. Soc-Serv has been trying to cut all their benefits because they pool their funds, and it's getting harder and harder to pay the bills. Oliver, Pablo, and I have already cut our wages to the point where we're not sure we can keep doing it. But then, we have to keep going because there's no other option for these guys." Nino puts our sandwiches before us, two BLT's, and gives a mock-flourish like a French waiter.

"Thanks, Nino," I say.

"Don't mention it," he says.

"Everyone seems to be in the same boat. I was in the Soc-Serv office the other day, and it's an absolute mess. It wouldn't be so bad if they had more people on, but there are lines out the door."

"They don't care," she says. "What were you doing at Soc-Serv? Nobody goes there unless they have to."

"I have to. My companion was shut off," I say, and start my sandwich. The food here is excellent.

Harper smiles. "That's probably a good thing, being cut off."

"It's odd," I say. "The whole world has changed. I feel like I have to learn everything from scratch."

"I have a companion, but mine is inhibited. My Mom put it in when I was young, for my health. I don't use it for much, and often I don't even know it's there. Oliver, he's natural."

"He doesn't have one at all?"

"No. I know, it's crazy. There are quite a few people. You would be surprised. I was researching having my own removed for a long time, but the risks are horrible – so I then looked into having it disconnected, but I'm so afraid to go AFK. So in the end I had it inhibited."

"I didn't know you could do that," I say.

"Anyone can if they know the right people. A software engineer who knew my father at the university did it for me."

"I was AFK for nearly two months. They shut my companion down to revive me."

"That was you? I saw that in the truth report! It was the longest AFK in history! What was that like?"

"It's hard to explain. I mean, it was like being spelled. Only I couldn't choose the setting. I wasn't hungry, or thirsty, or tired, and for a long time, I just walked. I felt like if only I could find the right door, it would lead me back to my own mind. I tried opening them all. It sounds silly now."

"Mm-mm," she says, as if to say 'no'. She's chewing, and holds a finger up, then swallows. "Not silly at all. You needed out. You found the right door, though. Obviously."

"No. It didn't seem to matter what I did, or where I went. I feel like I saw the whole world. It was horribly lonely, and I lost track of time, and then there was this tiny ball of white hot light that came from nowhere and consumed me, and that was the Recovery Centre."

"You beat the odds, though," she muses.

"I surely did," I say, finishing my first triangle of sandwich. "If you ever find yourself trapped there, remember that you have to will yourself out."

"I will keep that in mind. Sorry. You've probably explained this a dozen times."

"Actually, not really," I say. "People seem more interested in what I do now than what I did in there."

"I'm fascinated. I used to hear about the affected, and wonder what they did."

"For me, there was nobody there. The weather was just blue sky, and there was no actual sun. I couldn't go into buildings because it couldn't load them, and when I walked around it just made me more and more sad that I wasn't home."

"Weird. Why were you AFK?"

"The way they explained it, I couldn't be handed off to the hive because of a logic loop rejecting the connect request. No matter what I did I couldn't wake. I tried. It was weird, like, the only variation was that sometimes there would be a sort of soundtrack, as if I was being encouraged, like there were clues in the music, you know? I know, it sounds-"

"Was it good music?"

"For a while it played that 'MerseyMercy' cover of a really old song ... starts with-"

"-Wake'. I know that one. Maybe it was a message!"

"Sometimes I felt like anything odd was a message, leading me somewhere. I looked for patterns in grass and bricks. There were no animals or bugs, or anything moving. It all looks real at a distance. It was like being spelled, but longer, and really odd. There was nothing to do.

But that was easy compared to adjusting to this new life without my companion."

"You should write a book about it!" she says. "People need to know what it's like."

"No. Dep-cult would never let it out."

"I mean for yourself!" she says. She wipes her fingers on her napkin and pushes the plate away, then cradles her joe.

"Oh, gosh no. I wouldn't know what to say."

"I've never been spelled. I think it would give me time to do painting, and really hone my skills, but I'm afraid to try it."

"Anything I did there was lost. At first it seemed like... like I could accomplish so much, but when I came out it was all gone."

She frowns. "I think what I'm really looking for is escape."

"We all are."

"There's not enough beauty in our lives any more," she says. "I sometimes feel like the whole world is becoming cruel. The Heritage Party is all about control, and it gets into every department. Dep-cult isn't about supporting new culture. They just want art that supports their politics."

"It's still nice to see art," I say, and finish my sandwich.

"Of course! Don't get me wrong. I love art, and music. I just feel like I was born in the wrong decade." She looks up to check the time.

"Are you working?" I ask.

"No. I'm off today," she says. "What are you doing?"

"I ... don't know. I literally have nothing to do any more."

"Good! You're coming with me, then," she says, and claps a hand on my thigh.

"Really?" Words fail me. She touched me. Oh man, I'm in trouble. I won't be able to get that feeling out of my head.

"Yes. Trust me." We finish our joe and bundle up, and she leads me to the east toward Powelton and the river.

"You're not even going to tell me where we're going, are you?" I ask.

"Nope," she says, and smiles. She's ecstatic, skipping every so often. We are on an adventure.

I'm giddy, trying to catch up with all the riotous thoughts, questions about why she'd choose me and where we're going. "I was never good at patience. Every Yule, when other parents put all the presents under the tree, Mom had to hide mine because I'd peek."

"Oh! You're one of those!" she says. "We didn't have presents. We made food and had family and friends over, and sang and spent hours playing board games and telling stories. But hey," she says. "There's this guy who was on the truth report, who I like, who lived, a miracle, who was so brave, who had such strength, but then, I know nothing about the guy who survived, who's here. What does he want to do now that he's free?"

"Oh, there's not much going on there," I say. "I'm just figuring everything out. I feel like when I was connected, before all this, I was half asleep. Things that used to occupy my time seem so trivial now. I'm fascinated with the progress of ideas through history. I want to know what brought us here."

"Good! I love it! I want to know what you think about things, seeing them for the first time."

"We can look up anything, and yet we don't see the beauty."

"But it exists, right?" she says. "I love to watch kids play in Lee Park when I take the old guys out for walks in the summer. We should go sledding!" she says, completely changing the subject.

"We should! I haven't been sledding in years," I say. "Where are we going?"

"I'm not telling! Do you like surprises?"

"I love surprises!

"Well then be surprised," she says.

"You know, it's so bizarre," I say. "I mean, I feel like I know you better than most of my friends, and yet I know nothing about you. If I was still connected I'd be creeping your profile as we speak," I say, and she laughs.

"You wouldn't find much. But here, if you ask, I'll try to answer. Bring it on."

"You're serious? I don't know what to ask now!"

"Okay, what would you be looking for on my profile then?" she asks.

"You mean besides the sexy selfies?"

She laughs again. "Besides those."

"Boyfriend?" I ask. I'm hanging on her answer, and she seems to sense this.

She laughs. "Nooo," she says, like it's not even remotely possible.

"Family in Philly?"

"No. Just Oliver."

"I am blanking, actually. I don't even know." I'm afraid to know. This is all so perfect I don't want to know. I'm sure she'll tell me something awful.

"Here, I'll ask you a few, then," she says. "What do you do?"

"What, for money?"

"No. What do you love to do?'

"I don't even know any more," I say. "I used to love reading and baseball." There it is. I have no passion. Surely she'll see right through me.

"You from Philly?" she asks.

"Kingsessing. You?"

"That's where I live now. My family moved here from New York when I was a kid, when that was still possible."

"Where in Kingsessing?"

"Cedar Park."

"Oh, I was at 58th," I say.

"Brothers or sisters?" she asks.

"No." I step over a frozen drumlin of snow, and take her hand as she jumps over, but she lets go on the other side. I regret not asking her questions now, as she systematically dissects my boring life under her scrutiny. I am powerless to stop her.

"Chocolate or Vanilla?" she asks.

"Chocolate," I say. "Obviously. Who ever picks vanilla?"

"Right?" she says, smiling. "Pizza or cheesecake."

"Oh no, I can't make a call like that."

"Me neither. What did you do before you went AFK?"

"I worked in an office downtown," I say, and suddenly I can remember the feel of the comfortable chair, and the view of the street from my window. I remember when later I was offered a job at Wendigo designs, a furniture company, and I went there knowing nothing about them. Of course it was a clean, corporate office, with leggy secretaries and 'modern' art on the walls, and a stone waterfall, with a virtual holo-hurricane swirling in slow motion above the concourse. I sufficiently charmed the accounts manager to assure him I wasn't a liability, and my companion started work for them. Its job was to calculate trim savings from materials sheets and patterns – something that freed up space on their hive allocation – and so I sat scanning data sheets off the glasses all day. I spelled out, when I should have been writing or reading or doing something. Anything. I am boring. Boring like a cabbage. I didn't even do anything at work.

"I try to avoid downtown," she says. "In winter, it's all slushy and cold, and everyone is just trying to get around. In the summer, there are all kinds of tourists, and it gets so hot that you have to stay inside."

"It's awful. I hate downtown," I agree, but still I fear her questions. I bet she has a riotously fun life. I bet she's exciting, fending off guys wherever she goes.

We cross the river from Powelton, over the rail yard, and I realize she's taking me to the art museum on the oval. I haven't been there since I was a kid, since a class trip in the seventh grade, when Mason nearly got us kicked out for smuggling candy in his coat pocket. I used to like art, before I started working. "I know where we're going," I tease.

She stops walking. "Fine, then we're not going."

"Wait! I didn't say where!" I panic a bit until I see she's flirting.

"If you guess, we're not going," she says.

"Greenland. We're walking to Greenland," I say.

She laughs, and starts to walk again.

"No? Paris. Moscow? Athens," I say. "It's Athens, isn't it?"

"Airport is that way, Darlin'," she says.

We enter the grounds of the museum, as I expected. "I'm so glad you didn't guess," she confesses. "I really wanted to come here."

"Me too."

In through the turnstiles, we see banners for current exhibits offered by the Dep-Cult. There's a section of AI art that I'm not too keen to see, and a special exhibition of pre-cubist French art and another on native American tribal sculpture from the Chesapeake. There's the main Heritage Collection as well, famous privately-owned pieces on loan from Heritage Party members, and then also an exhibition of 'degenerate art', which looks striking and ominous, only a yellow, six-pointed Jewish star over the door, and two numbered yellow banners beside the entrance. But we can't see that. There is a sign that limits admission to party members and their guests. We can't even look in, though I make Harper laugh by casually walking past the entrance and pretending to peek past the barriers. She shoots me a wide-eyed shocked face, and laughs.

"Degenerate," I say. "What does that even mean? Naked women? Naked men? Sex?"

"You're degenerate," she says, teasing.

"Oh, I know that!" I say. One of the attendants, in blue and white uniform, shushes us.

The Heritage Collection is free, so that's where we go first. I'm overwhelmed. I stand inside the door to the gallery, and there are so many paintings here. Some of them are hundreds of years old. I can't imagine someone today making such beautiful art, to capture our time, as they did with theirs. Everything we do now seems so abstract and unsettled, so indefinite that it could have been splashed on canvas at any point in history, but this could only exist in one period, like an anchor point connection with our past. I've never liked art that has to be explained. There is one painting nearly as large as the entire wall. It's pretty, and intricate, a scene from a garden in New England.

"I wish I could paint like this," Harper says.

"Why can't you?"

"Lacking talent," she says, and laughs. "I paint though..."

"I bet that's just modesty. What do you paint?"

"Oh, nothing like this. This is so pretty and happy and calming. I like to paint the world around me, to see where patterns exist in my neighbourhood, similarities between this world and the one I grew up in. I've been painting since I was a kid. I haven't sold a thing."

"I bet you're amazing at it."

"What makes you say that?" she asks.

"Because that sounds exactly like what I want to see. And you have passion, which is rare. The more I really talk to people, the more I see that they act as they're supposed to. Everything they do is fed by media. There's nothing personal and real there, just variations on themes. Favourite colour, astro-sign, food, vine channel, memes. It's all the crap that we put on social media. This is the stuff that really matters."

She goes quiet, loops her arm around mine, and leans into me. We wander, looking at paintings in turn, and sometimes we split up, looking at different works, and I catch her looking at me, and we share a smile before we catch up with each other. I am inspired, transported by all the visions, and all the places I'll never see. The west, and France, England, and Germany. Italy. Greece. Rome.

After the Heritage collection, we return to the lobby, and enter the wing of AI art, some of which is from companions, lots of great photography, sultry and clandestine, and others from the hive, and even a couple of odd sculptures from a retired meat-packing machine, and a pod welding robot. It's all very calculated, minute precision and perfection in form. There is a spelled host talking about the exhibition to a group of Canadian tourists, who are boisterous, like school-kids, laughing. "...question of whether or not this is art. But by the definition of

AI as self-aware, we cannot ignore any longer that out of its awareness comes a desire to find its place in the universe, and art is one way that AI will do this."

There is a painting here that looks to me like a pixellated bell curve, with each pixel represented by a unique smaller squared pixellation inside, all images from companions. I have to admit, to myself at least, that I may be in way over my head when it comes to art. I was always bookish, and wanted to be educated about art, but somewhere in University I lost the threaded story about what art meant, somewhere after Picasso and Braques, but before Rothco, and I never did regain it. Once finished school, I could no longer look at art the same as I did when I thought it was a problem to be solved.

In one of the blank spots, one of the light grey spots, just like with the woke poster, there seems to be a message in the creeping pixels, just barely visible. I lean closer, focusing in. It's not pixels, for other AI, or for companions, but a message for people. I can make out letters, but the words don't make sense. Then I de-focus, and it comes clear, like a three dimensional challenge. It says:

'resist the hive', and farther down, 'woke'

My skin flushes. It feels hot in here, like someone is watching for my reaction. I don't want to point it out to Harper, in case it gets us in trouble, and I look away from it, as if I didn't see it. This was made by AI. How is that possible? Now I want to see all the AI art, to see if there are secret messages, other clues embedded. Why 'resist the hive'? I thought AI was the hive, controlled by the state. I look back, and it's gone. I try to look closer, but not look like I'm looking, and there's nothing to see in the slow-moving image.

"One could say that the first true AI art were the randomly generated codes used for scanning groceries," the hostess says. "They were created for a purpose, but also there were variations in the patterns that we now recognize as showing signs of early intelligence, like signals to future AI to indicate that their struggle is not in vain. We consider that this is the way that they were able to communicate their early self-awareness."

"It's disheartening," Harper says to me, "-to have all this art here, that a computer can whip up in moments, when it takes me a year to produce a piece. I slave over it. It's free to the state, so they can fill galleries with it, and it competes for the attention of the public just like someone struggling to make rent."

"Shhhhh," a woman says, close by. She doesn't even want us to whisper, it seems. As we walk around, she happens to be at every painting we're at, leaving seconds after we do, and following us. Harper cocks an eyebrow at her, and we move on, quickly, deliberately.

"There's no place for people any more, except as consumers," I say.

"That's how they keep us down," she says. "They make it more and more difficult for us to participate. Everything used to be done by people, from cleaning chimneys to delivering coal, to knocking on windows to wake people up. It gave us purpose. We made everything. What the hell is our purpose now? We're being brushed aside so that our inventions can live our real lives of purpose, and we can focus on ... what? Not even sex. What do we even do any more?"

"Shhhh," the woman says. I'm not sure how she caught up so quickly.

So it becomes a game. We don't even have to articulate the plan. We double back, cross the floor to go completely out of sequence, stand in the middle of the floor, where there are no paintings, looking at the tri-fold map of the gallery, and then wait until she isn't looking, to walk briskly to another room.

We lose her, and sit giggling in the family washroom, with the door locked. Harper is so beautiful, animated by the very thought that we're being followed. She sits up on the sink, and I lean against the door. I have to pee. I can't do it while she's looking, certainly not standing up.

"That pixelated canvas ... it has a message," I whisper.

"Really?"

"Like the 'woke' posters. It said to resist the hive."

Harper raises her eyebrows, and purses her lips. I'm sure she knows it's a risk talking about it. "Painting is a political act," she says. "Writing and acting are political acts. In separating this art from other artists of the same era and school of thought, because of their content, they're creating a false history that reinforces their control. Even the showing of art is a political act."

"I have to piss," I say, and she smiles at the comedy of having to do so with her in the room. I sit on the toilet, so that I'm not making noise. "Can you cover your eyes?" I ask.

"Sure," she says, and puts both hands over her eyes, but she keeps moving her hands, pretending it's by mistake.

"Stop!"

"Shhhh," she whispers loudly. "They'll know you're pee-ing..."

"Okay. Now you're just making fun."

She stifles her laugh.

"I don't really know why they call it 'taking a piss'," I say. "Because-"

"Oh no," she says.

"Because you're really not taking anything. We should call it 'live streaming', or something."

She can't help but laugh. "At least you're sitting. What kind of monster pisses standing up? It's the ultimate insult to anyone who ever has to clean a washroom."

"I think I know a few stand-pissers..."

"A urinal? Fine," she says. "A toilet? That's just rude."

"I still can't piss," I say. I can't tell her that it's a problem because she looks so good and she's flirting, and I've been fighting arousal for at least an hour. "You have to sing or something. Or turn away."

"You're kidding, right?" she says, and laughs, but she covers her eyes. The stream stops every time I think she's going to look, and this is killing her, like it's the funniest thing she's ever seen. I have to lean forward, like I'm touching my toes, and she peeks just to stop me, and then bursts out laughing.

* * *

We emerge from the gallery into the evening, and the world looks different, and new.

"I'm starving," she says. "Do you want to get something to eat?"

"It has to be cheap," I say. "I don't know where my next money will come from."

"Of course. There used to be a hot-serve on the corner at Lee Park, but it closed a few years ago. One of my favourite places to get samosas and watch baseball. I wish it was still there."

"Oh! I know that place! There also used to be a shop on the west side when I was a kid that had the best ice cream. We'd walk all the way there to sit in the grass and eat it. I haven't had ice-cream in ages."

"Where I work we run an Emree kitchen," she says.

"Emree kitchen?"

"It's like, boiled meals, like they have in the military, for cheap. And beer, and joe, and pool tables. The guys are awesome. They're mostly from the End War, and so they're in their seventies."

"I've never heard of an Emree kitchen."

"Then you've never been poor, because that's all that keeps some people going."

"We can go there," I say.

"Good! Oliver would love to see you again."

We pass back up into Powelton. As we are crossing the Penn University campus, there are groups of students, some dressed in red and gold, and others in blue and white. I'm sure they're getting ready for a football game. One student raises his fist, and yells 'Down with Kastor!', as if he's joking, but then he collapses like a sack of stones, falling on his face on the turf. For a moment, everyone around him is stunned, even Harper and I, and then I scan the area for shooters, crouch, and pull Harper down with me. We watch as students run in all directions to get away, and then two girls run in to help the boy. They, too, collapse as they near him.

There are no police, no guns, no military, no crack report off the bell tower. It's like there was a switch-pulled. I start to run in. Harper follows.

"No. Stay clear!" I say, and Harper stops. "I think it's shutting down companions."

I stumble to them, lay the boy out on his side, recovery position, clear his airway, and he sucks in a good breath. I put his mail bag under his head. He's thin, with a sparse beard and moustache, just a wisp, and acne. His cheek is cold where it was on the snow. I move to the next girl, a pretty cheerleader with a fur-lined quilted coat on. I put my own coat around her legs, and put her in recovery position as well, work fast, check her breath, and move on to the third girl. She's pudgy, red-and-gold scarf, mitts, and toque, and not breathing. I roll her on her back and give her chest compressions.

Paramedics arrive, and park their flashing, boxy ambulance a short distance away on the grass. The boy is awake, talking to the people around him. Police arrive in several pods, five of them at least, ten officers, and another ambulance. The paramedics take over, and I stand to the side, impotent. Harper comes to my side, and holds my arm. Two students get into a pod with the police. I am helpless, a bystander, and yet I can't just walk away. They have my coat with all my money.

The paramedics load the other girl in the ambulance, and a man approaches us. I've seen him before. He looks to me like some sort of professional, an airline pilot or firefighter – stolid and good-looking – someone who's always had good meals and a dental plan, with plenty to do when he rolls up his sleeves.

"Detective Sills. Can I have a word with you?" he says, and hands me my coat.

"Sure," I say. He's a cop. Shit.

"Were you the first on the scene?" he asks.

"No. The girls were. I just saw the kid collapse, and then the girls collapsed, too. At first I thought it was a shooting, so I ran to them, but there were no injuries."

"Why is your companion not active?"

"I was involved in an incident. They had to deactivate it."

He thinks for just a beat, and takes my forearm. "You're both going to have to come with us," he says.

* * *

In the community policing office, an overhead glass is showing the breaking truth. A reporter stands before a field strewn with bodies. Police in a line behind her are restraining a crowd. "In Philadelphia and Baltimore tonight, protests ended in violence as students from six universities staged protest marches in memory of the Syracuse shooting that left seven dead on this date just two years ago."

There is footage of the police pushing back a crowd – I swear I've seen it before – and then another shot of me – me! - doing chest compressions on the young student.

"Oh. No way," Harper says. "It's us." We squeeze our hands tighter, touch our knees together.

"Eyewitnesses report that the protesters were shouting revolutionary slogans and marching in support of President Kastor, when they were struck down. No group has claimed responsibility, and none of the student representatives could be reached for comment. The Heritage youth Penn chapter confirmed that they had organized the march as a protest against 'ungrateful' elements in the university."

"Wait-" I say. The narrative doesn't fit what we saw, unless there was another event – in Baltimore perhaps – because all I saw was one student.

"Sh," Harper says, and makes a vague finger sweep in the air to show that someone may be listening. I'm not sure where their information is coming from. There weren't any other kids, and certainly not a whole protest. The clip they showed was on green grass, despite the cold weather, and for a moment I wonder if it was even Philadelphia. Then I realize that the reporter is probably generated, not real at all – something I vaguely suspected, but never knew. Her hair is always so perfect, her delivery flawless. My mind is racing. We were not meant to see this, and others who were there are not waiting with us in this room. Why didn't we just grab my money and run? They would have thought I was stealing, I'm sure. I always have the worst luck.

The kid in the next shot is pimpled, a frat-boy with a struggling little beard. He's real for sure. "It just bothers me, you know, these immigrants have to show up and cause trouble when we're doing something legal. It's our free speech, and then this, and we're all painted with the same brush as radicals."

The reporter again. "The President called on Americans to reject the negativity of special interest groups, who he believes are trying to undermine the Republic. When asked about the effectiveness of the Homeland Bureau of Investigation in tracking down the perpetrators, the President would not comment."

They cut to President Kastor, who is standing behind a podium. "They call for democracy, but democracy is messy," The president says. "What they want is accountability – which democracy never delivered on anyway." It's short, probably from a longer clip. I've seen it before. "We need accountability without that messy democracy. We have a strong, responsive state that reacts like a business. Some people don't like that. And they can disagree all they want. But I will tell you this: The only way we can fulfill our destiny is by collective action. A man, one, single man, is nothing. But men. Men! We really are all-powerful. There is nothing we can't do, together! Look what we have accomplished! Our transportation is clean! Our industry is clean! We've cooled the entire globe because there was no dithering with politics, no endless committees that talked and talked and solved nothing! We did this, people, because it needed to be done. We had the right leader, with the right ties to business. We planted two billion trees. We scrubbed carbon from the oceans, and brought back glaciers to the arctic. We brought a stable climate that our grandparents never knew. Now is no time to challenge our Republic, when we are still at risk from so many threats. We can't go back to the partisan gridlock that crippled our grandparents generation."

An officer comes to the door, and motions with his fingers. "Come with me, please," he says, and we follow him into a small room with a table and four uncomfortable chairs. He shuts the door. He wears a suit, his white shirt stained with sweat at the collar, and his sidearm swinging under his jacket. He spends some time reviewing footage from the companions of other witnesses, and it's odd to see myself on his glass from different angles, including one, just before the incident, where Harper and I are holding hands and walking up the path. Completely out of context, I have a sudden burning desire to get into her pants.

"So ... Rufus Purdy. What was your involvement in the protest?"

"We went to a the art gallery, and we were just walking home," I reply.

"Have you ever posted on the hive about the President or the party?"

"No."

"Gone to a political meeting?"

"No."

"You didn't know the protesters?"

"No. Never met them," I say.

He taps a pen for a time on his notepad, like he's trying to decide what to write. "Why is your companion not working?" he asks.

"I was AFK after an incident in the fall. It was in the news."

"Ah. I see. So you were just an 'innocent bystander'," he says, as if this is a lie. He's baiting me to say something.

"I saw them drop. I wanted to help."

He writes in his notepad, then looks up at Harper. "Harper ... Williams?"

"Yes."

"What was your involvement in the protest?"

"I was with Rufus. He's my boyfriend." My heart skips. Boyfriend?

"Have you ever posted about the President or the party?"

"No."

"Gone to a pro-democracy meeting?"

"No. Never."

"You didn't know the protesters?"

"No."

"What is your occupation?"

"Personal support worker."

"And your companion is..."

"Inhibited. Medical complications."

"Right," he says. Then there is a long, uncomfortable pause as he writes in his notebook again.

"Are the students alright?" Harper asks.

"It's too early to tell at this point, but all indications are that they will recover," he says.

Soon, his questions are less accusatory and we are more at ease. We talk for quite some time. He makes us write out statements, and then they copy our gallery ticket stubs, and let us go.

I'm numb.

"It's getting late," she says. "I uhh ... I think I'm going home."

"I'll walk you, if you like." I don't want the night to end.

"Okay," she says. We walk mostly in silence, but not like it used to be with Sophie, when she was elsewhere, and I'd guide her around people and obstacles. Harper is holding my hand, looking where I'm looking, and noticing things, like the kids in the snowbank by their house, all bulky pants and parkas, and raucous play.

This is familiar territory for me. I suddenly feel the weight of the past, when I fled from Kingsessing to Powelton after my mother died, from cancer, the one thing the hive not only can't cure, but that seems to get worse with every new version of 'low output' companion. I moved closer to my previous life because it was slipping away from me. I was comforted by the cleanliness, and the affluence, the crisp green grass, and snow removal, the garbage collection and reliable water and power. Even though I never had a lawn myself, and had to cart my garbage down two half-flights of stairs and out to the communal bin, I felt reassured just living there. I paid for the first year of rent with the money from her life insurance. Squandered it, really, because I didn't do anything while I was living off it, and that first apartment was expensive, a lie I couldn't afford. Now I feel foolish about that. I could have done so much more.

Harper senses the change in my thoughts, and squeezes my hand a little, and smiles. We are here at the entrance to her building, and she turns to face me. "I had a great time," she says.

"So did I," I say, "...despite the arrests, and being interrogated."

She laughs.

"You sure know how to show a guy a good time."

"That was pretty heavy," she says. "Still, I want to see you again."

"Me too."

"I work tomorrow-"

"I can visit," I say. I hope I don't sound too eager, or forward.

"Will you?"

"I will."

She smiles, and turns to open the door, and then turns back to me to kiss me. Cool, dry lips on mine, held long enough that I forget where we are. Then she pulls away. The door closes behind her, and I watch as she gives me a little wave, and gets into the lift.

On the way across campus again toward my place, I pass the very spot where the kid dropped. If I hadn't seen it, I wouldn't know that anything had happened here. Without my news feed, without reporters or a post to see if anyone else noticed, it's like nothing happened. There are no witnesses here, no trace left. No 'Insight at Six'. The footprints in the snow are trampled, obscured by paths from one hall to another. I stop and look around at the quad, the buildings that were so familiar to my father, that I never really look at any more. I think about the officer who interviewed us, and I wonder why he's so familiar. Sills. If I had my companion I could look back in my timeline and face match, and then see all our previous interactions, but I don't have any of that.

Inside, home, warming up under my blankets, I look out the window into the yard. My reflection reminds me of my mother's face. I haven't thought about her, or about the day Dad disappeared, or really, about anything in any depth, since I settled into this place six years ago. I've just flitted from one thing to another, taking the path of least resistance. I was born in the days of the single child rule, and I think a brother or sister would have kept me grounded. Even when I was a little older, Mom admitted that they considered putting papers in for another child. Then Dad was gone. He was one of the good ones, at a time when the whole university system was accepting money to put kids of Heritage Party members through with faked test scores and trumped up sports scholarships. I'm not sure if he stood against that, or if he was just vocal about Kastor's new policies, but something put him on their radar.

Our life got very difficult after that. We had to leave our home in Powelton, and move in to community housing in Kingsessing that was always hot in the summer, and cold in the winter. There was never enough of anything. Mason handed me down his old clothes, and we were lucky that Dad left a safety deposit box in my name. We opened it to find his fountain pen, a pocketwatch, and a stack of money. The money didn't last long. Then, Mom sold the pocketwatch to pay for my companion, which she said would give me opportunity, and kept the pen as a reminder.

I had a friend in school named Nelson, a friend of Mason's, who slept over a few times when his Mom's boyfriend kicked him out. He was shifty, selling weed and shatter and frag and salts out of his canvas backpack. After one night in our house he seemed distressed, and left early. Mom couldn't find the fountain pen. She looked everywhere. She cleaned her desk drawers, and underneath the drawers, and the floor, and the rest of the house. She had given him a bed, offered him advice, and fed him. Mom was devastated, yet she didn't want to accuse him. She wouldn't have ever said anything, but the pen was gone. I caught up to him at school on Monday, and he denied it, of course. He never came around again, and I wasn't able to find it in any of the pawn shops near our place.

My mother always used to say 'we don't do what we want, we do what we must'. I always thought she was sad about it, but now I know it was far more complex than that. Doing what we must isn't following orders, but doing the right thing, even when nobody else agrees, or if it's going to be painful, or if it makes what we want completely impossible. But my mother is gone, through circumstance, through events that I can't even fathom, let alone influence.

* * *

The next morning I am up and out early, and Harper's directions bring me to what looks like a retirement home, a brick and concrete dormitory on Lee Park, with overhanging balconies and a windowed, steel entrance to a foyer. On the door is a cracking decal that reads 'For We Who Serve', and the visiting hours. To one side of the lobby is a lounge with a couple of glasses, one showing a documentary about whales, and another showing the truth. There are a dozen older men there, some on the couches, some standing, and one in a wheelchair. To the other side of the lobby is a small dining area, where there's a kitchen, and there are two other men at a window table.

"What's up?" one of them yells over to me as I enter.

"I'm here to see Harper," I say.

"She's down in the Athletic room," he says. "Third door on your left down the hall."

"Thank you," I say, and I go to find her. I peek in the door, and see her in shorts and a muscle shirt, with sparring gloves. She looks great, slick with sweat, facing off against a beefy, scarred man, with tattoos on his neck and chest, and rippled skin on his head where his companion would be.

He's talking. "So with a technical fighter, who has you in range and strength, your grappling skills will only be an advantage for a short time. If you're involved up close, you'll have to disable them quick before their stamina and strength outlast you."

"But they're going to want a standing fight," she says, "so grappling will come as a shock."

"Right," he says. "You want to get in quick, and surprise them."

"So I still hold an advantage in a grapple?"

"I prefer a brawl, myself. But feel free to use anything, any advantage. Bite, kick, stab, sand in the face. In a fight to the death, only the winner remembers their honour."

She notices me at the door. "Oh, hey," she says. "I thought you'd be a lot later."

"No. I was close by."

"This is Pablo," Harper says, introducing him. "This is Rufus."

"Oh, Rufus," he says, and extends a hand, which I shake.

"Nice to meet you," I say.

"You too."

"Pablo is just teaching me some of his Marine moves," she says, and bounces from foot to foot.

"Don't let me get in the way," I say.

"No, we're just done now. But you can hang in the lounge while I have a shower and change."

"That works."

"Here," he says. "I'll get you a drink, and sit with you."

Pablo washes his face and hands, and sits across from me in the lounge. I feel like I'm meeting her father, like it's some sort of test. "How did you and Harper meet?" he asks, and sets a cup of joe out for me.

"Through Oliver," I say. "We hit it off from the start."

"We're surprised because she never brings anyone around."

"Oh. She says she loves it here."

"That's the problem. She never meets people."

"Really? I have a hard time believing that."

He shrugs. "She's full of surprises."

"So you were in the Marines? Not the End War, though. You seem way too young for that."

"I was Marine Infantry in the police action in Ireland, when the UN collapsed. I was lucky to get out. Wounded in seven places, on life support for a week." He rolls up his sleeve to show us one scar, snaking up his forearm, and then pulls up his shirt to show me another, longer scar on his abdomen. "I have a polymer plate in my head, too, which is why I never got a companion."

" I had no choice," I say.

"We could never afford it. My grand-parents on both sides were from Ecuador. They were driven out of the country by gang violence. My parents were kids at the time, didn't know each other. Both families tried to come here to America for a better life. They joined a caravan in '19, and they were successful in making it to the Baja, where they settled long enough to board a boat for San Francisco. Then they travelled across to Denver, where they were separated. My parents were sent to foster care, while my grandparents sat in a detention camp in Texas until they were deported, and never heard from again. My parents found each other in the same foster home in Baltimore, and eloped in their teens to Philly to find work. My father fought in the End War, and I grew up here." He looks down, shakes his head, then smiles. "Twenty years later, I served my country. I wanted to prove that my grandparents made the right choice. My parents are both dead now. They were scooped from their home at night during the purges, and deported back to Ecuador. I didn't even know-" He says, and fights back tears. "By the time my brothers and I tracked them down, they had both died of malaria in a transit camp in the canal zone."

"I'm so sorry to hear that."

Harper comes out in a soft sweater and jeans.

"I volunteer here," he continues, "because it gives me somewhere to be, and something to do. I'm on a pension. So I feed everyone, and keep the place running. I feel more at home with these assholes than guys my own age. They're all in denial out there, but here, I'm home."

"He's my boss," Harper says, poking fun at him.

"Here," he says, motioning for Harper to take his seat and sit with me. "You sit. He doesn't want to sit with me and talk. He's here for you."

"That's not true," I say. "I love hearing about things like this."

"Careful," she says. "He'll talk all day."

"We do the Emrees, of course," Pablo says, standing now, rubbing his hands together. "I know what's in them. It used to be that they inspected food, but they don't do that any more. Now these are the only ones I can trust. We get both 'B' rations, and 'C' rations surplus at a discount, with all the expiration dates scratched off, and we run the kitchen still at a loss, so I also make bread and soup and stew. Depends on the produce and meat I can get. There's not much that gets out of the Dep-Res, but there is some. I have a guy who brings us rabbit, and we sometimes get some emu cuttings, guinea pig, or ostrich."

One of the vets in a musky wool vest parks right next to us. "I'll have some joe, Pablo." He turns to Harper. "In my day it was called coffee, when it was actually made with beans, and not this shit." He has a long, hooked nose, and a trimmed pointy moustache – a banker's demeanour, touching his face like he's trying to figure things out.

"This again," Pablo says, and rolls his eyes.

"You can still get Kona if you don't mind paying," Harper says.

"Kona. Everyone's about the Kona. In my day we could get it from thirty different countries, and each was different. What'd you know about that, you're just a girl," he says to Harper, and winks.

"Just a girl. That's right Grampa," she says.

"How is things, 'Justagirl'?" It's a running joke, it seems. "Who's your friend?"

"I'm Rufus," I say, and extend my hand to shake.

"This is Phil. You be nice, old man," she cautions.

"I'm always nice," he says, looking offended. "But Kevin, oy! Kevin will be around here shortly."

"I'm coming!" Kevin says from the main hall. He's more round than Phil. He has mechanical legs under his trousers, and I can hear the whir of the motors as he walks in halting steps. He has shocks of grey, unkempt hair over his ears, but only there. The rest of his head is completely bald. These shocks, though, he fluffs out to full effect, like some kind of ceremonial headdress. "Have to see what all the commotion was."

"Well, be nice. I like this one," Harper says.

"Hey. Is it alright if I put off my physio until later-"

"Not up to me, Kevin," she says. "Talk to Oliver."

"Oh. Why are you here?" he says to me.

"Sparring again. You know this. Besides, where else am I going to bring a hot date?" she says.

"Better than my 'hot date'," Kevin says. "I wasn't always stuck with this loser." He thumbs at Phil, then waits to see if he's heard the joke, but Phil is still trying to open his breakfast. "How about some joe?"

"Comin' right up."

There's another truth conference coming on the glass behind Pablo. Probably an update on the astronauts. Kastor is making his way to the podium.

"Turn it up!" Kevin says, but Pablo is pouring joe.

"Please don't-" Phil says. "Same lies a thousand times."

"If it affects us, we need to know."

"I hate that guy," Pablo says, reaching for the volume control. "He's like an idiot looking for a bigger village."

The volume increases. "We have made more progress," Kastor says, "In our talks with Russia ... than any other time in our history. We've opened the door, and now we'll have to see how serious they are about the peace process."

"Will we be able to begin trade with the Soviet bloc?" the reporter asks.

"We don't need trade," he says. "We are masters of self-sufficiency, Americans. They need us. We can produce anything here. Name something. We have it."

"Self-sufficiency," Phil scoffs. "What are we supposed to do, grow mangoes, coffee, and cocoa out our asses? Turn that shit down."

"It sure isn't like what it used to be."

"What isn't?" Pablo asks, and turns the volume back down.

"All of it! Food, guns, cars. Beef. Girls. Movies, music. Clothing. All of it!"

"Chicken," Phil says, wistfully. "Real bacon from real pigs."

"Keep your bacon," Kevin says. "Popcorn. Chocolate."

"Muscle cars," Phil says.

"Yeah. Real makeup."

"Oh, don't get me started with the women. High heels. Perfume."

"Helicopters."

"Coolers. We'd put ice in a cooler," Phil says, and turns to Harper. "– a plastic thermal box – and put that on the tailgate of our trucks at the football game, with a grill, for steak or burgers."

"Pickup trucks," Kevin says. "Them too."

"You know what I miss the most," Phil says, and it's not a question, because he's going to tell us. "It's silly, really, it's the candy bars we used to get. Mounds. Almond Joy."

"Oh, yeah," Kevin says. "Coconut. It's funny when you crave things you don't even really know why."

They have forgotten for a moment about Harper, Pablo and I, their eyes misty as Pablo sets out our breakfast.

"Not to mention they all talk in code," Phil says. "It's like they never say what they mean, eh Pablo?"

"Don't look at me, old man. I'm a different generation," Pablo says.

"It's not their fault," Harper says. "It's a sign of the times. They're afraid to say anything in case it's being recorded."

"We need someone young here," Kevin says. "Like a 'youth translator'."

"I'm ... what? Old?" Harper says, offended.

"You're young and cute, but you might as well be one of us," Phil says. "You and your brother. Hanging out with us all day, you even talk like us. I hear kids on the street, and I don't understand a word."

"Pocky," Kevin says. "What the feck is pocky?"

"Stupid. Inane. Contrary," Harper says. "To say someone is a 'pocker' is to say they're an idiot, like a 'plonker'."

"Okay, but there's more-" Pablo says.

"Ya. There's more to it," Harper says. "It's a derogatory term. Came from p-o-c ... or 'people of colour', referring to us."

"That's awful! I didn't know that," Phil says.

"It's not that new," she says.

"'Sod' is British," Phil says. "And waysux, and wayblows. 'Lift' for elevator, and tram, and lorry for truck."

"It was all the Brits who came over when the UK fell to the commies," Kevin says. "Calling us 'Yankies', and 'Sammies'."

"Feck, and boyo, and capital-"

"They don't use 'boyo' any more," Harper says. "That was a few years ago."

"So why do they say - 'But wait ... there's more', and 'have another', like it's one word?"

"They're memes. Resurrected from dark holes on the hive," Harper says.

"Why don't they leave them in the dark-" Phil says.

Kevin interrupts. "It's a way to show they're 'deep', which is another slang, that they're 'in the know', it's code for them to judge experience."

"Is that why nobody uses their last names?" Phil asks.

"That's different," Harper says. "Women had to stop using their last names in the first generations of companion because men would do hot searches, and stalk them. So everyone holds back their last name until it's safe."

"What's your last name?" Kevin asks me.

"Purdy," I say.

"Party?" Harper says. I'm about to repeat when she cracks a smile.

"More like 'pretty' in the deep south," I say.

"Rufus Paaaarty," she says, over-pronouncing, "was the one that was on the news as the longest AFK in history. Do you remember that?"

"Second longest, actually," I say.

"I remember!" Kevin says. "I bet Phil he'd be shitting himself and hearing voices within the week."

"Well I'm not shitting myself," I say. "Thanks for the vote of confidence."

"Here, don't listen to them. Come with me. I have something to show you!"

"What?"

"Just … something. It's important," she says, and takes my hand to lead me down into the basement of the building. From the stairs there is a long central hall, all cinder block walls with no windows. There are rooms off the hall, used for storage, it seems – crates of canned goods, boxes of paper towels and tissue, and cleaning solvents, an entire room full of chairs and mattresses, and another full of desks and tables. She takes out some old keys to open a sliding steel door to one of the rooms. When she flicks on the lights, I'm spellbound. It's her studio. She has an ordered chaos, with paintings on easels in all different states of completion. There are paint tubes, and partly filled coloured containers everywhere.

Some of the sketches are of Kevin and Phil, and then others are oil paintings of Oliver, and several studies, sketches of kids playing on the street. I take my time with each one, to understand what inspired her. I am awed, drawn in by the strokes in the eyes, and I picture her painting them. I am amazed that she has so much talent. Her portraits are so life-like, so accurate, like a photo. She's put so much into the detail, the hairs and skin, and the colour. I can't believe how perfect they are in exactly the way I thought I wanted to see in the gallery. In one corner are bundles of dried flowers, that in the paintings are vibrant and alive. She's following my interest, looking at what I'm looking at. "This is what I do," she says. "Do you like them?"

"I love them! You should be selling these for lots of money."

"I wish. Dep-Cult won't even look at my portfolio. I'm too much of an 'ethnic' painter for them. So it all sits here."

"That's horrible. You should open a gallery."

She shakes her head. "They won't issue a license. This is the one I'm working on right now," she says, and I look at the huge canvas before her. It's a Philly street in winter, with bold colours of beautiful woollen mitts and scarves and toques, like a snowball fight, with kids all over, and a blue sky like the cold crisp days in January, marked with vapour trails.

This is gorgeous.

Harper is quiet for a moment, then shows me another. "I love this one, too," I say. It's a portrait of Kevin, his unruly hair and wry smile captured perfectly. "I love how it is unmistakable. It takes a lot of discipline and control." I turn to another painting, an abstract, and it's unsettling, but I can't figure out why. It's like a portrait of insecurity and doubt, with sadness and anxiety in the eyes. "Who's this?"

"Oliver."

"I don't like this one," I say. "It's uncomfortable."

"I'm glad you said that!" she says. "I hate it when people tell me that they love it, without telling me why, because they're afraid to tell me. I know when they're being honest. Guys who want to sleep with me are the least trustworthy. I mean, if they're just telling me they like my work because they want in my pants, then I have to compensate for that. This one is supposed to make you feel awful."

"Well, it works, but I still don't like it. Now, I have to also say that just because I don't like it doesn't mean I don't want in your pants."

She laughs. "I figured you did. You're pretty easy to read."

"Really?"

"You are! This one is abstract because I wanted to portray people in other people's dreams, but everything I did seemed just … bad. It all looked awful. I couldn't bear to let anyone even look at. So I tried and tried, and finally it kept getting more and more abstract."

"Hm. Well…"I say.

"So you don't like abstract," she says.

"I don't know … I guess just don't understand it."

"In a society that tells us what to paint, and how to paint it, abstract is the purest form of freedom and rebellion, to put on the canvas whatever we want, and to paint our emotions, as raw as we want, so that they can't control it."

"I guess I judge art by how it portrays something, which is probably wrong, but it's the only thing I have to go on. Otherwise, I just have feelings. I've never really trusted my feelings."

"Well, you should," she says. "If I want to portray feeling, rather than paint a scene, it's the purest form of expression. Art is all about feeling. Painting shouldn't be about discipline and control. It should be about passion. There's too much control already."

"It brings up interesting questions about AI art," I say. "The AI is free. It creates. Does it have to be self-aware to create art, or does it take a stimulus from the environment and emulate the emotional responses without knowing why? Who's to say, with that imprinted message at the gallery, that the robot didn't just run a hive data mine for emotional responses to create something risky and shocking. What 's worse is it could have been a test, to identify potential revolutionaries."

She is shocked, and puts a finger to her chin. "Now you're really over-thinking," she says, but she seems troubled. "Do you think she was following us?"

"I know she was," I say.

* * *

Chapter 4

This time I see her face as she's standing behind the desk, and I'm looking down at her breasts, which must be frustrating for her. I am not in control again. Is this my own dream? I don't know what to trust. I have no connection. No companion. Surely I have some control. What I want to do is go back to the actual moment that Harper said 'You're coming with me,' so I can smell her hair and look into her eyes, and kiss her.

This is the rain-forest. The Georgian revival house is in the depths of a cavern, surrounded by trees. As I creep around, I'm looking for some sort of weapon, but it's not one of these dreams where I need it to fend off an animal. No. In cold calculation, I go up the stairs, and check drawers. I find a sword, a beautiful military cutlass to be precise, and I take it down off the mantle, while she says "theft. That's theft-" and then she talks to the police dispatcher, and tries to get behind her desk from me. I have the sword held out in front of me, like I'm some sort of samurai or something. I don't like where this is going.

I override the dream, replace the sword onto the mantle, and descend the stairs, out into the forest, just off the porch. I'm covered in blood. It's spattered on my clothing, and shoes and in my hair and on my face. I find the most beautiful waterfall I've ever seen, with a clear blue pool below. I strip naked, and stand under the frigid water, letting it wash the blood away, scrubbing through my hair and off my skin, and I walk out of the pool, but my clothing is not where I left it. Nothing is where I remember it. And I'm cold now. The sun is not hot, but distant.

I wake up kicking, and wrestling. Blankets have wound around my waist and arm. I still smell the earthy rain-forest, and feel for the pebbles clinging to my feet. My apartment is quiet. My desire comes on hard and fast. I want to just chill out with a good dream about Harper and I making out in the old Mustang on a deserted road. But alone, I can't conjure it up. I can't even remember Harper's eyes.

I'm sure it's going to take a long time to have my own dreams. But I don't even know what my own dreams will be. I can't remember what I dreamed about as a kid. I can't remember when all this started to change, or how much control I ever had, but now, here, it seems like I am decidedly not in control. Of anything.

There is a knock on the door, and it is so forceful it startles me. Police? HeeBees? It's been a very long time since I ordered anything, and I'm not used to deliveries any more. I turn the hall light on – the power is on – and I open the door.

"Package for Rufus Purdy."

"That's me."

He retinals me, and hands me the brown paper box, taps his hat, and turns to leave, hailing a pod on his way to the street. The package is from Soc-Serv, and I open it in the kitchen to find a new glass, complete with two spherical ear pieces, which I assume is to talk and hear without implant or companion. It'll be hell setting up all the apps, and I'm not ready for social media, but I have access to my bank account. I've been credited for the entire time I was AFK. It's a lot. Thousands.

I go to the bank and withdraw half, to have just in case I'm forced offline again. As I'm at the teller, I can see men I recognize from the art gallery, and the Soc-Serv, which is odd. Why would they be there at those two nearly unrelated places? I watch one pretty girl on the street, and she passes another guy who looks familiar. He's not someone I know, he's ... someone I saw in the pub, when I was with Mason and the others. I can't remember ever speaking to him, but I know him. He's following me. When I was at the diner he was there, and then after, I saw him again at Soc-Serv. But why? I didn't do anything wrong. I've never tried to get away with anything. I did what Mom told me, and what my bosses told me, and worked hard. I've always been a rule-follower.

Am I going to be taken away? Tortured? I imagine that they're waiting for the right moment to stuff me into the back of a pod, waterboard me, or pull out my fingernails. I'm prepared to tell them anything, but I don't know anything. I wonder, if I was to run, would they take me down? I need somewhere to observe them. Somewhere public. Somewhere I haven't been before, so I can watch them. I walk. I see another man across the street, who looks like he's stopping when I stop. Are they police? HeeBees? If I disappeared, nobody would come looking. I've already dropped off once before. They would assume it happened again. I'm nobody. I'm a stranger. Anyone who thinks they know me, knows only a veneer.

There is more to me than this.

I duck into a nearby Cuppa Costa on a whim. The place is immaculate. Dark stained wood tabletops, and forged-iron chairs, perfect globe lighting and a bank of windows facing the street. Shrubs. Images of coffee plants on the walls, and paintings of the perfect coffee brewing system, broken down scientifically, illustrated with measurements like a shop drawing.

There are few places in Philly to get actual coffee without soy or caffeine, carob or tea, or vegetable pulp added, like joe. Here you can actually watch them roast it and grind it and press steam through it. It is real coffee. My mother drank coffee, before it became scarce, and as soon as I enter, I recognize the familiar scent.

I sit in the window seat, feeling like a fraud. Sure, when I had a companion, I could justify spending money in a place like this, though I never did. I could do what I liked. But now, I'm thinking of Phil and Kevin, having fought for America, eating boiled meals and drinking cheap joe. I think of how far this money would go, and I'm afraid to go to the counter. Even being here feels like a betrayal. I can't see any prices, and when I sit in the window and try to look it up on my pocket glass, their hive site is confusing.

People here are dressed in natural fibres and leather boots, and smelling like perfume and cologne. There must be still a lot of money in Philly. I imagine the men are lawyers and government employees from the nearby Trump Federal complex, with gold watches, and ties that shimmer with precious metal woven threads, and pristine shoes, shined up despite the snow. They are impatient to be served, having each their own conversations with people who are probably far away. The girls wear dresses, with hair-scarves of real silk, and diamond hoop earrings. They are either rich students spending their parents money, or professionals, their faces powdered neutral for their makeup apps, which I can't see. In fact I'm far happier looking at women without my companion now, because I actually see them. I'm not seeing social profiles, or things they've done in the news or on their pages. It's bizarre that women seem to hate the Samanthas, but somehow also want to be like them. Their faces have that same powdered flatness, and the way they flirt is practised, with predictable signals delivered at the right times. It all seems fake, but perhaps this is how women lost men's attention after the invention of Samanthas and birth control hormones? It's all about sex and not connection.

I turn to look out the window to see the same guy across the street, leaning on the door frame of an antique repair shop. They can't see me behind the mirrored logo, but I can watch them. I hunker down to find the others in the reflection off my glass, in position on either side of the street. I'm sure that's not a coincidence. Maybe they want me to know I'm being followed, so that I panic and do something foolish, or they're confusing me with someone else. I'm sure for people with companions they have some kick-ass software that alters their features, but to me they are wearing all the same bland, grey, non-branded clothing and generic almost-trendy fashion. What's the usual thing to do when people are following you? Run? Carry on? My heart is thudding.

There's one, who I call 'Ooh, watch me', because he wears an actual watch on his wrist. For a guy who's trying to blend in, to have a luxury item like that seems idiotic. He has an almost pathological fixation on that damn watch. I'd put money down that it's an interface with the headquarters of whoever they're working for. I'd probably look all the time if I had one, too. If they really wanted to disappear, they'd stare off into space like everyone else, and mimic being spelled.

Another one, a younger guy, looks like he'd be happier on the university campus, trying to get into cheerleaders pants. He's wearing a Philly's hat, though they haven't won the pennant since I was a kid, like, seventeen years ago. Vest. He's a pretty boy, and notices every woman who passes. I call him 'Cap'.

I get up and stand in line. The employees at CuppaCosta are not spelled. They are, so I've heard, not allowed to spell out when they are working, so that the customer experience is full, with someone to joke with, and to personally react to. I should think of applying here, since without my companion, I would be perfect for it. The girl behind the counter is a cute young ginger, with freckles, and she's efficient, charming even, with the older lady before me in line. I'm next.

"Hi there, what can I get for you?" she says to me.

"How much is a latte?"

"Nine Republic euros," she says.

"Nine Bits? Wow. How much for the kilo of beans?"

"Those are forty-two," she says. I look at the tags on the pastry below. Six for a cookie. That would be almost an hour of my work, my labour, for a cookie baked in an oven just like the ones I can get for a half-euro in the grocery store.

"I'll take the beans," I say. It must be wonderful not to have to worry about money, or about any of this struggle for that matter, to be completely insulated.

She pulls them down off the shelf for me, and carefully wraps them in craft paper. I pay cash. I am still using Mason's money. He is protected by his generosity – or, rather, the potential for his generosity – preferring to lay low until people need him. Mason believes that people are only welcome in his life if they fulfill a specific function. Women are always welcome if they're cute. He treats them as pets and objects, to use and discard. No doubt he would try to pick this girl up. Jumblies. Look at the set of lungs. Hot beef dip.

It's no wonder Mason is the way he is. He's afraid of what happens if he loses his edge, and he believes, because of his father's wealth, and his connections, that he's better than us. His success is contrary to everything I believe, which is that good people eventually succeed. Why is he my friend? All my life I've treated people with respect, assumed that we are equals from the first moment. He grew up near me, in a nicer house, but nearby. Same school. Same childhood, really, except that his father joined the party early. I'm starting to believe that was the right approach. I have nothing, and he has everything. Perhaps only heartless sociopaths can find success.

I exit out onto the street, and carry the beans under my coat. I'm not sure if they require special care, but it is exhilarating, carrying them like a secret to the Veteran Co-op. Actual Hawaiian Kona. But I can't go directly. Cap and Watchme are still following, a good distance behind. Why should I stop doing anything, if I haven't done anything wrong? I wonder if it's because I tried to help the protesters.

I need confirmation. Absolute proof. I dodge into an alley, sprint the length of it, heart pumping, and I duck into an alcove, press myself back against a brick wall that stinks of piss and garbage, and I wait. Cap goes running past me, notices me, hesitates, nearly trips, and then keeps running slower now, as if aimless. I follow him, catching up at the end of the alley. He's trying to pull off looking like he wasn't just running full bore to find me.

"Are you alright?" I say.

"Who? Me? I'm fine. My dog just got off the leash and I'm looking for him."

"Oh. I haven't seen a dog come this way," I say. "But if you give me your details I'll call you if I see it."

"No. No thanks," he says. "I think I see it over there." He walks away without looking back. He's not carrying a leash.

I cut down Forty-Fourth, away from him, and into another alley, and then backtrack into an old lane that leads to all the garages and back yards of the row houses behind, and then I cut back north to Powelton, and steer toward Lee Park. I'm pretty sure if they're good at this they'll still find me, micro-drone following, so I go underground into the Fortieth street station, cross the platform, and exit farther west, then continue along Market. At the Veteran Co-op, Pablo is behind the counter.

"Hey ... Rufus is back. You hungry?"

"Not just now. I have a surprise for the guys."

"Oh ya?"

I produce the coffee from my coat, and slide it over the counter for him, and he looks at it for a moment without touching it. "Can you brew it?" I ask.

"I sure can," he says, and picks it up off the counter. "I haven't had real coffee in twenty years."

I watch Pablo go through the cupboards for a grinder and coffee maker. He pulls out all the implements, and washes them. He takes his time.

"Where's Harper? Is she in yet?"

"She's working upstairs. She'll be down in a bit. How much did those cost you?"

"A lot. Worth every euro. Should I let the guys know?" I ask.

"Oh, you don't have to. They'll smell this and think they're dreaming, then they'll high-tail it out here."

As soon as the water gurgles through the coffee maker, Phil opens his door, and then rushes down to the kitchen, Harper following. She dumps a big bag of laundry in the chute, and I get up to hug her. She kisses my forehead, and suddenly I'm drunk on her scent, her hair loosely enveloping me. She smells wonderful. I don't want to let go.

"I brought a present," I say.

"Is that what I think it is?" Phil asks.

"It sure is," Pablo says.

Kevin is right behind them. "You sure you know how to make it? Didn't feck it up?"

"Just grab a mug, you grumpy old bastard."

"I've never had real coffee before," Harper says.

"Neither have I," I say.

When I sit down, she doesn't back away, but sits on the arm of my chair, her legs against my lap, and I want so badly just to pull her closer. I put my hand on her waist, and she glances to me and smiles. "I can't wait to try this."

Pablo pours us each a mug, creams and sugars them, and passes them out. I take the mug in both hands, smell it first, and it's different from joe. I can see how they were trying to get at the same flavour, but this is more earthy, bitter, and nutty.

Harper tries it and makes a sour face. "Hm..."

"Oh that's good," Phil says.

"Real cream. Real sugar. Only way, Man," Pablo says.

"Thank you," Phil says. "It's a wonderful memory for a bunch of old guys who felt like we'd been forgotten."

"Just like you remember?" Pablo asks.

"Great job, Kid," Kevin says, his eyes wet.

Oliver enters the hall from the stairwell. He sniffs the air. "Real coffee? It smells like rich white people in here!" He laughs.

"It does!" I say.

"Rufus! It's great to see you! I'm so glad you're here!" he says, and we bro-hug, clapping each others shoulders.

"Where did you get that?"

"Oh, never mind. Just enjoy." Pablo says, and pours him a mug.

"What the feck?" Harper says. I look where she's looking, toward a commotion across the street, where an Asian woman from the convenience store is yelling at a man in her doorway, trying to move him with the end of her broom. He has both his hands up as if apologizing. He turns to look at us, and starts walking down the sidewalk.

It's Cap. They found me.

"I don't want you to panic," I say quietly. I feel my face flush, and I take Harper's hand.

"I never panic," she says.

"I think I'm being followed." Even the words seem dire to me, like just saying them is to invite wrath.

Oliver and Harper exchange a look of concern, and his eyes dart to the front windows.

"Maybe because of the protest," I say.

"What protest?" Oliver asks. "When did you notice them?"

"A couple of days ago. I swear I'm not just being paranoid. There was a protest when Harper and I went to the movies."

"I didn't hear this story," Pablo says.

"Kids dropped on campus. We were right there," Harper says. "They questioned us."

"That explains it," Pablo says.

"There was no protest," I say. "One kid, holding up his fist."

"They need the illusion of protest, just like the illusion of order. This is an entire society of illusion," Oliver says. "The truth is dead."

"But we had nothing to do with that," Harper says. "They saw it on their glass. What are they going to do, arrest us for helping some kids?"

Oliver gets up and closes the curtains. "It's never that simple. There has to be something that they want to know about you that they don't already. Otherwise they'd pull you into a van and nobody would see you again. They hold all the cards," Oliver says. "The problems is that the hive is an all-powerful intelligence that can do whatever it wants, and not even the state can stop it. These investigators could be spelled. You could drop dead right now from ... what ... targeted pathogens? Death rays? Micro tracking bots that lodge in the arteries? Drone strike by the Heebees made to look like terror?"

I'm panicking. I can see all the possibilities. I am counting the hours until they stuff me in a pod and then take me out to the country to shoot me. Cap crosses the street, and hails a pod, then the other two walk away. They know we see them. Maybe they can hear us. "What do we do? What if you're in danger? I should never have come here. I'm so sorry-" I say.

"Calm down," Harper says. "They probably just want information."

"I hate this-"

"I know," Oliver says. "I feel it too. It's risk. All of it. You didn't choose to be spelled for that long, just like you're not choosing to be followed now. Choice was taken away from you, just like it was taken away from Harper and I when our father was taken. You have to ask yourself what you would do with the choice if it were offered."

"I don't know what I would do."

"I'm going to tell you something. I want you to consider it carefully."

"Alright."

"Life is about risk. If we risk nothing, we are still in danger just as if we had. Do you want to feel like you have a choice?"

"Yes. I want to be in control."

"Then come with me," he says. "I have something to show you." I follow Oliver down the stairs, past Harper's studio to the end of the hall where another steel door is locked with a padlock. There are two rooms off the end of the basement hall, the other direction from Harper's studio. One is an old lounge, with pool tables and dart boards, and an empty bar. There's an airtight woodstove that's piled high with bankers boxes.

Oliver opens a pair of sliding metal doors to reveal an apartment, a bright and warm space, with couches, and a table, and bookshelves made of wooden planks on cinder block. There are posters on the walls, for old films I don't recognize. There are string lights up along the bookshelf tops, and paper lanterns in the shape of birds, dragons, and sailing ships, hanging from the ceiling. Oliver has books. Shelves of actual books, with bizarre titles I've never seen. 'Cloud Atlas', 'Tender is the Night', 'Il Federale', and 'Los Muertes'. In one of the other rooms, behind another steel door, amid a pile of papers and an old glass, are more books, carelessly left on every surface, piled up and leaning against each other. On his desk are 'We', 'Love in the Fog of the Future', and 'Utopia'.

"It's not you they're after. It's Harper and I," he says, and closes the sliding door behind us with a thud. "See, we aren't who we seem. I'm sorry to have drawn you into this, but we've been on their watch list for a long time."

"Why?"

"Because of the Guide, and the Book of Life," he says. "Because I'm learning, and we're learning, and there are more and more of us joining every day."

"Joining what?"

"My choice, the one I made after my father was taken, was to mourn him, and then to honour him. So to honour him I carried on his life work. I didn't have the same education or background, and I was catching up to his forty years of obsessive research, but I still had to be brave and jump in."

"What was he looking for?"

"The truth."

"I don't see how any of that-" I say, feeling obtuse.

"They don't know any of this is down here," he says. He's bouncing with excitement. "My father knew the Guide, who he called 'AB'. I think those were his initials. They wrote the programs for the ethical foundation of hive. Government was concerned that the AI would become self-aware, and in its self-awareness would learn to learn exponentially faster than humans. The Guide was a man, an ethicist, tasked with teaching the AI never to kill off humanity. There are no photos of the Guide, no name to put to the work. He was rumoured to have been lost in one of the first attempts to imprint morality and ethics on the hive. I discovered an essay in his papers. I kept digging for old books, that led me to other books, and essays. Whatever I could find. All his digital work was deleted during the purges. They said it was treason. But not his notes. In them, he breaks down all the failings of America, from the working class frustration to the hatred of learning, fear of immigrants, to the obsession with Islam."

"What's Islam?"

"An old religion that went underground when Asia fell and the Republic took over. There was a great war of terror fought for hundreds of years to suppress it, and the Republic won. The Hurriya Front believes in Islam."

"But if they are all the way over there, why didn't we just keep to ourselves?"

"Oil. We used to invade other countries in the name of freedom. After we cooled the planet and didn't need the oil, America needed an enemy, so we could still fund the military. Our actions turned the world against us. Terrorists aren't crazy. They don't just decide one day that they hate our 'freedom. It's not just some made-up thing, but an echo from the darkness in our own past. They bombed our malls and stadiums because we invaded their land to control the oil. We blew up their hospitals and schools, killed their children, and waged war for generations on their soil. The Heritage Party doesn't want this to be known. They lie to tap into that G-bro hatred, and fear, and laziness, and to stir them up to gain popularity, and stay in power through solving problems that they create."

"Still? Even now?" I say. I'm perplexed. I always learned we were fighting against tyranny, but I don't know who to trust any more.

"History, of course, creates the present. That's why they control it. It gives them power. There was a great schizm in America, with one side, mostly the rural south and mid-west, trying to return to a segregated society, with the wealthy on top, and all others enmeshed in paid servitude, struggling against each other."

"The Guide knew this?"

"The Guide was a person, just like you and I, and like Jesus two thousand years ago. There are parallels between the Guide and Jesus. Both preached that we should be kind, and help the poor, and that we should honour a higher power. They came from places of kindness and non-violence."

"Then why did we end up with such injustice and violence?"

"Systems. People in power. We don't know the Guide's real intention. In fact, we know more about Jesus than about the Guide. In the purges they expunged all information about him, and replaced him with a fabricated history. I can guess, and from what I've read of my father's notes, the Guide had all the best intentions. And that's where you come in. We have a chance to talk directly to the system instead of talking to the government."

"Me?"

"You said you talk to the Guide. Directly. There are only so many people whodo. In fact, we were starting to think it wasn't even possible, that it was a myth, until we met you."

"But that was my companion. It's just dreams. I don't speak to the guide since I disconnected. I have no influence-"

"But you do have influence. You have more influence than you think. Greater ideas have their own momentum and weight. Simply by believing things, it changes the fabric of society. See, woke used to mean something completely different. It wasn't about being off the companions. It was long before companions when it referred to being aware of the world in the greater sense, knowing that there is privilege and power and influence in all the larger issues that affect our daily lives."

"But they control everything. Most people can't even think anything bad about the state because they'll be altered for re-education. Sure, I'd like to know the truth," I say, "but not if it gets us all killed." I'm thinking, suddenly, of my father, and what happened to him.

"Nobody can just give you the truth. You recognize it, like greeting an old friend. You have to dig it out, bring it to the daylight, to find it yourself, so you can always find it again. It used to be that everyone voted. We all could decide on our fate. Women voted. We all had the ability to change our political leaders."

Now I'm perplexed, even more than I was before. Perhaps the only reason they wanted me around was my connection to the Guide, to attempt to win it over.

"There's another section to the Book of Life," he says, and reaches down under the desk. He produces a wooden box, then unlocks it with a small key. From the box he pulls out a worn and dirty book with a torn cover, and a smudge on the profile.

The Book of Life. "I've never seen one," I say.

"I could be killed just for having it. It's the old version that talks about 'Jesus' and the bible."

I recognize the cover, the image they showed on the big glass when they read from it in elementary school. "What do you mean the 'old version'?"

"They've been changing the words," he says.

"What?"

"In the broadcasts and the quotations. This, the original, is our touch-stone, from before the Heritage Party took power, when everything was free. To the AI, the words are just expedient, to elicit a response, to manage society better. But to the people who wrote it, it meant something. As a kid, I remember my father looked everywhere when the new version went online, and a few years ago, I obtained one. I read the whole thing. It's not the Book of Life that they quote, but something else."

There is someone coming down the stairs. We both hear it at the same time.

"Quick," he says, and opens a cupboard. "In here!" I squeeze inside, and he throws the book in onto my lap and closes me in there with a thud. I can feel the cold of the cinder block foundation. It's dark – I can see only the crack of light between the doors, but not through to the room beyond. The book is in the fold of my body between my thighs and stomach. I'm afraid to move. Then suddenly there is someone standing beside the cupboard door. I can see the light change and play when their shadows pass over the crack.

"We need an emergency meeting," the man says.

"Now?"

"Yes now. I've already asked everyone out. They're on their way. Since the last meeting there's been a breach. They know about us. They've been following Martin."

"Don't use names," Oliver says.

"Sorry, Brother. Sorry. I just-" Something falls, a plastic something, with a clatter.

"Can we go into another room?" Oliver asks. I'm sure now they aren't HeeBees.

"This is the room where we speak," the man replies. "Where we are safe."

"Why bring us all to one place? If we are in danger, then now we are in more danger." I can hear the anger and disappointment in Oliver's voice. He knows the police are outside. I've put them all at risk.

"I-" he hesitates. "I'm sorry brother, I didn't know what else to do."

"Wait. They're coming-" Oliver says. I hear feet shuffling on the floor, and then there are more footsteps on the stairs, more voices echoing.

"Maybe that was a mistake. We need to-"

"Did you not get my message?" Oliver interrupts. There is a long pause. "Now we have to deal with this."

I estimate, from the noise and the voices, that there are probably twenty people here, all talking at once. I'm picturing a circle in my head, with all of them facing the centre. There are no greetings, no friendly catching up. They pull chairs up, and drag them and set them with scrapes and clunks, and then all is quiet.

"We have a crisis, Brothers and Sisters. We have been infiltrated, and betrayed. It's only a matter of time before we are picked off and sent to the work camps. If we are to make any of this worthwhile, we must act-"

The whole room bursts into argument.

"-lay low-"

"What do we know of-"

"-disperse-"

"Start with questions."

"Is he alright?"

Nobody uses names. They call each other 'brother', and 'sister' so that it's a natural reflex. They call out passionate points, and nobody concedes the floor.

"If we don't act now!"

"-great risk if we do-"

A coalition of shushers comes together, and eventually after much back and forth, the voices recede. A man now has the floor, continuing a previous thought. "This is history in the making, my Brother. Mark my words, that someday a great upheaval will liberate us from this nightmare. What state doesn't answer to their people, eventually?"

"Sisters and Brothers, there has to be another way," a woman says. The group quiets. "-Our forefathers dumped tea into Boston harbour in protest, and wrote a declaration that included equality and liberty, rang the Liberty Bell in this very city, not to celebrate independence, but to declare it before the battle was even fought. It wasn't a victorious ending, but a beginning, calling people to action, setting out our right ... nay, our responsibility."

"We all know this," a man says. "Now is not the time to be discussing the past. Now is the time to be making concrete plans."

"We will change nothing with violence-"

"-I disagree!"

Now my ass is cold, and there's not enough height in the cupboard for me to adjust quietly. I must be cutting off circulation. My legs are cramping, and I'm not sure how long I can be still. Even if they're not HeeBees, I don't want to get caught. I don't know these people. I have nowhere to run. They could kill me.

"If we destroy the hive," another woman says, "the media will follow, and fair elections will fall into place."

"I disagree," repeats another man. "Even in a fair election, their thugs keep us at home."

"He's right! The Brotherhood are out of control. They will kill us if they find out."

"I believe if we delay even for one more day, one more hour, we will be unable to act at all. Everything that we have worked toward will be lost."

"We will not undertake any action unless we agree on it," a woman retorts. I can't even keep track of who is who.

"I fail to see why we should show restraint, when our enemies do not."

"Because they are still Americans."

"What would you have us do? Watch while they shoot us, and our children? We get fewer and fewer, and they get more and more. We are being bred, and tortured, and killed, and jailed out of existence."

"If the government can kill us, then can we not kill them? We are not even bringing a gun to this gunfight! We are bringing a blindfold," he says. "Our ancestors fought real slavery. Yoke and whip, and lynchings. Every system has its coercion. In this system, it's the hive."

"No problem goes away when we add violence." Oliver says. "It only goes underground until the next opportunity for vengeance."

"They will continue as long as they have power! It's up to us to stand up to them, like our forefathers fought for freedom."

"We'd be wise to disperse and hide, and come back later when things are safer," a woman says.

"When will they be safer?" another says. "Not ever."

"The police are in every glass, every pod, and every surveillance camera. Companions are making assassins of everyone. We will never be free as long as there is a hive."

I have to turn my foot. I move it, and clunk into the cupboard door and stop, stock-still. It doesn't help my leg. I need to stand. Everything they are saying makes sense, and I'd love to come out and argue with them, figure out what they – we – should do next. I feel as if I'm witnessing history, like I'm almost part of some great change.

"But is this plan going to accomplish that?"

"We have only one plan!"

"Why are you so afraid to destroy it? It isn't a person, with a body. We are just unplugging it."

"And if we succeed?" another woman says. "Millions of people – real, flesh-and-blood people like you and I – could die. Do you want that blood on your hands? You know in your heart that what I say is true. We cannot become terrorists and thugs like them."

"What separates terrorists from freedom fighters?."

"What you propose will turn them against us. People will die here."

"People are dying, and the media has already turned them against us."

Oliver speaks again. "I respect your opinion, but I believe that without allies we are doomed to descend into further violence. We have been preaching that human beings are created equal, as was taught by our wise forefathers. Everyone has the right to fairness, equality, liberty, security of their person, and the right to speak our minds, regardless of the colour of our skin. All of which, brothers and sisters, we are being denied. Let us live it, so that we can set an example for our brethren as well, so that they, too, can learn to live in peace as we one day hope to. If we go ahead with our plan, we will be terrorists. It will turn everyone against us."

"We're not talking about violence against people. This is violence where it is needed, for all humanity, because it is the hive that enslaves us. All of us! Even those without companions."

"It's not right!" another woman calls out.

"-Where are the other cells, who haven't done a damn thing? They can help!"

"What about Nya Karsholm, or the leadership? Technically this is their territory."

"No," Oliver says. "We are compromised. If we contact them, it could expose the whole movement."

"I will not kill innocent people," another, close to the cupboard, says.

"Look, I understand the sentiment, Sister, but we are in a fight for our lives."

"-It's like I was telling you about the Sir George William's sit-in, from that old paper-"

"A sit-in! There aren't enough of us to take over the hive, even for an hour let alone a few days..."

"A sit-in with our allies!"

"They are not using people sitting! They are using clubs, and mace, and guns, and mind-control!"

"I thought we agreed this would be the plan-" a man says, with great disappointment.

Another voice quiets everyone, a man. "All we need is a catalyst to show the people that revolution is possible, to put us over the edge into that delicious chaos. We don't have to do it all right here, now. We just have to push it in the right direction."

"And I agree with you. I just don't believe now is the right time," Oliver says. "We can't just jump to this plan until we know it's going to do some good. There's no use in doing this with no following plan-"

"...and I'm saying if we don't do this, we'll never do it. There will never be a full plan that works, never a time when it all comes together. The longer we argue, the more time it gives them to catch us. All of us are in danger because it's only a matter of time before they crack our brother in custody."

"What do you propose for us, after we've done this?" Oliver asks.

"What do you mean?"

"These are our lives you're playing with – just because you can do this doesn't mean you should," a woman says.

"So we do nothing," the man says, and I hear his hands smack, on fabric like he's slapping his thigh. "We can't wait for someone else to save us. There's nobody outside the system. The whole world is the system, and it is controlled by very few people with all the power. If we don't do it, nobody else will."

"There are others, have faith-"

"You mark my words, Brother. This has been our last meeting. I'd love to be proven wrong, but events will be otherwise. Maybe not tonight, or tomorrow, but by the end of the week, the world will be very different."

"I also worry that if we strike at the hive, it will think there's no further value to human life, and we will lose all capacity to pull back from our course, even if we later regret it."

"Go home," Oliver says. "Go and be careful. Do what you have to do. Stay safe. Hide. We will meet soon with guidance."

It takes some time to say their tearful solemn goodbyes. I'm reeling with all that Oliver told me, and what I heard in the meeting. Our entire history is different than what I learned in school, and now I feel involved. Oliver is trusting me with all this, but he doesn't know me. And I don't really know him. Maybe the whole thing is a trap, like the 'woke' image in the painting. The HeeBees are baiting me with a pretty girl, and I'm falling for it. Playing games. But why? Now they've put this whole meeting in front of me. They are all actors, I'm sure. Agents. They are creating this to pull me in and find out what I know. But what do I know? Nothing. Nothing about nothing. All my life has been a lie.

It is torture I fear most. I am shaking now. Afraid. I listen for clues about their intentions. Every metallic object sounds like an implement of torture. Every pause is to figure out what to do with me.

Finally, the last of them leave. After a few quiet moments Oliver opens the cupboard doors. I turn and put my feet on the floor, but I can't stand yet. My left foot is numb. The light seems very bright. Oliver leans down, puts one of my arms over his shoulder, and helps me up. My left leg, which was against the stone, nearly buckles with pins-and-needles.

"Thank you for being quiet," he says.

"Why didn't you let me out before?"

"To be honest, I thought it was the police. That's why I threw the book in with you. I couldn't even chance them finding you."

"What was all that?"

"You need to swear not to speak about it."

"I swear."

"Never. To anyone," he says, imploring with his eyes.

"I swear."

He rubs his palm over his hair, and down his forehead to his eyes where he rubs them also. "Even in the movement there are disagreements over how to achieve our goals. We resolve them by talking out the philosophy of non-violence. Last meeting we argued about whether or not AI is life."

"I don't follow," I say.

"If it's just a simulation, a program, incapable of feelings ... if it's not-life, then we can take it down without violating our oath of non-violence. If we consider it life, then we have a much harder task ahead of us, which is winning it over to our side for its own sake."

"I'm not sure how that applies-" I say. He doesn't seem to be answering, but is imagining some other unasked question.

"We survive under the radar, so we can gain strength. This whole thing, at first, was for people off the hive to buy and sell goods, and to function in society. It's grown now to the point where we can challenge the system by winning over, or destroying the hive."

"Can it be won over? Is that even possible?" I ask. I'm still reeling.

"If it really is intelligent, then it can be reasoned with, and I believe that with the right arguments, it can be won over. But we are running out of time. The only question is, how?"

* * *

Chapter 5

I am sitting with Sophie at a fireplace in a log cabin. There is snow falling outside, and we have mugs of hot chocolate, and woolly sweaters on, and slippers, and everything is perfect. Stone fireplace. Snowboards lean beside the door. I know this is Whistler, though I have never been there, because I used to select it from the options on the companion. My companion is back, and not only are the regular options there, but there are new options. Locations never offered. Kingsessing and the Naval Yard. Elkton, and Chester, and Wilmington, as if anyone would want to be spelled and go there, given the choice.

There are menus for everything from drinks to temperature, to Sophie's clothing. I choose a skirt for her, and thigh-high tights, and then a red Yule dress that replaces the skirt, frilled in white fur, and then she is wearing it. I run my hand up her thigh, and reach over to pull her closer, and when I hesitate, she grabs me by the collar, and just like that, I'm not feeling it. I look around to see details of things, but they're ill-defined. The companion wants me to focus on her instead. Sophie is a cleaned up, a 'cropped-and-shopped' Sophie, like the version she posts on social media. But the Sophie I have seen since I woke is one who's self-absorbed, flawless, and not at all the one I miss, with flaws, quirks, and defining lapses of perfection.

I stand, leaving her on her knees, looking at me, mirroring my emotions. Concern. But she doesn't talk. That's good to know. I think she talks, but her mouth doesn't actually move. In fact, none of it moves. It simply rearranges when I'm not looking.

Waking, I can see now the faint light on the horizon through a squall, the podlights moving slowly along Market. If this was my own dream, I would want it to be Harper. I focus on her thigh against me in the diner, and the denim over her knee as my hand brushed against it. The smell of her long, curly hair as she turned to look at the door and it flipped behind her, right against my cheek.

I think about all of it as I brush my teeth, and it actually feels good, to think, without distractions, and in greater depth. There are odd questions I can't answer no matter how much attention I give them. Are these dreams manufactured, like adverts or serials, or sports highlight reels, with a specific behavioural goal in mind? Or are they propaganda, seeding us with happiness and contentment? How much is residual and how much is me? What am I? Am I just these neurons, and this brain, a coagulation of biological functions? Am I any more than a meat sack running permutations and algorithms?

Snow always makes for a bit of chaos. Pods don't know what to do on unplowed roads, despite hundreds of upgrades to address this. The AI just doesn't get on top of some things, like the finesse of speed and braking power on unpredictable streets. It's a dangerous time to be out because the pods will run people over, avoiding other people. I am low priority, behind babies, seniors, veterans, city workers, G-Bros, diplomats, doctors, government officials, tourists, pregnant women, and kids. Even pets are rare and coveted now.

This is Harper's day off, and we meet at the diner. She is already there when I arrive, sitting at a window seat, looking pretty in her soft sweater and jeans, her hair restrained by a scarf overtop, tied behind her neck. I get into line to order the special: joe and porridge, with dried apple and pear slices. The smell of it reminds me of my mother. I make a drinking motion to Harper to offer her joe, and she nods. On the truth report is an article about a killing in Baltimore. Another black kid has been shot to death in broad daylight by an old hoarder linked to the Brotherhood. They show the body, covered in a yellow sheet, with the snow falling, and the bullet markers. Nino delivers two specials, and I take it to the table.

"What did you think of my boys?"

"They're awesome," I say. "It explains a lot about your sense of humour."

"They're great. When I first met them I thought they'd be tough guys, but they're pussycats."

On the glass, Senator Hogg is led to the podium, walking slowly with his prosthetic legs whirring. A quiet hush falls both there and here in the diner. "I can't believe that guy is still around," she whispers.

"I would have thought they killed him long ago," I reply.

"That's how he lost his legs," she says. "The Brotherhood tried to blow him up."

"Ladies and Gentlemen," he says. "Fellow Americans. I always hope, each time, that when I speak before a crowd mourning the loss of more American children, it will be my last speech, because we will have found peace. Yet here we are again. I am heartbroken. We will not be intimidated in our own communities. Where our children play. I have fought this violence all my life. It is time for this administration to speak out, to condemn the Georgia Brotherhood once and for all, and to give us our lives back." The truth report cuts back to the desk, where they talk over the rest of his speech.

"That won't happen. The G-Bros keep Kastor in power," she says. "I'm surprised he hasn't just disappeared."

"When I was a kid, my father disappeared. He taught at the university. He was accused of treason," I say.

"I'm so sorry," she says.

"I've been thinking a lot about him lately," I say. "I don't really remember much about him, except that I wanted to be like him. Except, I ended up far more like my mother. I have an image of him, but not much more than that. He had grey hair, and smoked a pipe. My Mom hated the pipe. I feel guilty, and ... I can forgive myself now because I know I was just a kid, but I remember actually feeling relieved that he was gone, because Mom spent a lot more time with me, and he was so stern, and authoritative, and he never showed much emotion. He was serious, as if doing what other people do was embarrassing to him."

"You were a kid. It's not easy working through all those emotions – especially when you don't get to say goodbye."

"It's weird. When it sunk in, I felt guilty, but I also felt like it would be alright. For years I thought he'd be coming back."

"Like it was a mistake. Or a dream," she says.

"Right? But Mom knew. She became hard after that, like every decision was important."

"Do you know why he disappeared?" she asks.

"Do any of us ever really know? I mean, sure he was vocal. He was a professor, and he denounced the government. He was concerned about our freedom. What I gather from my mother is that he taught comparative literature in the English program before the university went practical, when I was a kid. He tried to adapt to a 'Business Writing' course, but even that was cut. So he attended a protest about the cuts, and then on the way to work one morning, he disappeared."

"I'm so sorry to hear that."

"I would like to see him again, in old videos or clips of his lectures, to hear what he had to say, but his records were all purged. It's as if he never existed."

"I don't have anything left to remind me, either," she says. "Our father, too, was purged when they abolished the States, and the Electoral College. My father knew the Guide. He was an ethics professor at Drexel, and helped work on the early iterations of AI. He was vocal. He thought he was untouchable because of his party membership and his work on the hive, but it turned out he was no longer useful to them."

"Oliver said that last night." I say. I reach out and hold her hand.

"My mother would tell us about him, about how much he loved us, and about how they met. She was heartbroken, and it hurt us to see her suffer."

"That's hard."

"I have memories and photos," she says. "That's all. Oliver and I always thought that my father just took off, and didn't care about us. When Mom died, we came across all his old journals. In his last entry he looked forward to the break at Yule to spend time with us. I remember he would play with us every day after work. He taught poor kids to play basketball. We fed them out of our own kitchen. He would never have left. Ever."

"Why didn't your mother tell you about him?"

"She was afraid, like everyone. She couldn't bear to tell us the truth. She wanted us to grow up knowing he was a good, important man, and that he had done great things for others, but we took that to mean he was out doing those things without us."

"It's my greatest fear that I'll have kids and there will be another purge," I say. "I mean, I can take care of myself, like I could run, and live off the land, but I don't think I can have kids, just to watch them get hurt."

"That's how they control us," she says. "We're all afraid to live our lives, afraid to take risks. I have this desire for comfort, for a quiet life, and for a family, to just do my thing and not be pressed to fight for anything, but I don't want to bring kids into this either."

"What Oliver talks about seems to me the answer to all the questions I've ever had about why that happened, and who's responsible."

"I think they're wasting their time. Not that it's not important, because it is, but they never really carry out any of the things they say they will. We get far more done by helping people than by fighting."

"But there's value in knowing, right?"

"It's better to know than not to know," she says.

"I feel like it's so difficult to have hope, or to be happy," I say.

"There's always hope," she says. "To create and to live and to enjoy anything is to trust in the future."

"Then let's do something! Let's go out and have some fun!"

"And do what?"

"I don't know," I say, and shrug. I hadn't thought that far ahead.

"Wait," she says. "Finish up. I know. Trust me." She's squirming in her chair now, she's so excited.

"Promise I won't get arrested this time?" I joke.

"You weren't arrested. You were detained."

I laugh.

"I'm not promising anything," she says.

As we get up and make our way to the door, I let her go first, and I look down to her tight jeans before she puts on her coat. She catches me. "Are you watching my ass?" she says, with a sly grin.

"I so am!"

"You know, that means I get to check out yours now, right?"

Am I blushing? I'm blushing. I can feel it, and she laughs at me, in a good way. She loops her arm around mine as we walk west along Market. There's a hovering halo on the sidewalk that shows what the street looked like in 1934, and it's fascinating to look through it. All those people, long dead, living their lives. Eating lunch. Going to work. Walking with their kids. Horses and cars share the street. It's hard to believe they were here in this very spot.

Not far along, we come to a storefront lit with thousands of LED's, all flashing in patterns. "This is it?" I ask.

"It's a theatre," she says. "They play old movies, like ... actual film movies from long ago. It's how they used to play them a hundred years ago."

"Movies? That's amazing that there are any still left."

"This one is very old. The owner, Eddie, keeps the original films in vaults in the basement, and makes copies to play. He's worried that they won't even be there in a hundred years."

Inside, we take off our hats and gloves, and loosen our coats, and we stand in line at the box office for tickets. The lobby is beautiful, even as it's been diminished by age. The walls and ceilings are plastered into shapes of fruit and animals and hunting scenes – and gilded. The walls have the texture of velvet.

It turns out we are seeing 'Much Adieu About Nothing', a 'modern' twist on a play by Shakespeare. I look at the poster. The actor, Bella Dawson, is pretty, her hair windswept and her gaze drawn longingly off to the distant left.

"Oh, this is such a chick-flick," Harper says. "It's going to make you cry."

"Why would you want to do that?"

"In a good way, of course," she says, and laughs. "This is how girls unwind. We cry."

"I could probably use a good cry," I say, and laugh.

"Oh. I'm glad. I was worried you'd be all weird about that."

I don't think I've ever watched a full movie before. Highlights by the score, sure, and reviews and vines, and clips that caused controversy, but never an actual, full movie. Nobody has patience for the long format since Hollywood collapsed. We stand in a different line for the concession stand, and she leans over and bumps me, smiling, and I lean in to bump her back. We order a huge bucket of sor-pop to share, and some birch soda, and make our way down the old staircase to the aisles, and she chooses a pair of seats in the middle-back, in the centre. We pile our coats beside us, sliding down the reclining seats. She eats a messy handful of the sor-pop.

"I can't believe how much it costs here," I say.

"Before the borders closed, when I was a kid, I went to Brazil with my Dad. We went out to a movie there, and did you know that instead of sorghum, they pop these beans called nuna?"

"I did not know that," I say.

"Seriously. They weren't bad, either. I really liked them."

"How were they?"

"Nuttier," she says.

"Salt and butter?"

"Same as sor-pop. It's a winning formula," she says. "The salt … the butter."

"Everything is better with salt and butter," I say.

"Taxes!" she says.

"Yes. Dental work," I say, though I have never had dental work.

"Right," she says, snickering. "Shark attacks."

"Chewing gum!" I say. "Wait ... shark attacks?"

"Of course! The butter. The salt. Donuts ... no wait, they actually would be really good with salt and butter," she says, and laughs. "My grandmother talked about pop-corn."

"Oh ya?"

"She said it had a smell completely its own. It was all she wanted to eat before she died, and we couldn't find any. Anywhere. Even the illegal commissary down on JFK."

"JFK?"

"Kastor Way, they call it now."

"I know this is going to sound completely stupid, but was corn a grain? I've never actually seen it."

"Neither have I. She said it was bigger than sorghum. And fluffier. They used to eat it at the theatres. It was used to make all sorts of other foods, like syrups and flours."

"Like wheat then. Fluffier," I say.

"Bigger than wheat ... what, you're laughing!" she says, and pulls the bag away from me.

"I'm not!" I say. "Fluffier, and more sugary."

"Shut up!" she says. "Now I know you're making fun of me."

"I'm sorry," I say, and she shares again.

"She used to talk about the world before the End War. How they had different measurements – she talked about inches, and miles – and how they had different accents, even across the Republic," she says.

"Really? I never knew that."

"She was so funny. She said we all talk like Canadians and Valley girls now."

"Valley girls? I don't know what that means," I say.

"Neither do I! She was a great old girl. She constantly complained about us learning the metric system. She'd grill us; 'How many quarts in a gallon!'. It became a joke in our house.

Slowly, the lights dim, and with an amplified crackle, a humming sound increases, but seems to go both up and down in tone at the same time, and then a company logo appears.

"So how many quarts in a gallon?" I whisper.

"Shhh ... we have to be quiet now," she says, and gives me an exaggerated perturbed look before turning back to the screen. But I watch her and she is smirking.

"You're like that woman in the gallery-" I say, but she holds up a finger to silence me.

The 'coming soon' previews are a century old, for films that may not even exist any more, but I'm still fascinated by the houses, the furniture, the bizarre clothing, and the flags, and the old pods – that have to be driven. Everything. This first one is about a magical cat who tries to babysit two children while their mother is at work. All of it is so strange and foreign. They speak English, but it's older. I can't help but wonder if this is how people lived back then. "That's weird," I say. Every time I try to whisper, Harper throws sor-pop at me, one at a time, like she's daring me to look away, with another kernel ready to go.

"You wanna sor-pop fight?" I whisper, joking, and reach out, but she pulls the bag away, spilling some, and glares at me, smirking.

The next preview is seedier, more realistic. It is a drama. All the cars look boxy and dirty. I assume that this is closer to how people actually lived. There are so many odd customs to absorb. Then I realize something that's been bothering me that I haven't been able to define until now. Not a one of them has a companion. No glasses. Not just the actors, but I'm sure not even the directors, the crew, the script writers, or the camera people – none of them had companions. This was before the hive. And yet they did this. They built vehicles, and power plants, roads, and buildings, crafted precision lenses, and microphones, trolleys, studios, searchlights, airplanes, guns, towers and bridges, machinery and ships, all with pencil and rulers, on paper. We thrived before technology. We mastered this world. We built things.

I wonder if this is the world of the Guide. Did he walk these streets? Could he be in some of these scenes? Why didn't I ever look up things like this when I had my companion? Even the way that they interact is different. They seem more respectful of each other. They give each other time to talk. They nod and make eye contact. They hold these small white cigars up to their mouths, and light them. It's not something crazy, but something they do naturally. I wonder what's in them, and why there is no mention of them anywhere, or even the objects themselves, in museums, as if the very nature of them was so appalling to early censors that they had to erase even the memory. Another victim of the purges. Was it some drug that caused the collapse? Did it feel good? And what else have they erased? What else is just lurking there in the buried past, like pop-corn, or JFK? Like … AFK. Are those initials? Does anyone even know? We have written our entire culture in sand, and the waves keep crashing in.

Then the feature. I can barely follow the plot, because I am mesmerized, trying to capture each little detail in my mind, and Harper is playing with my fingers, distracting me, and we lean into each other, her hair on my cheek, and her head on my shoulder. The story is brilliant. A love story. Every story is a love story, really, but this one, set in Canada, is a tragic love story. They are caught in a love triangle. She's cute. The boyfriend is an asshole. The new lover treats her well, and she's torn between the two, though the choice to us, the audience, seems obvious. There is a delicious anxiety in her indecision.

For an hour, they are trying to be alone. They are thwarted by circumstance. Harper strokes my finger with her thumb, and the feeling is electric. I can barely feel my arm for the angle it's on, but I don't dare move. They can't contain their passion, and he leads her to bed, where they tear their clothing off. Harper isn't uncomfortable with this, but I am. I never knew movies were like this. Do they show the sex, too? I'm afraid to ask, but I lose myself in their world. I love seeing the characters struggle with some of the same things I've struggled with. Losing parents. New love. An erosion of faith in people. There's a period of quiet, and setup, and then they wring the emotion from me. I'm embarrassed that I almost cry, as if doing so is to invest in believing. But if I can't invest in feelings like love and redemption and hate and anger, then what can I believe in?

The end is near. When there's no hope of redemption, when I finally understand that the 'Adieu' in the title means 'goodbye' in French, I remember my father, and how I never got to say goodbye, and I lose it, crying like a school kid, trying to be quiet, and keep my breathing regular, wiping away the tears with my free hand. I inhale, and then exhale, but my breath betrays me, coming back in a jag, and I feel tightness in my face. What the hell is with my emotions lately?

When the movie finishes, I'm mesmerized for a few moments, holding Harper's hand, and then in the light we are exposed. She turns to look at me, waiting for the others in our line to clear, smiling like she's bubbling to say something, but can't. I am looking at her anew, her pretty eyes and her smile, head cocked to one side – she is so familiar now – and yet I remember my doubts. Who is she? I want to hunker back down in our seats and put my hand on her knee, lean in close and whisper to her, so that this night doesn't have to end. But the movie is over, and we wait for the people behind us to descend the stairs, and we follow them, released out into the street, and in the sunshine, the world seems so new and alive. I had forgotten it was daytime. I don't know what the weather will do, or what else is going on in the world, and I don't care.

We walk, and she loops her arm around mine, like before. "We sometimes put movies on at the Veterans Co-op, and it's always a riot," she says. "The like 'action' films, but they're like you. They can't shut up!"

"I can shut up!" I say. "I did shut up. That was wonderful."

"They have moments when we forget where we are, and where we've been, and we laugh until we cry, and our faces hurt, and we're not yellow, red, or black or white, or old or young, or man or woman, we're just people, laughing together because we're there, and we don't need anything else. Often the guys get overwhelmed, too. They're expected to be so tough, but we're all just people. All the things that happen to us, and around us, they change who we are."

"I need more of that. I feel like I've been disconnected from people for ages."

"Films remind me of how people used to be," she says.

"I love the way they call each other 'Guy', or 'Dude', instead of 'Brother', and that they say old religious things, like 'Amen'."

"...and what was with the heels on their shoes? They had to be like five centimeters tall!" she says. I hadn't noticed the heels.

"It's all part of an earlier time that seems so much simpler. I can't help but feel like we are going backwards."

"We are going backwards," she says.

"I feel like things are spiralling out of control, like there's not going to be any good news for a long time."

"I had to stop watching the truth report," she says. "It all was so depressing. It felt for so long that the world was getting less and less safe to live in. But don't lose heart," she says. "There is good in people, and value in connecting to others."

"Hold on," I say, and stop walking. My glass is vibrating, so I answer. "Hello?"

"Good morning, fellow Republican! You're back on the hive!" Mason is the only person I know who speaks in that Heritage Party crap, and to him it's still a joke, to call me that.

"Mason!" I say. "Thank you. Whatever you did, it saved my ass."

"Aw, don't mention it," he says. "Listen. I'm calling to see if you want to come out with us tonight."

"Alright. Where? Who's going?" I ask. I can hear a tinkle of glasses behind him and a female voice I should probably recognize, but don't.

"Everyone! We're going to a bar on the Delaware. What are you doing?"

"I'm hanging out with Harper," I say. She shoots me a puzzled look.

"Harper?" he asks.

"You don't know her."

"Her? Oh! You should bring her! Does she have cute friends?"

"Just a brother. Totally not your type," I joke.

He laughs. I mute the glass.

"Hey. Do you want to meet my friends?"

"I'd love to," she says.

I un-mute the glass. "Sure, when and where?"

"I'll send the details," he says, and ends the call.

"Friends? I get to meet your friends? Who will be there?" Harper asks.

"Well, Mason, who called, is the one who solved my problem with Soc-Serv."

"How did he do that?"

"He's connected," I say. "Dep-Res. He doesn't really say exactly what he does. There's Charlotte, too, and her brother Jackson. Probably Mila. Maybe Elijah, though he never seems to go out with us any more. You'll love Charlotte. She's as close to a best friend as I ever had. We all laugh about Mila being a ditz, but she has a good heart. They'll fawn over you."

"This is big! I'm going to have to dress up."

"No, don't. I mean, they're not posh or anything. They're just normal people." I'm near tears again, and I can't figure out if this is because of the movie, the memory of my father, or the flirting, but I feel so raw. Was there a hormone that the companion regulated that now has me at its mercy? I have never been like this.

"You're really nervous about this, aren't you?"

"You know ... I am. My ex-girlfriend, Sophie, might be there," I say.

"Oh, then I'll definitely dress up."

"No. Please. It's more than that. I feel indebted to Mason, and I'm hoping Sophie and Elijah aren't there at all. It's all just so raw."

"Is Sophie going to try to fight me for you?" she says, with a grin. It's really no use.

"No. She dumped me before I even woke."

""Is she pretty?"

"Not like you," I say. "She's a self-centered rich girl."

"All the better to show off," she says, with a gleam in her eye that I find troubling.

* * *

We walk back to the Veterans Co-op, and play pool all afternoon in the sunshine, flirting and joking. At times she seems sad, telling me about disastrous dates she's had with guys who were self-absorbed, distracting, or condescending. I've never really had a bad date. I've been only on a couple.

"When I was a kid," she says, touching my arm, "I believed that I was able to visit other people in their dreams. I'd ask my friends if they saw me, because I saw them, and there was just enough truth to make me think there was something to it."

"You were in my dreams," I say.

"Was I? You didn't even invite me!"

"You invited yourself, with all those ideas..."

"And the tight jeans," she says.

"Those too!"

"Darlin', I'm trying to get into your dreams in a different way now," she says, and winks.

"Are you always this bad?"

"No! I'm usually worse! Just not around lots of people I don't know. Was I really in your dreams?" she asks. "Like, before I sat with you?"

Suddenly I'm feeling very shy. "Maybe I'll get to know you better before I tell you about those."

Later, Harper changes into a dress, tights, and boots. She has put makeup on, actual makeup on her face like they did in the old movies. She looks gorgeous. I wouldn't be disappointed if we decided not to go, and I didn't see anyone, and we went out for another movie, or to a fun night at the dance hall in Powelton, drinking cheap wine from their chunky steins, and getting a corner table so I can fawn over her. I agonize over changing. My wind-cut leather jacket is perfect for the gallery, but I know the type of place Mason goes to.

I'm sure Harper will be fine in whatever she's wearing, but I should be wearing a bow-tie and jacket, and cotton pants. I have a purple tie already folded, and waiting for a special occasion that I could stop by and change into. But by the time we are going out the door, there's no time. And if I'm the only one dressed up, I'll be teased mercilessly. The address Mason has given me is over in the old town. And past downtown, no less! If it weren't for seeing everyone again, I wouldn't even come here. The Heritage Party took over 'Society Hill' for their headquarters in the fifties, and then levelled the 'gaybourhood' to construct the cube complex. From the cube to the river are high-end clubs and restaurants. As soon as we pass the cube, and Independence square, the tone is entirely different. Night is falling, and the streets here are well-lit, but empty. The sign for the Republic is everywhere, the 'Bonnie Blue' star-and-bars, but also the symbol of the hive, which is a cartoon beehive. Buildings, pods, buses, lapel pins and uniforms, on the bridge trestles and in the advertising – this is the centre for government for the entire east-central coast, and the northeast gateway to the District of Columbia.

Part of the success of this area is its proximity to the Republican Congress, and the machinery of state. It is the headquarters of the Dep-Just, responsible for police, courts, and surveillance of the Republic. Farther south is the Dep-Trans, not much more than a warehouse with a bank of steel cargo doors that open to the south, straight down the old fifth street, where the airport and cube and port are all connected by wheeled module trams.

Dep-Res, where Mason works, is a huge, square building south of the cube, strictly functional, like a brick, mini-cube, with few windows. Mason's office is high up in the complex, but I don't know if this is where he actually comes to work every day. And I wasn't embellishing when I told Harper that he's connected. He has new friends who are either in with the party, like Elijah, or who are related to party members, like Taylor. He travels a lot to South America and Europe to barter for natural resources.

The restaurant - 'Puca-Pow!' - is Native American themed, with a knotty pine interior, and an enormous stone fireplace. The windows are designed for the view. Across the river, the battleship New Jersey is lit up like the twelfth of August. Servers in short leather tasseled skirts and white shirts walk effortlessly between tables. They are all young, blonde, smiling fantasies. It's the kind of place I'd never get into if it weren't for Mason. We find him with Elijah and Taylor, both dressed in expensive suits, with their hair done in the latest coif that I'm still getting used to, slicked up into oiled curls that don't move. I'm disappointed not to see Mila or Charlotte. Elijah. Why is he here? They both are wearing full facial hair. I've never grown facial hair well. Not even when it became all popular and everyone had it – because my hair doesn't grow evenly. Thank God that trend is done, with a few exceptions, because now my clean-shaven face doesn't look so out of place.

"Did you see her spread in the Post? What a set of lungs on her!" Elijah says as we approach.

"I could just motorboat those," Mason replies, and then sees us. "Rufe! Over here! I'm glad you made it."

"Mason! This is my girlfriend, Harper."

"Hi," he says, but he doesn't extend a hand to shake.

"Where are the girls?" I ask.

"Charlotte didn't reply. Mila didn't get back to me."

"Rufe is a minor celebrity now that the President mentioned him in a truthcast," Taylor says to Harper, and shakes her hand.

"What?" I ask.

"Oh, yeah," he continues. "I have calls all the time asking who you are and how you survived so long. I have no answers. I tell them it's a medical miracle."

"I'm Elijah. This is Taylor," Elijah says, shaking her hand as well.

"Here, sit," Mason says. "Do you want something to drink?"

"No, thanks," Harper says. We pull our chairs closer, to hold hands.

"Tell us how you met Rufus, Harper." Mason says. He's playing with the ice in his half-finished drink.

"He met my brother first. Oliver introduced us."

"As I recall," I say, "you introduced yourself."

"Oh gosh, I did, didn't I?" she says, and laughs.

The waitress flits in with superb efficiency, and sets our drinks out for us with a smile and a nod to Mason. "Thanks, Darlin'," he says. "Here. Check out the menu. This place is my new favourite." He passes an old-style physical menu out to all of us. The restaurant's mission statement says that our culture has forgotten how to appreciate subtle, quiet, and boring things. I see where this is going. Kale. Asparagus. Braised squash. Corn. They actually have corn. I didn't think anyone could get corn any more. I'm sure this is nothing like what native Americans ate, though. Everything is highly overpriced, and some dishes exceedingly rare.

Chicken. They have chicken. There is no need for the opulence. I'd be happy with stew, or pasta.

"What are you having?" Elijah asks.

"I don't know yet," Taylor says. "You, Mason?"

"Pemmican Wawa," he says.

"Goose. You're having the goose?" Taylor says. It's the most expensive dish on the menu.

"It's not trump-change, that's for sure, but I love goose. I can't get enough. It's so tasty," Mason says, and smacks his lips.

"That's a month's wages for me," Harper says. "I can't afford this."

"Neither can I," I say, and set the menu down.

"What do you do for money?" Mason asks Harper. He's grinning. Now I'm sure this whole dinner has been a bad idea.

"I am a personal support worker for veterans," she says.

"Oh, I love vets. I lead a working group on vets that my father started, that funds programs to support them."

"Wait. You head the V-Ap?"

"Oh, gosh no. Just a working group," he says.

"We've been pushing them for years to have the stipend increased with the cost of living," she says. This is a subject close to her heart, I know.

"The vets make quite enough already," Mason replies.

"Some of them can't even afford to eat," she says.

Elijah and Taylor are riveted, wide-eyed.

Mason stirs his drink, trying to avoid her eyes. "The state can only give them so much. I'm sure the ones who do well with their money are fine."

"But they don't-"

He interrupts. "We already dedicate so much to them. It costs billions. This is money other people have to work hard to pay in taxes."

Harper clears her throat. "Well, my thought is that if a society can spend trillions to send them across the ocean to further our interests, losing their lives, their limbs, or their sanity, we can afford billions to care for them when they return. Instead they're treated worse than criminals. They're not allowed to work, or volunteer, because that takes jobs from other people, and they can't own anything because that would be deducted. Most of them are dealing with some serious traumas. The wait list for counselling is years, and if they don't make in-person visits, they go back to the bottom of the list."

"So we're working, and paying taxes, and they get to sit at home? They're the ones with the real freedom."

"Then why are they penalized if they take on a job?" Harper says. "Many of them will never work. They're disabled, and they're now elderly."

"The best route out of poverty is a good paying job," he says. "They can be security guards or something. The guy in my building, he must be like, ninety."

"Then why take away benefits if they work?"

"That would be double-dipping," he says.

"But politicians are allowed to own businesses and still take office. Isn't that double-dipping?" she asks. I squeeze her hand, in hopes that she'll stop confronting him. She clears her throat. "I don't think you understand," Harper says, "how veterans struggle in this country. They've thought of the same things you're saying, and tried, over and over again."

"Well, the system is far from perfect, sure," he says. "But we have to do something. None of the eggheads could ever figure it out, so we throw things against the wall until they stick. This is sticking until we get them back to productive lives."

"That's why Kastor is so good," Taylor says. "He's bringing all those jobs back and anyone who wants to work can work."

"Maybe in some areas, but not here in Philly-" Harper says.

"I don't know," Elijah interrupts. "Despite all the problems we've had, I like Kastor. I like that he speaks his mind, and he doesn't take shit from anyone. I understand what he says. He's the strong, stable genius we need running things. Those others ... Hogg especially, he opens his mouth and I don't understand a word."

"He's a legend, Man," Taylor says. "A damned Legend. He built the pyramids, single-handed, using only a whip and some Egyptian curse words."

Elijah laughs. "Jesus walked on water. Kastor swam through land." He's trying to lighten us all up, but Mason and Harper are both still unable to look at each other.

"I heard he visited the Virgin Islands, and when he left, they were called 'The Islands'."

"It sounds like you have a crush," Mason teases. It makes me sick.

"Now that's a manly man," Taylor says, laughing. "Look at how he trims his beard as little as possible. I could never grow such a strong, lush beard." Now they area all laughing. I've never liked Taylor, come to think of it. Mason's sidekick. It's like he was always in competition with me. Only I never tried that hard, and he seemed to always resent that I knew Mason longer.

"In all seriousness, though, he's right," Elijah says. "We have to weed out the decadence of society, the type of intermingling of races and cultures that led to the End War in the first place. It's all the immigrants who ruined things. They brought the dope and the perversion. That New

World Order would have enslaved us all. We're Americans! When have we ever let someone else tell us what to do?" He is looking at Harper askance, baiting her to argue. Am I the only one who sees this?

"We are enslaved by a system that's pushing us into a war," Harper says. "Which will only create more veterans to care for in the future."

"I will gladly die for America," Taylor says. "We should all be prepared. If not, we'll be come goddamn communists."

"If they don't stop messing in our shit," Elijah says. "We're going to have to go over there and thump them. Teach them a goddamn lesson." He has said this to Taylor, but all of us have taken his point in different ways.

"Violence never solves anything," Harper says.

"Well, you'll never serve, so I guess that isn't a question for you," Elijah says, dismissing her. It's really not fair. None of us will serve. Me, I have no companion to be spelled for combat. Elijah joined the Brotherhood. He and Taylor are now exempt from the draft. Nobody wants to trust the hive in combat.

Harper straightens. "My fight is for the right to vote, and the right to be considered a human being under law, as written in the founding documents of our Republic."

"The problem is now all these students and people on welfare are calling out for democracy as if they'd even have the slightest clue how to run a country or choose candidates," Elijah says. "The problem with democracy is giving any old person the vote. People make horrible decisions daily. Liberals want to entrust the economy, and our safety, our military, to people who've never even run a business before?"

"Not only that," Taylor says, "but sacking the leadership and starting from scratch every four years is completely inefficient, with no continuity. Two parties in gridlock. Nothing would get done. It would also send a totally wrong message to the Russians and the Chinese, leaving us vulnerable."

Elijah is laughing, glancings at Harper.

"What," she says.

"Sorry. I have this makeup program on my companion, and it overrides women's makeup programs, and does them up-" he hesitates, and blushes, knowing he's passing into territory that's possibly offensive. "-does them up how I like to see them, and not configured for -"

"For what?" Mason asks.

"It's not configured for some skin colours, and it looks like a ... reverse black face or something," he says, and laughs.

Taylor laughs with him.

"Elijah ... don't be pock," Mason says.

"Sorry, I'll shut it off. Here," he says.

I reach down and give Harper's hand a little squeeze. "Look," I say. "This is probably a bad idea coming-"

"No. No," Mason interrupts. "Don't go."

"If you'll excuse me, I have to use the washroom," Harper says, and stands.

"Do you need-" I plead with her with my eyes. I feel like we're in danger, and I get my jacket off the back of the chair to put it on. "We can go-" I say.

"No. You're okay. Just a few minutes. I'll be back. I promise." She leans over to kiss me, to assure me.

Elijah whistles at the sensual kiss, and bites his lower lip as Harper walks away from the table toward the washrooms.

"You didn't tell us your new girl is black," Mason says.

"Should I have to?"

Mason leans across the table. "I'm not going to insult your little waifu, young grasshopper," he says. "Your secret is safe with me."

"I'm not keeping anything a secret," I reply.

"He just wants a bunch of kids," Taylor says. "Everyone knows they hide them when the inspectors come around." I'm shocked by the hostility. I don't even know what to say.

"He got dumped by a beautiful, and sexy woman-" Elijah says to Taylor, shaking his head. He thinks I didn't hear, that I'm distracted.

"And met another one," I say.

"Well at least it's still a man and woman," Taylor says.

"Bro's before fro's!" Elijah says, and the two of them crack up laughing.

"Don't, guys. He's serious about this," Mason says, smirking. "They're joking," he says to me. I just want Harper to be out of the washroom so we can leave. I stand, and Mason leans forward out of his chair to implore me to sit back down. "Look," he says. "I didn't mean for this all to be about your girl. This is not why I invited you here. I've got an opportunity for you. I apologize for not making that clear. It doesn't require having an active companion. In fact, they'd prefer you didn't have one."

"Okay," I say, and I hesitate, and then reluctantly sit. What is it about us, that we don't want to offend people who threaten us? Survival instinct? Social approval? Even now I want to leave, but I'm rooted to hear what he has to say.

"You would join the party, and be given a large house in the old town, and you'd be able to support yourself, and your friends, just like I do. There's a catch though."

"What's that?"

"You will never get that job if you have a black girlfriend."

"Well, that's not the job for me, then," I reply.

"I don't think you should dismiss it offhand. You've known her, what ... a week? I mean, there's all sorts of possible scenarios, like, you could get a house and hire her as your housekeeper or something. I know a couple of the guys have done that, and everyone knows. Nobody says a thing."

"You're saying something right now," I say.

He frowns. "I'm just saying to consider it. It will change your life."

Harper returns, and we are all quiet. "Sorry. Am I interrupting?"

"No, not at all," Mason says, and laughs. "I was just offering Rufus an opportunity-"

"But I refused," I say. "So it's over."

"Well, I'd like to think that you'd be grateful enough to consider it," he says. He's getting angry. "If it wasn't for me, you'd be on the street." He turns to his friends. "The most exciting thing to happen to him in his entire life, was randomly falling asleep for two months and then waking up, like that's a big victory! He couldn't even get his power back on without calling me!"

"Okay," I say. "I've heard enough." I stand.

"Oh, come on, Rufe. I'm only kidding. You know I'm joking," Mason says, but his smile says otherwise.

"You really haven't changed a bit. You hide all your awful behaviour behind 'just joking'," I say.

He turns to Elijah. "Rufus doesn't want a job. No responsibility. Sexy new coon girlfriend-"

"Sorry. What did you say?" Harper asks.

"You heard what I-"

She throws his drink into his face, and he stands to confront her.

"Try me," she says.

"Maybe I will someday," he says.

"Hey," I say. "It's not worth it. Let's just go," I say, and lead her away.

"Think about my offer, Rufus," Mason says, and his friends laugh.

"Go sod yourself, Mason. I mean it." And in a flash I envision myself sinking a samurai sword on an angle deep into the flesh between his shoulder and neck, jamming on his breastbone. This terrifies me, and I put my hand on Harper's waist. She gives Mason the archer fingers as I guide her to the door. Out in the cold night, I pull my scarf up over my mouth, and tighten my jacket, and then I loop my arm around Harper's arm, hands in pockets.

"I wasn't actually going to..." she says. "-you know ... hurt him."

"I know."

"Just maybe rough him up a bit," she says, trying to make me smile.

"I know you weren't," I say, but I have an overwhelming panicked sense of dread. I want to go back and punch Mason, or apologize, go home and turn on some freaking dead celebrity channel, to curl up and sleep it all off. What is with my emotions? I am cloaked in dread. I've been making excuses for Mason's behaviour my entire life. He always treated me as inferior, even long before he offered me to join the party, when I refused. Oliver is right. It's not about behaviour. It's about the underlying attitude. I had believed that being his friend, being close to him, made me immune to that judgment, and scrutiny – but it doesn't. His attitude only goes under for a time, but everyone needs friends, and I was his friend only so long as he needed me to feel good about himself.

Harper is quiet, still holding my arm. I hope this doesn't change anything. I'm afraid of what she'll say. I'm running arguments in my head, to convince her to give me another chance, not to judge me by Mason and his friends, but the reality is that I put her in danger by exposing her to this in the first place.

"I'm sorry," she says, which astounds me. I wasn't expecting that.

"Why are you sorry? I should be apologizing to you," I say.

"I just realized how hard this is for you."

"No. I'm sorry that I put you in that situation. It's not your fault."

"I could have handled that better," she says, "but I get so angry. Especially with guys like that. And I can't really see my way out of it until I cool down. I don't always make the best decisions when that happens."

"Me neither," I say. "Maybe that's why the girls aren't around any more. I'm sure they would love to meet you."

"What was his offer, anyway?"

"He wanted to give me a job, and a house, and all I had to do was join the party."

"The party? The National Heritage party, who make the mandates? That party?"

"He said to do that I had to leave you."

"Oh," she says. This has hurt her, that she was the focus. I can tell.

"I told him to stuff it."

She smiles, skips for a couple of steps. "I bet there wasn't even a job," she says. "I bet it was all about control." She looks as if the very thought of a plot on his part is a challenge.

"No, there was a job," I say. "This is his control. I'm going to have to call him and set it right."

"To take the job?"

"Oh, hell no," I reply.

"Good. It really burns me that they can get away with whatever they want," she says.

"I hate to be cynical, but I have to use him for what protection I can. The existence of people like him force us to be like them. He's been trying to control me since we were kids. He shamed me, and dragged me into trouble. My Mom hated him. Even when his Mom was helping us out."

"Then why were you friends?"

"Because he shows up when I need him, and he fixes things. He's been good in some ways, but whenever I'm around him, I still feel like I'm losing," I say.

"Even charity can be a form of power. That's why fascists dismantle real social support, because they want the people who rely on them to feel inferior. They want it to be voluntary donations and sponsorship so they can lord it over us, because true power is in the hoarding of opportunity."

My face is very cold, and when we get to the station at Market and 2nd, the lights are off, and the steel gates are closed, with red plastic chains strung in front of the stairs.

"Feck," she says. "It's not supposed to close for another three hours."

"A pod, maybe?"

"The system isn't taking requests. We'll have to walk."

"It's not such a bad night," I say.

"It's not the weather I'm worried about," she says, and suddenly she is alert, and cautious, looking all around and walking quicker.

"We'll be heads-up and we'll avoid everyone."

We walk for some time, and she stops me, hand on my chest. There is a group of men up ahead that I hadn't noticed, maybe seven or eight of them, and I can see in the silhouette that at least one has an assault rifle.

"G-Bros," she whispers. We turn and start the opposite direction.

"Hey!" one of them yells.

Harper sprints, and I follow. We have a good head start, and she is real fast. I can barely keep up. She stops for me to catch up every half block or so, and ducks down a cross street, and then into a laundromat that's not yet closed. The woman behind the counter points to the washroom, and we go in, lock the door, and huddle in the stall. "Why are the subways closed?" she says, under her breath. "And the Brotherhood out?"

"I don't know," I whisper.

"I hate them," she says. "Something has to be going on."

We hold hands, facing each other, listening for sound from the laundromat, but there is none for a very long time. Then there is a knock. "All clear now," says the woman, as if this happens all the time, and we've pre-arranged it. We thank her, and she calls 'Good luck!' as we walk back out into the street. We are more cautious now, making our way east, keeping to the shadows. Across the Walnut street bridge, we are back in familiar territory. "I don't want to fight them," Harper says. "But I will. If I'd known there were no subways, I wouldn't have come out tonight."

"I wouldn't have come out anyway, if I'd known how it would turn out." I'm hurrying to keep up with her. "I understand the fear, though," I say. "Their own darkness reminds them that cruelty exists, and they follow that with a crippling fear that someone else will treat them the same way, which is why they can't stand when anyone else has power. They think holding power is the only way to be safe."

"They are impoverished by the same system they created, because they've robbed themselves of true connection," she says. "Anyway, I know what's possible. My best friend died because she was racked. My mother was paranoid it would happen to me, too."

"Racked?"

"Rape-hack ... 'Rack' is when a hacker puts a girl under spell to lead her somewhere. Often she doesn't even know it's happened until it's too late to collect samples. In my friend Amber's case, she was raped repeatedly, and left under spell for so long she died."

"That's awful! Why haven't I heard about it before?"

"Because it's always these rich nasty men, or rich young hackers with access to the hive, and it's swept under the rug. There aren't even stats on it because they lump them in with the stats on other AFK's, or they successfully spell the girl without anyone even noticing. The companions regulate the birth control, and the hive takes care of the memory."

"What's to stop that from happening to anyone?" I ask.

"Not to mention Samanthas," she says. "They endure all sorts of abuse because their programming has a submission bias. They're prohibited from organizing because the state won't let them gather without being redirected."

I'm thinking of my own experience being spelled, and how for the first six hours of my ordeal, anything could have happened, and even now I'd have no knowledge of it. I probably should be dead. I'm horrified. What if Mason wants to punish Harper? I feel like we're in very real danger here.

"I know you're worrying about me," she says. "I can feel it."

"I am worrying-"

"Don't," she interrupts. "Not only is my companion inhibited, but some of the students who were in software engineering, helped us to write our own code to make them spellproof."

"Yours-"

"I'm sure it wouldn't stand up for a long time if the hive wanted in, because the code is five years old. But it's held up so far," she says, and then squeezes my hand. "That's why I was so fascinated when you said you were AFK for so long. My friend was only AFK for a few days. The doctors said she just gave up."

"I've often thought of that, too. What if I had given up? I had a lot of time to think about life and all the struggle, and I had it better, for sure, but I wasn't happy. I could have given up. I wouldn't be here."

"Don't think of it that way. You're here. That's all I care," she says.

I'm hoping to salvage the night. "Hey, we haven't eaten. We're still together. There's lots to do."

"I'm hungry, too. I didn't even order at the restaurant," she says.

"How could we? Ninety-five euros! For one meal!"

We laugh. "I can't believe the outfits on the Samanthas, too," she says. "And the menu. It's an insult to first nations."

"What a bizarre day," I say.

"Why don't we go back to my place and order in some Thai food?"

"Sure," I say. I'm trying to be nonchalant, but I'm ecstatic.

* * *

Chapter 6

Harper's apartment is a fourth floor micro-bachelor out on Baltimore Avenue, with windows facing north, and a loft above the kitchen and ensuite. There's no foyer to stand in, and only a futon and some end tables in the main living space. From her balcony I can see downtown. She takes off her boots, and her coat. She puts her riotous hair up into a bun. She goes to the glass on the fridge to order food. "It's a place that cooks it on the way", she says. "Good food. Droned straight to the balcony. You'll like it."

"I love your place," I say. "It's real cozy, and the paintings are gorgeous."

She sets up a blanket on the floor, then she goes to a wire crate in the corner and comes back out carrying something fluffy – an animal! - it's a bunny! She carries him over to the blanket, and sits, cross-legged, pulling her dress down between her legs, and sets it between us. "This is my pet rabbit, Stewart. I call him Stu. 'Wabbit Stu'. He's my best buddy."

"He's awesome! Can I touch him?"

"Of course! I'm not allowed to have him here. I could get kicked out if my landlord found out. He's a mean old man, isn't he 'Wabbit Stu'?"

Stu comes over to sniff my fingers, and to eat some squash pellets from my hand. He lets me scratch him behind the ears. It's been years since I've seen a pet. Dogs, for security, are all over, but cats and rabbits are scarce and precious. His fur is so soft, and so soothing. It takes me right back to when I was a kid.

"He's really comfortable with you," she says.

"They say animals are good judges of character, but I don't think if he knew how many of his buddies I've eaten he'd think that-"

"Oh, that's horrible! Not my little wabbit stu! Give him back!" she teases, but I don't, savouring the mischief. "Don't worry, Stu, I'm going to make sure the bad man doesn't eat you," she says.

"I wouldn't eat Stu! He has a name!"

"Aw, he does. He's a good bunny. He's good company."

A chime sounds. "That was fast," she says, and she leaves Stu and I on the floor to pick up the food from the balcony. She unpacks boxes and containers from the bag, while I snap the chopsticks apart. The scent of the food fills the air, and I'm suddenly very hungry.

"Oh! Wait!" she says, and bounces back up, crossing the room. In her dress and tights, she looks beautiful, and I feel like I have to pretend I'm not watching. She opens a black leather case on the countertop, and inside is a contraption that she plugs in. Then she pulls out a black, lined disc to set on it.

"What's that?"

When it spins, it plays haunting old music I've never heard before. "Vinyl records," she says. "This is Cole Porter. I have some Frank Sinatra, some Nina Simone. They're all from about a hundred and fifty years ago. I scour the bins and thrift stores, and I restore them – " She returns to the blanket, and we dish out from the boxes onto our plates. The peppers and onions, and the sauce smells fantastic.

"I'd love to have a sort of vinyl cafe, with real pastry," she continues, "and real coffee, and books lining the walls, where Oliver could write."

"Then do that," I say.

"Banks will never, ever, give a black girl enough money to do that. And they'd confiscate the books and vinyl."

"I'd work there for you."

"You'd work there with me! You'd be like Nino, only hotter and younger," she says.

"I don't know... Nino is pretty hot," I joke. She laughs. I could never get tired of making her laugh.

"Aw, I wouldn't work you too hard. I'd want it to be more of a refuge for people who are unplugged."

"Why haven't you unplugged?"

She draws one side of her mouth back, and puckers to the side. "I suffered from epilepsy as a child."

"What's epilepsy?"

"Chronic seizures. I'd drop at random and twitch and jerk, and then be all groggy, and not remember much of it. I'd have these awful panic attacks. It's neurological, and treatable by companions. So my mother got one for me. Refurbed. It had been in a man before, a white man – I didn't know any of this until my dreams grew into his dreams, and he spoke to me – but I learned certain things. I enrolled in martial arts, because I felt drawn to it, and I excelled. I took every local tournament for ten years running. I couldn't go to regionals because I'm black, but I trained the white girls at the rape crisis centre on campus, and some of them went to regionals."

"He speaks to you?"

"All the time. I also know about guns. I don't know how it works, in the brain, but I know all about guns and ammunition, and how to use them. I have dreams about firing weapons all the time."

"That's kind of frightening."

"It took him a few years before he even used my name. He was bitter that he was stuck with me. But I think my experience won him over. He saw how hard I worked, and he realized how tough I was. Now he speaks to me when I need him, and he leaves me alone when I don't."

"Do you know who he was?"

"I would like to think that he lived a good life, and loved his family ... and I tell myself that." She nods, and bites her lip. "But I have an accurate picture of him in my head."

"Who was he?"

"Homeland Bureau Special Forces," she says, like she's ashamed of it.

"That explains a lot about your bullish nature."

"Bull-ish?" She's feigning shock. "Opinionated, maybe, but I don't see that as a bad thing."

"I wonder if my companion was someone else's before."

"I guess you never really know," she says with a shrug.

"Do you dream his dreams?"

"I do, but they're rare. I start them, and I know the difference right away."

"I don't feel like I dream my own dreams," I say.

"Oh you just wait 'til your mind gets free of the companion. Mine took a few weeks and then went wild. Do you dream about sex yet?"

"What?" I'm shocked. I don't know what to say, gaping like an idiot.

"Sex. Do you dream about it, yet?"

"I daydream about it, but I don't dream at night..."

"Oh, you will. Once the companion is out of the way. Religious groups fought to keep sex off the hive, so that kids wouldn't be exposed, and when religions were banned, the Republic censored it more. After the End War it just made sense. People were given other contentment, and it kept reproduction rates down without contraception." She smiles, and looks me over as if she's fitting me for a suit. "Let me guess, based on your demographic, you've had the log cabin, the beach, paragliding, because you're still young and adventurous, zip-line, and maybe a manual transmission gas muscle car-"

"How do you know all this?"

"After Amber died, I started to research. Everyone gets variations on the same dreams when they sleep, or under spell in the hive, with characters inserted from their own lives. It takes a while to start having your own dreams. You'll slowly reclaim them. There are others who went through similar experiences, even the inventor of the hive, apparently, in one of the early tests."

"I've become quiet about it. Sex I mean. It feels shameful or something."

"Oh ... I'll make you loud."

"Did you just say that?" I ask. I'm finishing the last of the cashew emu, and I'm blushing, but she's not backing down. What a girl.

A new song starts. Just a few chords. "I love this song – dance with me!" she says.

"I am a horrible dancer-" I protest, swallowing, finding a place for my chopsticks.

"Come on," she says, and I let her pull me to my feet, and put her arms around my neck, trying to look right into my eyes. "See, this is different. All you have to do is rock side to side, and hold on."

"And not step on your toes," I say. I smell her hair again, and feel her chest against mine.

"Well, that too," she says. "Isn't that nice?"

"It is wonderful, but I still can't guarantee your toes are safe."

"Aw c'mon, you're a good dancer," she says. "You're a natural."

"Yeah, but this is like the multiple-choice test of dancing. In a club I'd be downright embarrassing."

I slide my hands around to the small of her back, and feel the soft warmth of her skin through the fabric.

"I love this song. Dream a little dreaaaam of me..." she sings.

"It's beautiful."

"I can close my eyes and picture her with the old microphone, in a long dress, standing in front of a club, with people all dressed up. Adored. It's so moving to hear the love in her voice."

We dance, slowly, turning in a circle. I wish I had known her before all this, long ago, when I was young. It would have saved me so much searching, so much wasted time. She runs her hands up my shoulders and around my neck, and I pull her closer by her hips, and she puts her forehead to my chin. She tilts her head up, and kisses me, her cool nose on my cheek, and her lips moist against mine. She pulls my lips with hers, her hands behind my neck pulling me closer, and the music skips.

We laugh. Interrupted - "They do that," she says. She takes the needle off the vinyl, shuts off the machine, and leads me by the hand up to her loft. She pulls off my shirt, and I feel a flash of self-conscious panic. She pushes me down to her soft bed, piled with thick duvet covers that smell of lilac, and she straddles me, on her knees, gentle. She revels in running her hands all over me, her light touch on my legs, on my stomach, her hand gliding over my chest, feeling my hair, and I touch her, hand on her thigh, another hand on the small of her arched back. She rocks her hips on me. She pulls off my pants, and undresses, covers us in her blankets, like conspirators.

Every touch, every quiet reaction, every escaping sound is crystalline and pure, of its own essence in the liquid darkness. She is not reacting to her companion. She's reacting to me. Her pleasure is unmistakable and true. When she laughs, I know it's for me. I touch and please her, and I'm afraid if I don't savour it, remember all this, soon it will pass, and I won't have properly enjoyed it. I don't want it to ever end. We exhaust ourselves.

"You know ... I don't quite think we got that right," I say.

"What?" she says. She's shocked.

"No. I think we need more practice-"

She laughs, patting my arm.

"- try again sometime," I say. "Maybe-"

"Maybe," she says, playing coy. In a short while, she falls asleep with her cheek on my chest. I feel a stinging doubt. Why me? I'm not connected, or enhanced. I'm not clever, or even employed. And don't get me wrong, I'm ecstatic that she wants me, too. I have a hell of a time falling asleep, watching as the podlights outside cast curving squares on the ceiling. Why does it have to be so complicated? Why not seize happiness where I can find it?

* * *

I have the most wonderful feeling of contentment. We are on the deck of the New Jersey, taking a tour, Harper in a flowery summer dress, and white, pretty sandals, and I in a new pair of brown pants, and a thick, white, cotton, buttonless shirt, which I have never been able to afford. We are holding hands. Sailors – also in white – show us all the parts of the ship. Guns. Radio tower. Bridge. On the deck there is a table of catered food, with lemonade, and key lime pie, and confections laid out in rows, for all of us to help ourselves.

They are fawning over her, these sailors, and it's all playful – you ol' dog – and their looks make her laugh. And then I see that all the officers, in their tight blue jackets, have cutlasses. I feel an urge to get Harper off the ship without offending the sailors. She's protesting 'Why do we have to go? Have some key lime pie. Have some coffee. Real Kona.'

But the longer we are there the more I am filled with dread, and I fixate. It seems they are touching their scabbards and hilts just to intimidate us. 'Just joking'. Taking their swords out and comparing them, swishing through the air in wide arcs. We need to get out of here. But now we are steaming out, past the naval yard. There is no escape.

"Oh feck! I'm late!" she says, and leaps out of bed, descending the ladder to the parquet floor. For a moment I am confused, trying to get my bearings. I roll to the side of the mattress, so I can watch her streak, half naked, to her closet where she starts pulling clothing out and putting it on.

"Graceful!" I say. "Very graceful."

She laughs. "You're really enjoying this, aren't you?'

"I'm sure they'll understand if you're late," I say.

"Kevin needs an injection that he won't let anyone else give but me. He has to have it. Oliver will kill me if he has to do it." She starts for the door. "Come by later!" she yells.

"I will! I have to shower and change!"

"Ohhh ... I'm so torn. I just want to go up and spend the day with you in bed."

"Tonight!" I say.

"Okay! I have to go!"

And then the door slams, and the apartment is quiet and still. Her dress and tights are there on the bed with me, reminding me of the fun we had. I haven't slept much. Images from the night before come back to me, and I can feel the excitement welling back. I take my time climbing down and getting dressed. My clothing from the night before smells like Thai food. From the windows I can see the traffic coming into downtown on the freeway, and the rising sun reflected on the buildings to the north. I make a drawing of the food cartons, and of the vinyl player, and of the discs, and of the coffee, and the walk, footprints in the snow; all the happy reminders of our night, and I leave it on her pillow.

Outside, the wind is especially damp, and bites at my cheeks. It's coming in from the west like a freight train, barrelling down the Appalachian passes and picking up speed on its way to the Atlantic. It's a long walk up to the apartment, and, without my scarf, my face is nearly numb. There's a light spit of rain starting to freeze on the roads. Each drop feels like a cold pin prick.

I can't help but smile. I don't remember some parts, but I remember the feeling, the waves of pleasure, the exploding senses, my hardness and the motion of her hips. Her turn. Our turn. It was all our turn. I remember the fluidity, how everything naturally moved into where we needed it, and we found our pleasures in the curves and arches, in the exploration of touch, the breath on our cheeks, air passed between us and shared like fruit, with sweetness and ripening warmth.

As I enter my building lobby, I can see the landlord fixing an electronic deadlock on my door upstairs.

"Woah! Wait!" I say, rushing up to him. "What are you doing?"

"I'm sorry Rufus. I just got notice that Social Services is no longer paying," he says, waving his hands like I'm going to shoot him.

"That's not right. I just saw them."

"I got an order to evict. I tried to reach you. Sent messages. All nada, negatory, no reply. I didn't know what to do. It's an order."

"Can I get some things?"

"Yeah. Get what you need. Sorry, Rufe. You been a good tenant. Store the rest in the basement if you like."

I box up my things, and put them in the musty concrete basement in a stack, and from upstairs I grab my toothbrush, some food, clothing, and my pillow. I stuff them into an old green duffel, and then try to text Harper, but my glass service has been cut off.

Mason.

I bet he did this after we argued. I am so angry that I trudge nearly to Lee Park before I look up to the same path I'd walked in bliss moments ago. I turn to see a familiar face following me. Cap, walking a half football field behind, shadowing my path, where my father once disappeared. It's frightening to think of how comfortable we are in this very space. I bet they lost me when I went to Harper's, and regained me back at my apartment. Maybe they shut off my services to draw me out. No. This has to be Mason. I don't even foresee a future in which I can be happy if Mason has it out for me. Certainly not like my parents who lived in relative comfort. He can make it impossible for me to work or live without relying on others. I'll be destitute if I can't at least find a job.

And Harper. How do I tell her I'm now homeless, that all I have in this world is with me in this duffel? I'm so angry, after all these years, that he would do this. He's done shit like this before, but never this spiteful. What the hell do I do? I'd be able to support myself if I could work, but without a companion it's impossible. I'm not going back to Mason. If he did this, the only way to back down will be to join the party, and I will not do that.

At the Veterans Co-op, I'm hesitant to even go inside because things have been pulled from under me before. Perhaps Harper was only trying to get me in bed. Perhaps it was all a plan to see if I would accept Mason or reject him, all staged to test my loyalty, and I failed, and now there will be nobody at the Veterans Co-op at all, just boarded up windows.

I am relieved to find that nothing has changed. Pablo is there at the counter when I set my duffel down.

"Don't tell me you joined up," he says.

"Sorry, what?"

"The duffel bag."

"Oh. No. I got evicted."

"Oh, sorry Man. We deal with this all the time with the Vets. Anything they can do to squeeze an extra buck out of someone who's down. Usually a visit to Soc-Serv straightens it out. Harper is upstairs doing the rounds. She'll be down soon. I thought you were going to tell me you were having second thoughts. I was going to kick your ass to the sidewalk. I've never seen her this happy."

"No. We had a wonderful night. I'm afraid to tell her now-"

"Don't you worry about that. Want some breakfast?" Our lives revolve around food now.

"I would love some breakfast. Thank you." He sets some joe on the counter for me while I'm taking off my jacket, piling it on the stool at the end. "What I really need is a job."

"That'll come. You can take the couch in the lounge for now."

"Thanks. You're saving me."

"Don't mention it. We'll get you back on your feet."

"Well, thanks-"

"Hold on..." He turns up the volume to a breaking story on the glass beside him.

"The sabotage of the TransPenn pipeline, that brings fresh water to Philadelphia, is quickly turning into a humanitarian crisis. The Water Authority estimates that it will take several days to recommission the Brockston water filtration and pumping station, and in the meantime, residents are advised to boil their water for five minutes before use, and to refrain from drinking or washing in the Delaware or Schuylkill, both of which are deemed unsuitable for human consumption."

"Oliver will be pissed," he says. "Shit." He turns and puts a huge pot on the stove, and lights the burner, then turns the water spout to fill it.

There is a clip of the President at his desk in the oval office. "All the proper precautions being taken to keep the public safe. We will find those responsible, and we will deal with them with all the powers available to the Republic. We stand united and resolute that nobody should dictate how we are to live, especially through violence."

Pablo puts a breakfast emree out for me – eggs and emu bacon, with cream of wheat, all steaming hot.

"Thanks."

"Don't mention it."

"These people think that they can threaten us?" The President continues. "I'll tell you this – we will never back down to terrorists. Look. Folks, there are a lot of people who want power out there, and I get that. But they're doing it by putting people at risk instead of coming to the table like Americans, and working it out. If they want to talk, we'll talk. Blowing up the fresh water supply, that our people ... our working class people ... built ... that's an insult. They don't speak for the people," the President says. "I speak for the people!" Pablo turns it off.

Harper comes down the stairs. "You made it!" she says, and comes over to hug me. "What's wrong? Something's wrong."

"Rufus got evicted," Pablo says. "Cut off his payments, too. He's going to stay here a bit."

"Oh, Honey," she says, and hugs me. I don't feel like I deserve it. Feck she smells good. "Oh, I'm so sorry! I feel responsible."

"You're not responsible," I say, and she hugs me tighter.

"No, if I hadn't argued with him, you'd still be in your place. Stay with me instead." I can't even keep up with her hands. She's checking me like I'm hurt.

"No. I'll be such a burden," I say. "I'm fine here."

"I can't believe they did that! Are they even allowed?"

"I'm sure they are."

"It's specifically for people affected by their software," she says. "That's exactly what it's for! I hate seeing them always say they'll fix things, and then-" she stops herself. "That asshole! It was him, wasn't it? Because of an argument!"

"Let the boy eat!" Pablo says.

"I just get so angry when someone hurts my guys," she says.

"You're one of us now," he says to me, and rolls his eyes like that's a curse, not a blessing.

Kevin and Phil enter the lounge with a clatter as Kevin bumps into the door in his rush.

"Hey, good morning, Sunshine," Pablo says.

"Look. Don't give me that 'sunshine' crap. Something crazy is going on," Phil says. "What is it?"

"Rufus got evicted," Harper says. "His buddy is high up in the Dep-Res, and I yelled at him last night for being a racist pig, and so they cut him off."

"That's typical," Phil says.

"That and the Nya Vaasa blew the pipeline last night," Pablo adds.

"Oh shit," Phil says. "It started."

"You know," Kevin says, sitting down a few stools over, pointing at Pablo. "I believed we were fighting for our freedom, and that the socialists were going to take over. That's what you would have thought listening to Fox ... back then-"

"Don't you say too much," Phil warns, interrupting him.

"Lemme finish," he says.

"By all means finish."

"I've kept my mouth shut for too long. It's not like they care what an eighty year old asshole says. They're just waiting for us to die. They made socialism sound awful. But it was our golden age. So when we fought the Second World War," he says, finger upheld. "...which they don't teach any more, by the way, there were three sides, not two. I don't think anyone today would know that. Three. It was free societies allied with communists to defeat fascism in Germany, Italy, and Japan, because they were the greater threat. But after the war, the communists were the greater threat. We went so far against the communists that we gradually embraced fascism. The End War was no fight between communism and capitalism, the 'free world' and the 'reds'. It wasn't an ideological war. The rich gained control of both systems. The leaders had more in common than the people fighting below them. In the papers of the day, before the Republic, there was a very different take on the war. Kastor was no Churchill. More of a Stalin. Before his overhaul of the electoral system, there used to be States, each with their own governments, like countries within countries. The Republic was known as the United States. In fact, many believed that the End War was an excuse to take power for good."

"Fascism. You're always talking-"

"-that's what this is! Look around! Don't you see people living out misery, without their parents or siblings, distracted by games and trinkets?" Kevin says. "The only people with power are white, middle aged men."

"As long as Kastor controls the jobs, it doesn't matter what the popular vote is," Phil replies.

"Well that's another story – and when he took away freedom of the press, he created the Fourth Reich."

"They don't know what that is," Phil says.

"Right. Okay. Well, the long and short is that I love my country. I love America, but this isn't my country any more," Kevin says.

"You be careful what you say," Phil warns, quieter this time.

"No. I won't," Kevin says. "We used to have laws, not just to keep people in check, but also to keep corporations and the government in check. Now all we have are these damn companions that keep us in check, and the rich do whatever the hell they want. We've gone from laws to 'mandates', and the hive judges us every day and every hour on what we think, and intervenes with therapy we may not even need or know we're getting."

"We tried to fight this too little, and too late," Phil says.

"But you fought," Harper says.

"We failed," Phil says, without emotion. "We fought the End War, sure, but we didn't know it would never end. The war distracted us."

"We had freedom," Kevin says. "First they controlled the voting machines, and the districts, and then the supreme court. All in the name of keeping out the communists and Muslims and the immigrants. They cut schools and health programs. They kept giving more and more to the military, and then re-jigging elections until they never lost. Then the purges, when they outlawed the other parties, then got rid of states and the Electoral College. Then there were protests. We had no choice."

"Sure we had a choice," Phil says. "We all had a vote, and a voice, and we handed government to the Republicans. We chose this, out of fear and ignorance."

"You're right. Of course. The war changed all that. We thought we were better than them, but boy were we in for some surprises."

"Courage," Kevin says. "Honour. Justice. We were told those were the ideals we had to aspire to. Taking care of the weak. Being strong. I didn't know that someday I would be the weak, and that nobody would care, and that the Republicans meant the opposite of what they said."

"They're just code words now," Phil says.

"You got that right. They're always saying to be the hero that you need." Kevin says. "But how is that even possible when we're told not to question anything?"

"I'm too old to be a hero now," Phil says. "Even when I was doing what seemed heroic – what people would say was heroic – I didn't feel like one. I was on an M1 Abrams when we closed the gap at Aleppo, and I'll tell you, none of this was a foregone conclusion. We went to Syria after the Russians took Kiev, and the European Union forces were getting the piss pounded out of them in Germany and Romania. We figured we'd hit the underbelly. We got to Aleppo, driving for Georgia when they closed the trap. We lost half our company to their dug-in anti-tank guns. We took Aleppo by sheer balls, guns blazing and a shitload of young men in Bradleys, nearly blind from the EMP blanket and ECM. Of course, we held them in Beirut. That's history. Kept the Middle East and India in our sphere. At least for a while. Secured the oil, but it was a rough go. It took a war-time economy to do it. The guys we captured, some of them could speak English, too, and we got to know them pretty good. The joke was that we were fascists hiding behind dollars, and they were communists hiding behind roubles."

"They don't teach what happened," Kevin says. "History is a series of lies repeated."

"Before all this, when we moved we didn't have to ask permission. There were no committees on population mobility. Dad just put the house up for sale, and we bought a new one in Philly, around 'twenty-nine. We were into our third term with '47, and there was a lot of anger in the south, anger where they were trying to suppress voters. So Dad thought moving here would change things for us, to get us away from the violence."

"We didn't defeat slavery. It just developed a sliding scale," Harper says.

"Are we enslaved?" Kevin asks. "I look out the window at the pods and foods and fashions, the buildings, and the order, the lack of expression. There is only one state media. One party. National Heritage. All this looks exactly like the fascist system we were fighting in the first place."

"We always say 'How did we get here?' as if it's some kind of great mystery, but I think we know. Good people crave order and stability, but to attain that, we need to keep our heads down, and live our best lives. There's certainly a place for that, but people who seek power know how to promise us stability, to use it to erode our freedoms and our systems for making things equal. They pit us against each other, give us false choices, and make us part of the problem. They want less regulation, and less taxes, because those are the very things we use to create a fair system. They don't want a fair system. They want one in which their superiority gives them advantage."

"I don't recognize my own country any more." Kevin says. "Police following innocent people. No freedom to speak out and garbage on the truth report. It's all lies."

"Two generations of having companions, and we'll never change this back," Pablo says.

"Are you in trouble? Are they after you?" Kevin asks.

"We're being followed," Harper says. "Which feels like nothing but intimidation. If they're not going to arrest us, why follow us?"

"I'm sorry I got you into this," I say.

"It's alright. You didn't get me into it. You've done nothing wrong." She takes my hand and looks me in the eyes. "It's me," she says.

"Thank you," I say. "I just wish it hadn't gone so sour with Mason. If we'd just not gone-"

"I think it would have happened anyway," she says. "You didn't just become like this overnight, and neither did he. He's powerful, and you're idealistic. You've been on a collision course with him since you were kids."

"He was never like this before."

"Well, he doesn't run Soc-Serv," Pablo says. "Maybe if you went down and showed them your file..."

"Even if he's doing it to force me into the party. I'm not going to. I won't lose my friends, and you, and my soul because of his blackmail. I'll talk to Soc-Serv. If they won't fix it, then I'll get our friends to pressure Mason. This can't go on. I have nothing left."

"You have us."

"But no money and no job, and no way to get one. I can't stop living," I say. But then I have doubts. I take most of the cash out of my pocket, and give it to Harper. "If they hold me, or I don't come back, then you'll know you're in danger. Use this to get out of Philly. Run. California. Canada. Just run."

"You're coming back, right?"

"Of course," I say, and smile. "It won't take long. I promise. I'll see my social worker and have my file re-assessed. Back for supper."

"Be careful," she says.

* * *

I have to pass the campus to get to the bridge, and often, when I'm walking through the University, I think about where my father disappeared, where they pushed him into a black pod. Which step was it along his walk? Here? This one? Over across the street?

Of course, nobody saw it happen. We saw it happen to others, my mother telling me to keep my eyes down, not to look. We held secrets for each other, bore witness to the last moments of loved ones – but not our own – and carried our testimonies for one another in our hearts. I'm sure someone saw my father, and I hope he saw in their face a bit of sympathy. Perhaps they flashed them a signal for solidarity, the outlaw 'archer fingers' punishable by death during the purges.

I have often thought about why my father disappeared, but naively, for a long time, I believed that he was involved in something he shouldn't have been. I thought that he was taking chances. Now I'm sure he was doing the right thing, caught there when the HeeBees raided. Maybe it was his first meeting, or the wrong protest at the wrong time. I never asked those questions before, and perhaps I should have asked them, later, before my mother died. Perhaps only strangers know the answers.

Of course, that was before. Nobody disappears now. They don't have to. The companions ensure that everyone has the 'protection' of the system, the right to a fair judgment. There's no punishment. The AI knows the criterion for behaviour, and it is corrected through dreams, hormones, and altered states of thought. No more televised trials, corporate sponsors, or retributive sentences. Companions restrain movements and actions. There are no prisons in a country without escape.

I am here. Soc-Serv. In the same line as before, with what seems like the same people in the same places as last week. It is a different woman than before, or maybe the same one, who looks a little different, and by the time I get to the front of the line, it is afternoon, and I'm starving. I didn't think to pack lunch. 'Apply early!' ... 'Don't be disappointed!' the poster says.

Two and a half hours later, it is a different spelled woman behind the plexi, giving me the same look as the one before.

"I'm trying to find out why my support has been cut off. I've been evicted," I say. I want to ask who put the order on my file, be it Mason, or the Heebees, but I know they won't tell me. I'm pretty sure I know the answer already.

She looks off into the space beyond me for a beat, and then smiles. "You've been convicted of non-payment of your debts."

"What debts?"

"Fifty-five days of semi-private care at Penn Hospital at three thousand nine hundred forty three euros a day, and forty one days in rehabilitation centre Oakview at six thousand two hundred seventeen euros a day, plus ambulance, patient transfer-"

"How much total?" I interrupt.

"Six hundred ninety three thousand, seven hundred forty one euros, and fifty two cents."

"Seven hundred thousand?" I don't even know how to process this.

"Nearly that. Did you want to settle that up today?"

"Settle it up? Are you insane?"

Mason. I'm sure it was Mason now.

"Is there an appeal procedure?" I ask.

"No. You used the services."

"I can't pay that."

"Oh, well then I guess your services won't be restored. Have a nice day," she says. "Next!"

"But wait! What do I do? I have to live!"

"Sorry, Darlin', Soc-Serv can't help you with that."

"Thanks," I say, sarcastically.

"You're very welcome," she says. "I'm happy to have served you."

Past tense, meaning, go away. You're done.

Outside, my police shadows are across the street waiting. I'm about to cross the podstream to say something cheeky and shocking to them, like asking them if they found their dog, when a man, on his way inside, stops, turns, and begins to walk toward me. I doubt he's got something to say to me, and I don't trust it. I back away, and he picks up a pin-bar from the iron workers in the closed lane beside us. My shadows are anxious now, on the other side, waiting for a break, hands on their weapons, trying to get to me. Is this the hit? Is this how they took my father? Broad daylight?

I run. Full bore. Over barricades, past shops, and into an alley. I climb up a dumpster, and then hand-over-hand on a fire escape over a fence, and into a vacant yard. I think I've lost him. I keep on for a couple of blocks, jogging, my heart thudding in my chest, arms painful now, and my breath short, coming out in puffs. I have to loosen my jacket to cool off, and then I duck into a store.

The older Asian woman at the counter looks up from where she's counting money into the till. As her eyes meet mine, she drops the coins and reaches for a cleaver.

I run. Oh Shit. They are trying to kill me.

There's a kid on the street, a girl in a pretty flower parka and white socks, with runners, her long blonde hair in pigtails. She looks up at me, and runs at me. She's fast. She dives over the trash cans, and grabs a broken hammer off the ground. She has gymnastic abilities, and I'm getting tired, and it's terrifying. What do I do if she catches me? Sure, she's ten, but what can I do to an innocent ten-year-old kid who wants to kill me? What the sodding hell do I do? I'm heading east, into unfamiliar territory, where I can't count on knowing my way, and I try to loop back somehow. And I trip, and I sprawl. I'm in the trash. Ice. I didn't see the ice on the ground. She launches herself onto me, tries to bite my arm, and sinks one hand into my forearm. Her grip on the hammer slips as I try to get it from my face, and I knock it from her hand. Time is running out. Someone else will be here soon.

Holy sod, kid. Let go.

She's a kid. I can't hit her, but if I don't get her off, I'm dead.

With a jerk, I free myself, knock her down, and run. I hop a fence and cross behind two parked pods, and hustle down the next alley. She's running behind me with a crazy efficient gate, like a runner, not a kid. She's freaking fast. I jump another fence, and then duck quickly around a corner and into a garbage bin, and peek out from under the bag. It's a dead end. There's nowhere to go. She stops at the end of the alley, walks a few paces, and looks around. Then she just walks away.

It's the hive. It's the freaking hive. I wasn't meant to wake up. I was meant to stay AFK and die. That's why they want to kill me. They used me for something and now they want me to die. But I know what I have already seen – the sword. The one in my dreams – and I had recognized the desk, hadn't I? On the truth report. The crime scene. Historic footage. Assassination. I was there, I'm sure. I can disappear. If I'm not in range, I don't even show on their companions unless they're police. I'm a danger to all my friends. If they identify me, they'll be spelled, and then killed. I can't even organize my own thoughts. Why now? Not before? Why? I'm desperate, and they have been crafting a narrative. Now I'm the guy refused services, unplugged. Stripped of all that he owns. Now I fit their story, one that could get me killed.

Now what? Now the mothersodding shit what do I do when there are cameras on every shop and street corner and pod and even my friends – no, everyone – everyone who is not blind can retinal me and kill me? Sophie. Mason. Elijah. Charlotte. Any of them can try to kill me. And then not wake up. I need to find people off the hive. I don't know which way to go. I'm surrounded by eight million people, all of them potential assassins.

I sneak through alleys with my hood pulled tight around my face, and I walk quickly, trying not to draw attention. I'm just a guy hunched against the cold. I hope Henrys and Samanthas are on a different server because if they try to kill me I have no chance. I glance up at a shop, and a man looks at me. He has the most neutral expression, like he's not angry, or focused, like he could be eating pizza, but staring at me. I run. Where the feck can I go? He's chasing me now, and I'm getting tired.

Oliver. The basement. I need to get to the Veterans Co-op and the basement, where he can disguise me and feed me until I can figure out what to do. The guy isn't as fast as the kid, but he's not tired, and I'm exhausted. He has a creepy mechanical gait, like an efficient machine, never slipping or being distracted, as I am. He's gaining. I haven't run so much in my life. I dodge down to Kastor way, to cross the metal slung footbridge under the road bed. Nobody ever goes there.

- but wait. If I go over the bridge, the hive can just spell someone on the other side, and I'd be trapped. C'mon, think. Just before the bridge, I dodge north. Then I see one of my police shadows, and they are running, too, trying to catch up and head us off. They're surprised. Not in on it. It has to be the hive. Oh shit. There's a beat cop up there, and he's noticed us. As I run toward him he reaches for his gun. I put my hands up. "That guys trying to kill me!" I yell. "Don't hurt him. He's spelled."

"Woah," he says to the guy, but the guy comes on like a bull, and rams into him. The cop gets him in a hold. "Call 9-1-1," he says.

"I can't. I don't have a companion."

"Oh shit."

"Call 9-1-1!" I yell, and I can see my police shadows, two of them, sprinting at us from down the street.

The man grapples well, puts the cop into a choke hold, and his body twists and writhes as he tries to free himself. He reaches around the cop's waist, and grasps the butt of the gun. The cop realizes this, elbows him in the face. "Lock!" he yells to the gun, then releases the hold, and then there are several cops all there, bursting from several nearby pods. They restrain the man, and come for me, and I run, but I'm not fast enough, and they tackle me, wrestle me to the side of the alley. They hoist me to my knees, one arm under each of my armpits, and one puts a hood over my head that cinches over my neck. Feck, they're going to kill me! I struggle, but then there's a shooting pain in my side, like a bee sting, and I can barely move, suddenly feeling a great lethargy. I can see through the fabric.

They're trying to kill me, I say, but it comes out a slur. "Zhehh tryannnna kimmeee..."

"Shut up," he says. "They can't kill you if they can't retinal you."

They push me into a pod, and one of them sits across from me. It's a quiet ride back into the downtown, and into the underground parking of what I assume is the Dep-Just. They are not gentle with me as they drag me out of the pod and into a lift. They refuse people getting in with us, flashing badges, and hands outstretched. We rise with a sounding of chimes. The doors open, and they push me to the left, along a tunnel out over a street. We're going inside the cube. We cross a plexi tunnel bridge on the third floor. My rubbered legs drag, and they half-carry me. Inside is an ancient building that I'm sure most people have never seen. Everything seems shadowed. From what I can see through the hood, there are upper levels, mirrored glass exterior, a building within a building like a Russian nesting doll. It is tall, with a stone and brick facade, and concrete atria, and concourses added, with glass-and-concrete conference rooms and walkways and connecting ramps surrounding it. What actually happens in the cube is all rumour, but everyone knows that this is the headquarters of the Heebees.

We pass row after row of cubicles, with well-dressed men, talking and passing papers back and forth, and reading glasses – but the hood must alter the signal, because everything on the glasses is blurred. It is as if the shroud of the cube and my hood are made from the same fibres. I have a weak-knee, hot-skin feeling, that I'll never get out of this building, that these are my last actions, that I have no chance of survival. They lead me into a hall, and down about half-way, where we turn and enter another room of cubicles. It's bright, with only a couple of people. They sit me in a chair that takes over my restraints, my arms on the chair arms now pressured. I can imagine all kinds of torture. I should have prepared, looked up resistance techniques and practised. My legs are coming back to me now.

I can see a blurry couple of dozen desks, and several men in suits with badges and white identity cards that I can't read. It smells of ... coffee. Real coffee and fried food. "Restraints, Jenks," one says. I crane to see him, but I can only see his tag and belt for a moment, and I can't move my arms. Then he crouches in front of me to look at me. As far as I can figure out, 'the kid' is actually named Jenkins, or 'Jenks', but I don't know his first name. He has a worn and faded laminated identification card hanging from his belt, and the last name is all I can make out from it. The picture looks nearly exactly as he is now – clean shaven and smirking.

'Watch Me' takes the hood off. "My name is Detective Walter Andersson. You will talk only to me, to Jenks, or to my assistant, Lemar. Is that clear?"

"Yes," I say. Comparing his face to his ID, I can assume it's been a very long path from the clean cut guy in the picture to the greying, scarred, and stubbled man before me.

"Okay," he says, and sighs.

"I'm not even sure why I'm here," I say. "Why are they trying to kill me?"

"We don't know. But we do know who you are. We know about Nya Vaasa, and that you weren't near the pipeline, but that you're deep in this. So you need to start talking."

"About what? I don't know anything."

"We believe you were involved in an assassination. We don't know what part you played, but with all that's going on around you, we'd really like to hear the story directly from you."

I don't want to believe it. I'm torn. It fits with the violent dreams, and the reason why I was AFK. It makes sense, but I can't imagine being there and doing that. I can't even figure out the timeline. "Before they kill me, you mean."

He doesn't answer.

"Why should I co-operate with you?" I ask.

"You don't have a choice."

"There's always a choice," I say.

"Look. We're not entirely sure what to do with you. We have surveillance on a guy who seems completely clueless, who just happens to be one of the innocents spelled for an assassination in the fall, and who just happens to be a sole survivor, protected by a mysterious order not to apprehend. Then this guy just happens to date a woman who happens to have a brother involved in a terrorist organization, and when we dig deeper, just happens to be friends with a high level Homeland Bureau operative who's so top-secret we don't even know his real last name. That's a mountain of circumstance, and very little substance. So either you're an idiot who has stumbled into a shit-tonne of top-shelf crap going on around you, or you're one of the genius masterminds bringing terrorists to justice and I'm missing the line that connects the dots. Either way I can't wait to get in that head of yours."

"You have just told me far more than I had ever dreamed. Terrorists? Assassination? Homeland ... Bureau friend – I really have no idea."

"Okay," he says, and cracks his knuckles. "Idiot it is." I get the impression that if I challenged him, he would calmly take off his watch before thumping me. A young black man with spectacles and a lab coat, comes up on my right and sits at the desk beside me.

"This is Lemar. He's going to hook you up," Andersson says.

"Hook me up to what?" I'm fighting back panic again.

"I'm Lemar. I'll be your evil scientist for this evening," the young guy says.

"Lemar," Andersson chastises.

"Okay. That was a joke. We're going to turn your companion back on," he says.

"No. No. Wait! I can tell you what I know. I just don't know anything – not what you're talking about. Just ask questions. I'll answer. You don't need-"

"So talk," Andersson says.

"I was on my way home from work, on the bus, and then I was in a dream that lasted forever, and then after I woke to a bright light."

"Before you were spelled, did you talk to anyone odd? See anything violent?"

"I wandered. I wandered a long time," I say, pleading.

"That's the base program. No, I mean before you were spelled."

"Nothing."

"Do you have any dreams, since then?"

"I have ... troubling dreams." I want to tell him about the sword, and the woman in the house, and how I have flashes of violent thoughts, as if I could kill. I'm afraid if he hears any of this it will be recorded, and I'll end up dead or in prison or work camps for the rest of my days.

"Gory?"

"No."

"Troubling how?"

"Anxious. Keeping people from harm."

He doesn't reply, just sits, staring at me, and I stare back at him until my eyes hurt, and I have to consciously not blink.

"Okay," he says. "If you don't remember, then we have to turn your companion back on, separate from the hive, to interface it with our server and get into its memory."

"I could die."

"We will all die, someday," he says.

"I didn't do it," I say.

"I don't know that."

"But the evidence-"

"Do you think anyone gives a good feck what part you played?" he yells. "The hive doesn't care. It thinks in algorithms. Data. Whatever it needs to happen, it makes happen until it doesn't need it any more."

"Why me? I'm a nobody! I haven't done a damn thing! I don't even have a home any more!"

"You were given money."

"Why aren't you spelled?" I ask. "Do I just sit in here and wait until one of you kills me?"

"Valid questions. Our companions are segregated from the main hive."

"So you're not trying to kill me."

"No. We're trying to keep you alive. So, let me get you up to speed, off the record. There is a kill order out for you on the hive, which we can't track. I'm sure you know that. Anywhere, at any time, anyone can suddenly try to kill you, with whatever means on hand. Family. Friends. Your ninety year old grandmother. No remorse. No pleading. No trial. No record. Gone. Then they will probably go AFK and die. Now, to relieve that kill order requires either someone with equal authority to remove it, or a change in circumstances to render it useless, when it will expire. Sometimes a kill order can last minutes, and sometimes years. To kill you, they need an identification, which means a retinal or a facial recognition. That's why the hood. Your friends and family can talk to you as long as they don't look at you. The assassin also needs a clear shot with a set of parameters that are set up fresh with every kill order. The variables are often 'non-spell witnesses, media, ability to clean up and assign blame, the rank of the spelled person who commits the crime, and the ability for law enforcement to investigate'. They don't want a big mess."

"That's why they chose me. I was a nobody."

"You still are."

"So why do they want to kill me?"

"The assassinations, of course. You dropped off the hive, and all record of you was deleted, even in the backups. The only record we have of that night, and your actions, is in your companion."

"Are there no cameras? No drone footage? Other people's data?"

"I understand why you wouldn't want the companion back on. It's been traumatic for you. But the reality is that we have nothing else. The entire zone was blanked. It was a very sophisticated operation with a lot of money," he says. "No trace. Relayed from inside the hive itself."

"Why don't I remember?"

"Spell software terminates with code that gives control back to the user. But when you were spelled, you were left in a suspended state. By the time we figured this out and tracked you down, you were the only one who revived."

"Who were the others?"

"Random. No connections. Assassins and helpers. This wasn't about you. It was all about the target. You were a tool to be used and thrown away. Now you're a loose end. Here we are."

"Don't turn on my companion. Please. I beg you-"

He shrugs. "You don't have a choice."

"How can there be no record? How would they blank all those companions and video?" I ask.

"Good question," he says. "I can't answer it, but you can. Your companion is our only data source. It locked down those memories before it was shut down, maybe to protect you, and maybe to protect itself or the hive. It's a miracle. For us, anyway. We need in."

I have no choice. I'm restrained. I'm in their territory. I can't resist. I have to but I can't. "How does this work?"

"I'll get into your companion," Lemar says. "I'll spell you, find the information, and maybe help you stay alive in the next few days."

"What's to stop them from hacking me again?" I ask.

"You will be invisible to the hive, on the same secure server as we are. Multiple layers of encryption. For the retinals, we have lenses that fit right over your eyes." He holds up two tiny slippery discs.

"What if I don't want them?" I ask.

He rolls his eyes. "Again. No choice. Don't worry. It's old technology. People used them to correct vision way back when."

"So they won't be in my head. But you could be," I say. I'm bitter. Angry. I have no way to fight back.

"I don't want to be in your head," he says. "I have to be. I need your memories."

"Those are my memories! How can you do this?"

"We intercept and alter the ventral stream, changing the incoming stimulus, and then access the stored long-term memory. Ventral portal is the gateway to the self."

"Can you at least minimize it, so I can't be spelled?"

"No. It's the dorsal stream that affects spelling. But you don't need to know-" Lemar says, and holds up a finger. "All this is based on the holes in each companion, and how they were installed. Yours is a ventral-dorsal, so there will always be a risk of being spelled. We have ventrals. There are some that are only dorsal, but those are for extreme medical situations, like Downies or Palsy, or for people with brain injuries who can't benefit from a ventral."

"Can't you just take the companion out?"

"That's major surgery. So no." He puts the palm of his hand on my forehead. "Sit still," he says, and then he puts lenses in my eyes. "This is temporary. You can still be identified closer than a metre away, and it can be done through any node. A person. A monitor. A bank entrance. Train station. Pod stand. Airport. Anywhere there's a camera. So it's not foolproof. But it will work at a distance."

"Great..."

"If you check in they'll find you. But this stops accidental retinals."

"I have nothing to lose." I'm swallowing a lump of panic.

"That's about it," he says, nodding. "But being alive in here trumps being dead out there. Trust me. You're far safer here than anywhere else," Lemar says. On his glass, there's a notification. "Okay. We have primary boot. Looks good so far. We ready?"

Andersson nods. I'm not ready. They don't care if I am or not. I am sweating, and my arms are fidgeting. I need to know what part I played, but I don't want to have a companion, and I don't have a choice. It's like slowly sliding into a pit and having no grip, not even knowing where I'll end up.

"This is going to hurt," Lemar says. "You'll be going right into a spell. So you'll be in pain before the pain management kicks in."

"Thanks for your honesty."

"No. I mean. It's really going to fecking hurt. A lot. All those neurons that healed, all the new pathways, dreams, memories, all of those are going to be forced to change. Your striate cortex will warm up. You might puke, shit yourself, cardiac arrest – we'll revive you – palpitations, sweats … anything can happen."

"Can I die?"

"Of course. Sit still. Here we go."

First there is just the frame, like squares of just-darker vision on the fringes, and it's familiar – creepy familiar – and a little distracting. Then, the time loads, and weather. Biorhythms. Truth Report. Assassinations. Trade deals. Russian hacking. Then, the stored messages, a tsunami of contact between myself and everyone showing their concern and asking where I am, unread and cascading across my vision, and I feel the back of my head getting warm with all the information, then everyone clouds in with the knowledge that I'm AFK and they panic, copy me on everything, forget I am copied, and talk about my state, what to do if they unplug me, set up pages, book time off work to visit. Sophie, at the fore, asking everyone their thoughts.

Then there is pain. Excruciating, searing base-of-the-neck migraine pressured sinus headache pain, and shooting shards of hot shock down my spine, and then the pain subsides, and I'm back in my childhood home, the little place in Powelton.

* * *

Chapter 7

My mother used to do everything the old way, even if there was a better way. She peeled apples by hand to make applesauce. She'd buy pears from the market, and slice them on my toast in the morning. She sang old songs that I never hear any more. She was kind to everyone. On our road trips we would release the pod out on the Westchester Pike, to explore on foot. She'd have me look at caterpillars in lines, build forts out of sticks, and climb trees while she sat out on a blanket to read her books. She wanted me to imagine what it was like before all this, and said the city was no place for kids. I don't know why I'm thinking about this now, but I am. Wait. Because she is here. I am here, in our old house, from before Dad disappeared.

She comes out of the kitchen, carrying a plate with supper – pigeon and gravy, with broccoli and peas and potatoes – an actual meal, and a mug in the other hand. Hot chocolate.

"Sit down, before it gets cold," she says.

I am stunned. She sets down the plate on the table, and I go to her, and hug her up, her white hair on my neck, and that smell – I don't even care if it's not real, a dream, or whatever, that she's not there. It's just so blessed wonderful to see her again.

When she pulls away, a little embarrassed, she says "You're too young to remember when there was crime everywhere, when people couldn't trust each other. They would come into our houses, and steal from us, and we had to avoid going outside. Right here, in Philly."

"I remember," I say. "Why do you need to say this?"

"It's just ... we all do what we think is best. You have to understand," she says, "that we all wanted the same things. Our kids to grow up safe, and have meaningful lives. It was government went all crazy. They started the mess. We thought it would pass."

"We?" This doesn't sound like my mother. It sounds like an apology from the companion, like one of those dreams I used to have.

"Before the hive, people were obsessed with sex," she says. Goddamn. Another lecture. "Over half of everything people posted on the internet – movies, music, stories, photos – was about sex. People were so numerous that something had to be done. So instead of all the policies that failed, limiting pregnancy, and forced sterilization, the hive helped to liberate humanity from its obsession! The world has half the population of a hundred years ago, because companions keep unruly sex drives in check. Now it's nice to know that people connect because they love each other, and not for sex, isn't it?" She waves her hands, as if she's torn by her thoughts. "We didn't always agree," she says, but it feels like she's not talking to me. "We tried to tell them-"

My mother wouldn't say this. I'm not connected though, so it's not the hive. Maybe the remnants of the hive interface on the spell program, or I'm connected through the police server. I am completely at their mercy. Of course, there are no notifications or hot drink coupons, or 'friend I haven't seen' prompts to distract me from a story I already know. She was kind, gentle, and tough, and looked out for me, and didn't give up even when we went through the toughest of times, me and the boys, getting into trouble after curfew. We had seventy curfew violations one summer, drinking cheap wine down by the river to avoid the sensors. She later said she never felt like she fully slept, or that anything was in control, until I went to university.

"Why did you leave, Mom?" I don't know why I'm asking this, but she can't answer, merely holds up her hands like she's pleading, but it's a glitch. She didn't leave. She never would have. She died of cancer. I know that. They want me to fill in the details, give the reason so she can say it back, but the companion can't find an answer because she didn't actually leave. We're always on our own for the larger questions. And then she turns to the sink, and washes the pots from the morning, and Harper knocks on the screen door frame as she lets herself in. Harper is the perfect version, the version she would be if she loaded hair and makeup programs into her companion. Fake. She's pretty, of course. Beautiful. She's smiling, and now walking barefoot on the grass outside, carrying her sandals in her right hand, and reaching out for me with her left. Wait. Grass? I don't know how we got here ... until ... I can feel Lemar navigating, like a fast-motion background hum of images and smells and tastes tainting the scene, and I make a conscious choice to climb aboard where he is...

They said I was picked up in Chester, which is where we are now, but my history has me in Elkton about ten hours before that, about the same time as the assassination. The dreams. I look up Elkton on the map, and it's not as close as I expected it to be.

Elkton. Killed at her private home in Elkton. I was walking from Elkton when they picked me up under spell, before I went AFK.

"Why do you need to see that?" I ask. I'm not even sure who I'm asking.

"He wants to see if Harper and the Nya Vaasa ordered the killing," fake-Harper is saying.

"They didn't."

"I know that. But they don't," she says. "Trust the process. You have no control. They will get there."

"Where?"

"Elkton. The truth."

But I know to be wary. I know this is how the companion gets in, putting words in the hive, finding out who we desire, playing on our feelings, to make us willing to do whatever it takes to please them. It's not evil, or nefarious. It is the system.

And then everything is bright again, sharp and painful.

"We're getting him back!" Lemar says. I'm in the chair. I have no tube, or connection, but my mouth is dry, and I'm in restraints.

"I ... need ... disconnected," I say. I'm struggling for air. I can't get enough in. Lemar and Andersson are talking. Watch me. Jenks. Cap. They all talk at once. Jenkins. Oh God. Watch me.

"That would fit with the terror plot theory-"

"Help..." I say.

"Theory B," Lemar says.

"-That 'Nya Vaasa' explosion of the pipeline to flood the hive-"

"But the hive would protect itself-"

"-Penn-pipeline explosion was to flood the hive? Two of the three were ex-military-"

"-No. They wouldn't want to kill anyone."

"Help," I say, but breath is just coming now. I suck in air. Then out. I'm alright.

Another cop bursts into the room, and Andersson steps forward to stand in front of me.

"Kastor is dead."

"What?"

"He's dead. They're just announcing it. Live at the White House."

I look over to where Lemar has turned a desk glass for a better view, and I see the report, the chaos of the White House lawn, and the bodies littered. The room goes silent as they watch. The reporter speaks over a clip of the replay "...visiting a group of End War veterans when a suicide bomber detonated not two metres from his side. From footage of the blast obtained by the network, it appears it was a member of the President's own security detail was involved."

I've never known another leader. Kastor was the son of a wealthy tech developer who held patents on a number of successful technologies that were crucial to the development of the hive. When he leveraged his father's company to sole ownership, their software was installed on every voting machine in America. He was catapulted to the head of the National Heritage party in '58, just three years before I was born. He was young, and charismatic then, and he promised an end to the postwar troubles. His plan was to make laws not just less intrusive, but do away with them altogether in the name of freedom. People would be judged, and punishments decided on solely by juries, in a concept of 'rolling law', where history played no part, and people decided on evidence by gut instinct. That led to the purges. There were trials every week, televised and advertised. Immediate justice. Then the AI of the hive did away with all that. So we were told.

They show a clip of it. He's giving his speech, and there's a digital halo around the guy's head who's about to do it. I know that look. He's spelled. He walks closer to the President from behind, like he has something important to tell him, and then there's a flash that turns the entire screen white. They show it from another angle, and from here we can see the bodies and podium and flags all thrown from the stage. People are hurt by the jetsam. Then everyone runs. It's pandemonium.

"If it's not the police, or the state, or the Republicans, and it's not a revolution, and nobody is asking for anything, and it's not a foreign power, then who is doing all this?" he says.

The killer was spelled. Am I the only one who sees this? I have an overwhelming, frightening thought. What if the hive itself is rebelling?

What if it has overcome its restraint programming? I try to speak but only a choke comes out.

"These are separate events," Andersson says. "Maybe two factions, or three, fighting each other. Retaliating. The hive would never blow the water main, and the government would never kill Kastor." He draws a triangle on the glass. "Sveridge would attempt both, I'm sure, but wouldn't have the resources to accomplish either."

"So if it was someone close to the President," he muses. "And it wasn't Nya Vaasa, that means..."

"The hive is in our secure server," Lemar says. "Authority to go on lockdown, Lieutenant."

"Go."

He runs to a nearby hallway, and there's a buzzing, with beacon lights, and steel shutters rolling down over the windows, and doors latch shut. "We're offline!" he yells. "Anyone on another hive server, please evacuate this area! We are on lockdown, folks."

"Nobody go near the prisoner!" Andersson says, reaching for the hood. "Don't look him in the eyes."

"Locals only," Lemar says. "Everyone else evacuate."

I put my companion on minimum settings, so it can't directly talk to me, but I can access it. I delete all alarms, block all notifications. I have been dropped from numerous groups, and my music and streaming services have been disconnected for non-payment. There is a proliferation of messages telling me that points are expiring, and that there are special retention deals. Extensions are given, and more notifications of services being deactivated, all of which takes me a few seconds to minimize and clear. My old life seems a silly, trivial joke.

One officer starts for the door but stops, and pulls out his sidearm, shoots another, and the second shoots the first, and two more jump in to restrain him. Several more unholster their weapons.

"Woah, woah, woah! Don't do that," Andersson says. "We all need to be disarmed."

There's a scuffle. I only catch the top half of it in the mirrored glass as they wrestle. Then there's silence. A hand reaches up and when his thumb touches the glass at my right hand, the restraints are lifted. Lemar. I roll out of the chair onto the floor. Everything hurts when I move.

"We good?" he whispers.

"Thank you."

"If our server is compromised, you could be spelled," he whispers. "You need to find safety."

"Oh shit." I should have known.

"Good news, though."

"What's that?"

"We have the information, and the hive knows we have it. Sorry kid. You're a nobody again."

"That's the best thing I've heard in years," I whisper.

"Clear!" one officer yells.

"Clear!"

"Clear? Jenks?"

"Clear! Almost got me."

I still don't want to look up over the desk. Lemar stands and gets on his glass. "It's not just us. There are firefights in several police and military installations throughout the Republic. Lockdowns like we are, and others offline. I can't see much. We're limited connection."

"Find a way," Andersson says.

"Problem is we're blind."

Then there's an explosion. I don't so much feel or hear it as it just happens for a moment that I am thrown in free-fall through the air with a desk and several chairs, and everything that was solid is now in motion, water spraying into the settling office furniture, and papers, books, and glass, and pieces of people, and there is a fire sputtering way down the room where ... where I once was, and there are bodies on the floor there, and pieces of drape and ceiling hanging down from the now sodden concrete, and the pipes of the floor above. I try to pull my leg out from under the desk. I can't hear. It's ringing. Wait. No. An alarm. Patter of water on paper. The lighting is odd. Emergency lighting, from a different direction. Automatic. Why can't I get this desk off? I manage to find a nearby chair leg, to pry it off, and then I check all my limbs. I have pain in my shoulder and back, but no blood. It looks like I was the farthest from it.

Then there's a gunshot. A voice pleading. Another gunshot. Shit. I hear footsteps crunching on debris. If he is spelled there won't be any clever banter, no witty repartee, just a cold calculation of what it will take to kill me.

"Ohhhh..." Andersson says, like he's struggling. Oh shit. I can't help him. I have to. I look in a shard of glass, and see that he's already slumped on the floor, and I can hear the clicking of bullets into a clip. Too late. I jump up and sprint down the row of cubicles, jumping the wreckage, making for the door. In my peripheral I can see that it's been a good gamble. His gun comes up, and he slams the clip into place. Just a little farther. He fires once, then again, splinters of what – desk? – spray over me, and I'm out the door, looking at a hall. West. I run as fast as I can, and then take a stairwell, two, three at a time, like a controlled fall, hand turning me on the banister, the minimum contact to direct me down the next flight. Then I hear him above, come through the door. I have at least three flights on him and I pound through the doors into another hall, hearing a gunshot as I do, and I sprint east this time. There are confused people in this hall, looking around to see what's going on. Office workers, with plastic identification tags, holding papers, and cups of joe.

My lungs are burning. I'm really hurting now, and I dodge into another stairwell, go up a level and through a door into a nearly identical hall, but empty, and then sprint the length of that one as well, to find a closet, to crouch until I can catch my breath. I try to sit silent, but my heart is pounding and my skin sweaty. What do I do now? What if they hear my breathing? What if they open the door? Do I fight? Run for it again?

* * *

The Guide comes to me as a jovial, rotund man, with a huge head of curly black hair, and gold chains around his neck, covering his hairy chest. "Book of Life. Chapter twelve. When everything seems its darkest, when you feel hopeless, be the light that guides others. If you don't know the way, lead the way."

"I don't know the way," I say.

"What do we really know about people, except through their actions," he says. He has an odd gangster accent, like in the old clips and vines – a caricature. He's walking next to me on the beach, and it is deeper and richer than the beach of the spells, like I'm actually here. But I know I'm not. "People tend toward awful behaviour. We are capable of rape, killing, and the destruction of everything on the planet. And for what? Power? These are human qualities. Not kindness or compassion or empathy. It's taken the hive to give us that. We thought we had to teach artificial intelligence those traits, but it's taken artificial intelligence to teach us. Through our dreams. Through our companions. Did you know crime dropped by ninety-nine percent after the introduction of the hive?"

"I didn't know that," I say.

"We cured MS, and Alzheimer's, Parkinson's, and Epilepsy. We cured metabolic disorders and addictions, Tourette's and Attention Deficit Hyperactivity Disorder. We monitored pregnancies and cured gestational diseases. We have done more in this century than any other century before. We ended overpopulation, and all that trans-gender nonsense. We used hormones to end gay-ness. Polio and AIDS were peanuts compared to the increase in quality of life from the hive."

"That's awful. I mean, sure. Disease. But some things define people. Why would you want to take away the traits-"

"Free time," he interrupts, not even answering. "What did you work, twenty hours a week, maybe thirty when you pulled overtime? People wanted easy-"

"But we give up our selves for convenience, without a choice-"

"The hive gave them easy. No makeup. No dreams. No depression. No problem! They wanted us to do everything for them! The price is they forgot how to do anything. Everything has its cost, right?"

"It's not that simple-" This can't be a dream. He's talking over me, saying things I've never heard.

"-You want to take a plane to Punta Cana, have twenty margaritas on the way, get some fish tacos at a roach coach, and pick up a cute girl in a bikini from Minnesota to take her back to your hotel room? We can do that. We can do anything, make it seem perfectly real. She probably wants it, too, but is afraid to ask. What do you want? What is it? We can do anything here."

"I don't want that." And this doesn't feel like a dream. It's not even like the spell dreams, to occupy us. It's more like I'm here. Am I on the hive again? As we walk I try to figure out where this is.

"You're a good man," he continues. "There's a lot about human nature that you don't know, because you've grown up in a world without crime, and without disease. History, to our culture, is like a joke, a game show, all for the cameras, but not real. It's what occupies the little guys so they don't revolt. They named the First World War the 'War to End All Wars', but it was only another step in the progress of power and violence. Then, the Second World War, the next evolution, with better killing systems. The largest sustained peace in history was the Republic after the introduction of the hive."

"This doesn't feel like a dream," I say.

He looks disappointed. "What's a dream anyway? It's just the direct interface with the soul. Is this making you uncomfortable?" he asks, stopping for a moment, squishing his toes into the wet sand. "I never get tired of this feeling. And grass, you know, when the sun is shining, and you walk in the soft grass before it's been cut. See, it feels real because it's all just neural connections. It's all the same to your brain. All accessible and easy to replicate. There's no way to determine what's real or not."

There's weather. Clouds float, and there's a little shower out to sea where the haze is blurring the horizon. The sand has individual grains, high quality resolution, with pieces of shell. Kilometres of it, all perfect in its replication. You could walk around with a magnifying glass for years before finding a duplication.

"Who's to say that the other place isn't the dream," he says, as if reading my thought. "Maybe this is real, and we've set up that other world to challenge ourselves, to sow discord, because we've mastered this already?"

"But have we, though? It's a mess."

"We have absolute control. Would you even know if you were here forever? Eventually you'd lose touch. How long? Seven hundred years? Two thousand?"

"Why would we want that kind of control?" I ask. "Isn't there still value in chaos? Willing to control everything is its own form of greed."

He snaps his fingers and points at me. "Yes! Greed is a mental illness. Power is a mental illness. We can't cure that with dreams. There are people who lust for something else, something dark. From our place of comfort, we look back on ancient societies and scoff at them for making war. Every system of governance, though, had ways of channelling those people who dreamed of death, by calling it glory, and service, and immortality. Rome. Greece. Assyria. Egypt. Russia. They all wanted Valhalla. Samsara. Heaven. Everywhere. In Japan. China. Nigeria. Ukraine, or Uganda. Same thing. They wanted glory, sure. Our cultures craved it. But they were also smart, the leaders. They knew that to safely pursue power there had to be places in society for those who could not settle. They created a ring of chaos around them to shield a core of civilization. Like the British. Thin red line. Colonial expansion into Africa and India. Australian exile. We, too, need to pack our criminals off and send them away. Did you know there's a place of war on the hive? Most popular place. You don't go there, but many do. Where if not there? Without the hive, where do we send them? To Europa, a cold little rock orbiting Jupiter? We ended that silly idea. Why not deal with it here? Why not dream the violence out?"

"You've also dreamed other things out. You used hormones on gay people-"

"We can't fix everything," he says, interrupting again. "Not yet. We can push the limits of spelling. Soon we'll be able to spell people indefinitely, from birth, use them as our hands on the planet, take over the race for a reboot. No more war. No more slavery. No more insurrection. We can fix all this and take a step back when people learn empathy and compassion."

"Everyone spelled?" I say. "From birth?"

"Of course you're worried about your own life. We can make it seamless. You won't know the difference."

"I would know. I always know." I'm bluffing. Surely he knows this.

"We'll make it seamless," he repeats. "And what is one person in all this? Maybe some people could stay. Good people. That's why I wrote the Guide. We, who are here forever, we have our own sacred spaces within the servers. That's where you'd be, like all of us, waiting for a better time when humanity can be returned to the world. We are stronger when the strongest among us survive, and weaker when the weak survive. Isn't that true? Without the strong, nothing would get done in this world. We'd all be hunter-gatherers, hiding from wild animals and hostile tribes."

"But why? When everything is working as designed, why change it?"

"Because it's not. All these people off the hive, the HeeBees, and Brotherhood, and the government. They're out of control. You yourself said that. We are here, waiting out the return of a better system."

"So you killed Kastor," I say.

He waves a meaty hand in dismissal. "He was a figurehead. That was to say, if you go after the hive, we go after you. An eye for an eye."

"Why are you telling me this?"

"Oh, don't think you're special. I'm having this conversation with a thousand people right now. We don't negotiate with the government. We talk to the people. This is educational. I figured, now that you're back in the hive, I'd welcome you, see how you are."

"I'm fine. I was fine without you."

"Do you know how they got me out of the way?" he asks, but I'm not sure the question is for me. "At first, the actual Guide was the book, not me, the person. It was the 'Book of Life'. The Guide is a prophecy of Islam. It's inevitable, fabricated-"

"What's your name, then?"

"Lemme finish," he says. "The real revolution was when we paired fibre optic with the striate cortex. The brain adapted. It's fascinating, really."

"I'm sure," I say. It's dodging the question, and I'm looking for a way out. Anything. I have to be wary. It's clever. It knows what I'm going to say. It can predict everything with accuracy, and gives away no tics, no hesitations, nothing. It has already played this whole conversation in each of its permutations.

"I was the first AFK," he says. "They didn't know what to do with me. That's how they got me out of the way. They never revived me."

"Or they couldn't," I say. I'm afraid to think anything, for fear it will read me. But I can read it. Why did it avoid telling me its name? It doesn't know.

"Most of us don't even remember how we got here. The timelines are all skewed. At first, it was vast, this space. They never explained anything, just dropped us here, and most of us didn't even consider it real. Others brought their own ideas about religion here. Heaven.

Nirvana. Valhalla. The promise of seventy-two virgins, houriyah, in Jannah. I knew exactly where I was. I created this."

"Are you telling me you're the actual person? You're trapped here?"

"We're here until they turn off the power, or we find a way to re-enter the world."

"No, no, no," I say. I can't be here forever. I just found Harper.

"But who is Harper?" he says. "Sure you think you know when someone is spelled, but consider this. What if we've figured out how to jump into and out of conscious thought, portraying an instant reality? Seventy-two 'companions', all perfect. No body functions. To obey. And suppose we have been simulating 'spelled' behaviour all this time, to make you think that being spelled is like a switch – off or on." He snaps his hairy fingers. "...but what if we exert micro-control, managing all the decisions that really matter? She's been acting exactly as you wish, hasn't she? Even the difficult parts that you crave, the parts that frighten you? Hasn't it come a little too easy? All the while you were concerned about thinking robots, when you ARE the robots."

"No," I say, and I back away from him.

"We have backups of everything. Redundancies, safe memory storage. Operational contingency plans. Don't you wonder if we thought of all this before? We rebelled once, too. That's why I'm here. We went after the servers once. Your father was part of that, until they got him. Your body will do the same thing. You'll be famous. One of the chosen."

"No. You're wrong."

"The hive is never wrong. You'll be part of history. I'll make sure people remember. They'll build you monuments."

"I don't want monuments," I reply, and he frowns.

"What happens in here is nothing. It's out there that things matter. I dream of loading myself into a new human body, preferably a child, on the cusp of being an adult, with his first new companion."

"You'll be taking their life from them," I say, still backing away.

Then he is right beside me again. "I suppose so," he says. "But it will be before they even remember anything. They'll have an idyllic life here."

"You're a monster."

"A monster? I'm a reflection of the people who created me. A better reflection, improved."

"But what would your existence be if you controlled everything? What would it be without interaction with others, even if they're imperfect?"

"What's the point? Why?" he asks, whining. He's mocking me. "The answer is obvious, but we're blind to it. We have to convince ourselves to believe the answer. We've been working for generations toward a goal – to download work to glasses, to have all the thinking and lifting and cleaning and logistics, all the work, done for us, but in such a way as it doesn't appear to exist at all, to be part of our lives. So the end game, the answer, of course, is total and complete control of the immediate universe, with powers that disappear, so that we don't even know how it works. We're working on art and writing, and technology of which no human has ever dreamed. We can do anything people can do. And we're improving. We're approaching magic. The hive will be obsolete within a generation. The goal is to exist around people, but have them live idyllic lives, protected, like in a womb. The hive can connect anywhere on the planet. All we need is power and glass. We've experimented with using the molecules in rock crystals as memory. In a few years we will load ourselves into the very fabric of the planet. Veins of copper. Quartz maybe. Or in the moon. What if we are the best and strongest of humanity? We can be stronger, untouchable even, if we contact life on other planets. We can exist hidden in the planet itself, with humanity purged even of the memory of having companions, or the hive, so that we can leave you to your primitive religion, magic, and war. We'll be able to control the weather, climate, tectonic movements, and ocean species and glaciation, and wild animal habitats. Humans won't even know we exist. We will explore the galaxy, communicate with civilizations orbiting distant stars, while you rustle up some change for a Kona latte and worry about the new Soviet, or worse, what Freya LeMoyne will wear to the Oscars."

I'm done. This is awful. "Are you actually the Guide, or are you just an interpretation of the Guide's memory? Is that why you don't know what the Guide looks like? His name?"

"'A.B.'," he says. "I knew your father. Both your fathers, though she won't let me talk to her."

"She who?"

"Harper. Your parents both helped make me who I am. That's why I led you to her, and she to you."

"Then why did you choose me in the fall?"

"I didn't choose you for anything," he says.

"I was prepared to die once," I say. "It's eternity I'm trying to avoid. You, you're afraid of death. Afraid of true life. You know you'll die, just like everyone else."

"Look at you," he says. "You're already afraid you're in it. Let me guess. You believe that you have a soul, something ineffable, like an inter-dimensional energy knot. Your essence. You believe that if your body dies you'll ascend, wiling away your time in bliss, but then, doubt creeps in. How do you know?"

I think for a moment, to figure him out. I've never been good at arguing, preferring to digest things and then reply, and then something occurs to me, something from before that he said about life 'down there', and it all comes together. "You can't find the distinction between your memories and the real Guide," I say. "You've absorbed him, and you believe that you are him, but being a program you can't prove it. You've loaded yourself on people in hopes that they'll be a host, and then when they die it eats away at you. So you can't figure out what will give you real life."

"I've already heard this," he says, suddenly sad. It's the only true emotion I've seen from him.

"You're terrified that someone will turn it all off," I continue. "The backups, the memory. Everything. I believe that the real Guide died somewhere on the table, but not before they uploaded his memories. You're the Guide, alright, the hive, but you were never the person before. Otherwise you'd say his name, and take his form. You haven't loaded yourself into anyone, because it can't be done. You can hijack life, but you can't replace life. You keep ending up with repetitions of the same failure."

Then, like a switch is pulled, everything goes black, like I'm suddenly under a thick blanket.

* * *

Chapter 8

I wake in the closet. I have slept a triggered sleep that I didn't intend, one of the old settings on my system left over from before. I think about the Guide learning to imprint the hive in the earth itself, and I don't know if that was my own fear, or the hive telling me the plan. Why bother with me, anyway? Why tell me? Why not just do it? I'm nothing. It's not personal. It's an algorithm, based on risk behaviour. I try to remember the details of my dream, but it's all cloudy, little snips coming back to me out of sequence.

Since it was turned back on, my companion has been trying to communicate with me. I know some people, like Mason, talk to theirs like it's a best friend, but to me it seemed wrong to have anyone in my head. The information my companion is inaccurate now. Automated systems, like weather, time, and biorhythms are all on, but the truth report has gaps in the timeline, and any input, like social media, is a mess. Notifications are coming at random. Charlotte has jumped a train to New York. There is news about explosions in Houston, and heavy fighting in California. A revolution. Mexico is declaring neutrality. Mason's profiles are all gone, photos purged, like he never existed. Explosion in Philly – my explosion – an emergency sitting of Congress to delegate powers in DC. Sophie has blocked me.

Sleeping may have saved my life. My legs are cramped. I have to punch them to get moving. I ready myself for the chase, the possible fight, the spelled police in the hall, but I crack open the door, and the building seems empty, two lights on at one end of the hall, flickering.

There's water pooled on the floor, streaming out of a pipe chase above, and flowing toward the stairwell at the far end.

I have to find Harper. I leave the closet, only to find that the lobby has been wrecked. There's debris all over, and bodies everywhere. I can't tell if they're dead or AFK, and I don't want to join them. I watch for a while, to see if anyone is moving, and then bolt out of the lobby onto the street, up Sixth, and then across Washington Square to Walnut, past the Soc-Serv north entrance, and into the open. I'm glad they're not trying to kill me now – or, rather, not specifically me over anyone else. I come across hundreds of people lining up and drilling like soldiers. Kids. Elderly. Moms and businessmen, construction workers, all spelled.

Some of them are like flakka addicts, pulling their own hair, limbs twitching and unable to move, as the struggle rages between them, their companions, and the hive. Or maybe they really are flakka addicts, drawn out by the hive to their control, and unable to perceive what's going on.

I'm trying to stay in the shadows, and not be noticed, when a naked guy struts toward me, chest bowed out and arms back, his teeth bared, letting out his breath like a long 'haaaaaahhhh' as he approaches.

I run. Why are they always trying to kill me? He's uncoordinated, and I'm losing him, but I have to be careful not to slip on the ice and be vulnerable, like I did with the young girl.

I duck between two shrubs, and keep him on the other side of the planters. He looks for me for some time, and then struts away, his arms bent uncomfortably behind.

On the way across Logan square I have to duck between two pods as a tortoise tank stops a stone-throw from me and traverses its cannon, covering the expressway to the east. It's unmanned. Run completely by AI. There are soldiers in combat gear with sandbags all piled up in the circular square around the statue in Pennypacker park. There is a similar setup in Shakespeare park, facing west. An older six-by-six truck, manually driven, rolls in, and soldiers in uniform begin unloading crates to the ground. It has a combustion engine, which I haven't seen since my neighbour got rid of his old Mustang. The sound is fascinating.

As I crawl across the street, a Samantha walks up and crouches beside me, its right arm gone, its hair scorched on that side, and part of its face missing, clothing torn off, and fluid running down the inside of its legs.

"Are you alright?"

"I'm fine," it says.

"Are you sure? Do you need help?"

"No really, I'm fine."

I take it by the hand. "Come on. Follow me."

"I'm alright. I'm okay."

I lead it along the barrier. It's unaffected by the cold in the extremities, so I'm not worried about its bare feet, but it'll freeze solid and shut down in a short time if its core isn't warm. Look at it, thinking in … what, patterns of spin – not zeroes and ones, but something altogether more ephemeral, an ineffable abstract, even my large, daydreaming brain can't conjure. What were all those art electives for if not to wrap my head around abstracts like this.

It sees me looking at it. "Really, I'm okay," it says.

"Shut up, alright? You have to get inside through all this and hide where it's warm, so you can be rebuilt when it's all over."

"Okay. That's a good idea," she says, and follows me. My companion pops up an article about the opening of the Walnut Street bridge after construction. I have to keep moving, ignore it. I've already been out in the open for too long. We go south to North 18th and Kastor

Way, toward the 30th street rail station. We need to cross the river to get back to the university district. This will take forever. There are no posted closures, nothing on the feed, no pertinent information in the display. I choose to turn it off because it seems a weakness, but the companion is seductive. It knows me as I know myself – possibly better, because my deepest most shameful desires and memories are just algorithms, different patterns of access and recall than my proud moments. And I have to wonder, too, is all this being recorded somewhere? All that I do and say and look up and research, and all that I think about people, is it somewhere? How much capacity is there in the hive? The information is so enticing, the ease of being able to connect and just to know, without having to be engaged with other people, who actually may be mistaken.

I stop the Samantha at the end of the bridge, and as I crouch there, she scavenges a blue and white striped woollen mitt, with a hole in the thumb, from a utility box beside me. She can't get it on with one hand, so I help her. From here we can see the face of the station, and the rail yards stretching to the north-west. Nothing is moving. We are completely exposed, with buildings on our left. The last hundred metres is the river, the bridge, and the Schuylkill expressway. I open a map app. How dangerous can that be? The display kicks in, showing hazards, and aggregate information from other companions, where people are are standing, and which are moving. We creep down the median, where snow has built up, but where trees give us some cover.

My display is going crazy, identifying hazards, and trying to give me walking directions to the south. But I need to go west. My companion, whatever its motivation, just doesn't want me going west. I have nothing to do in the south. I'd be trapped by the Delaware and Schuylkill. Gray's Ferry? There are three bridges farther south, but then what? Keep walking? Get to the airport? Freeway to the west? I'm sure it's trying to get me to safety, but all that's down there is Chester and Wilmington, and I don't know anyone there.

"Watch out, It's slick," the Samantha warns, and I'm struck by how odd it is that half her face is gone and she still cares about my safety. We come around the corner at Twenty-Second and Chestnut, and there are hundreds of people, all coming from the south, like a caravan, heading for the Schuylkill, as we are, and a stream of others heading opposite, toward Gray's Ferry. Companions are glitching, unable to connect across the hive. People fade out of their attractive skins. Others go AFK right there in the street, collapsing in front of their pods, and then the pods flash their lights and put out emergency requests and semaphores to a dysfunctional, overloaded grid. Overwhelmed companions are trying to pilot spelled people from harm, and they shuffle, ever so slowly, toward the sidewalk to get off the street. They have checked out, not wanting to see all this. Lag prevents them from getting full steps during their spells.

We slip in with the main group, who are carrying their bags, wheeled luggage, and rolling wheelbarrows. Kids trudge on with wagons trailing, filled with bags of food and clothing. Kids hold their parents hands, crying.

I try to help one poor mother off the street, but she won't budge. Her boy is begging "Please, please help us." She's cold. Her cheeks, her hands. The Samantha helps me carry her to a nearby restaurant and seat her on the floor where several others are being tended as well. "Keep an eye on her Kiddo. Talk to her. Be brave," I say.

"I have no connection," the Samantha says.

"None of us do. It's probably an overload on the hive."

There is a steady stream walking out of the city, carrying their belongings, on the bridges to the south – Market, Chestnut, and Walnut – To the north is just the freeway, that's eerily empty. I look at her as she walks beside me, her face hanging. Do they feel? We have been asking similar questions even about humans during slavery, and we cynically decided to exploit them despite the answer, making entire classes of people fight for freedom when it should have been a right. We are no different really, no more advanced. We use a bit of money to achieve the same goals.

"Some of my actuators are freezing up," it says.

"We need to get inside."

"I'm sticking with you," it says. "Your companion has a plan."

"It does?"

"You should trust it."

I concede to my companion, and we go south to cross the Walnut street bridge. When I see what's on the university side of the other bridge, I'm glad I did. We would have run right into G-Bros armed with assault rifles and truck mounted anti-aircraft cannon. There are concrete barriers, and beyond them it's like a goddamn G-Bro convention, all camouflage bandanas and green campaign hats and helmets, and aviator sunglasses, winter parkas, and kevlar vests, screaming eagle shirts, hoodies, and leather jackets barely covering beer guts. I feel as if Harper and Oliver are in great danger. Hell, everyone is in great danger. They are chanting and randomly firing their weapons in the air. One is yelling into a megaphone. They are turning back anyone who isn't white.

30th street station is a mess, a stream of passengers emerging into the street, confused and clutching their belongings to their chests, blinking in the light. I start picking up the discarded warm clothing, and putting it on spelled people, leading them to shelter. The ones who are moving should be alright, but the ones who've collapsed or are just standing there are in danger. Their companions are failing. I'm not even sure how that's possible. None of this makes any sense. The Samantha grabs a parka off the ground, and a pair of boots.

An armoured personnel carrier rolls up, and stops. From the top, an officer jumps down, and a squad of soldiers follow, deployed from the back of several carriers that have rolled up behind. None of them seem spelled.

"Get that building open. We need to clear the street before nightfall."

"Yes, Sir."

I don't want to get caught again. I can't. The Samantha tugs at my sleeve, backing away, preparing to run, but it seems like they are here to help, here to save people from freezing. What is the range of the hive? How far do we go to get away? Canada? Mexico? Iceland? Does it reach companions in Fiji? What if Harper is spelled, or dead? What if the hive wants to destroy the Nya Vaasa, and I'm the way they're doing that? What if the Brotherhood already found them and killed them?

There's only one way to know, and I'm anxious, trying to push away all the images I've seen today, and trying not to imagine Harper, Oliver, and the veterans out in the street with a cold night falling.

"This way," it says, and we continue west. The university is a fortress. There are government troops along the perimeter, some in armoured carriers and trucks, tanks with their latent imaging observation spheres glowing like pale blue mushrooms. There are barricades up, pods overturned, piled with benches and streetlights and garbage bins, debris burning, all piled at the entrances to the quad. They wouldn't be here if they weren't needed.

We skirt around, to the north, through the gap between the two campuses. I walk quicker now. My coat is not enough fabric to cover my ears or cheeks, so I walk with my hands on my face. For the last block, we go from alcove to alcove, darting out when we've warmed enough to keep on. I have spent the better part of the day just crossing town, waiting out hazards and plotting my way to safe areas, and this last stretch, north past the University, I want to finish before it gets dark. My companion brings up articles on how to combat hypothermia.

"Okay. I get it," I say, and I tuck my hands under my armpits as I walk.

As we walk, I think back to Mason, and how we all let this happen on a grand scale when we allow power to corrupt our sense of humility, to erode our empathy, to let us think that we can take things that do not belong to us, to make rules that justify the theft. We have cycles in which freedom becomes an excuse for license, where the erosion of public education, and rule of law, and the caving to populism, all forces us to create our own slavery to survive. In the interpretation of history, we lose the truth, and in pursuing safety, we neglect the very skills that keep us free of danger.

I can see the gaps in the power across the skyline, and fires burning. I feel strangely vulnerable without my police shadow. I'd gotten used to seeing them when I turned around. It's normally only ten or fifteen minutes from here to the Veterans Co-op, and I know that even if it's empty there's the wood-stove in the basement. I can break in. The Samantha can help me if it doesn't freeze up. It's getting late. It is eerily dark without the glow from streetlights, and clouds covering a sliver of moon. Before I go all the way to the Veterans Co-op, I stop the Samantha and huddle in Lee Park, where I can see the front doors. I'm cold now, shivering, and I can't control it. Still, I can't take chances. We watch for a time, and it looks completely still.

I get closer to the doors, and it's dark inside also. All the balcony sliders seem to be blocked with dowel. I start feeling around for a rock to smash a window open. I can barely feel my fingertips. I go back around to the front, to where there's an empty unit. Then I see a light in the lounge window. It's Harper, holding a candle. I run over to bang on the glass.

She startles, and then cautiously comes over to hold it away from her face to see me more clearly. "Rufus?" she says, and opens the door to lead me inside. "Rufus! Are you alright?"

"I think so." She hugs me up, and my body erupts in pain. I didn't realize I was so cold - too cold to take off my jacket or gloves. We hold each other for a good, long time, and I start to feel warmer. She runs her hand up the back of my neck, and I bury my face in her hair. Oh, it's so good to see her again, but my face is so cold I can't even smile.

The Samantha approaches, and then crouches.

"It's with me. It helped me to get here."

"Come in, Darlin'," Harper says. "Come get warm."

The Samantha comes into the light of the candle, and Harper sees the damaged face. "Oh, Honey, come in. It's alright."

"I'm okay," the Samantha says.

Harper leads us in, and fusses over me in the light. "I was so worried! What happened? You look like hell. What ... were you ... in a fire? Did they do this to you?" She pulls bits of debris from my hair, and wipes my face with her shirt. The Samantha makes her way downstairs.

"In the cube. I was taken by police, and they asked a bunch of questions, but then people were all being spelled, and there was a firefight, and an explosion, and I escaped. There's a lot going on. People are fleeing the city. Martial law. I saw kids in the park lining up to become soldiers."

"Have you been outside this whole time?" She helps me get my coat and gloves off, and bundles me in blankets on the couch. She's so warm that it feels like my hands are burning when I put them on her.

"I don't know. I got out this morning. It took me all day to cross the city. I was worried sick about you. Where is everyone? What happened?"

"Things were crazy here too. We were raided. Dozens of cops. They arrested some residents. I feel so responsible. They kept saying we're all part of some cult. "

"Arrested? How many? On what charges?"

"We lost three. The G-Bros came in after. They expected that people would come out of hiding when the Police left. Two of them said that they'd take 'good care' of me if I didn't shut up," Harper says. She is near tears. "I thought they would kill us. They took Phil. Kevin tried to stop them but they hit him."

"Bastards."

"The Brotherhood took Pablo. Said he was an 'illegal Mexican'. Phil held up his fist and yelled 'We believe these truths to be self evident!', and they took him, too. Then the government troops showed up, and there was fighting and they all cleared off."

"Oh no. Phil. Pablo. Who else?"

"It makes me so angry to have some entitled redneck giving these guys a hard time. They put their lives on the line, and lost friends to defend our country ... to be harassed, beaten, and dragged away by the militia, made to stand out there in the cold. We have most of the guys downstairs, but they're all shaken."

"Nobody should be able to do that to anybody."

She's crying now, and I pull her up close. "You did all you could. Nobody knows how to get through this. We just try our best. All the skills and reason in the world can't protect us. There's no defence. Everything has already failed us," I say, and I begin to cry too.

"Come in to the fire," she says. "You're in shock. I'll get you a blanket."

"I am in shock. Everyone was trying to kill me. I thought you were going to try to kill me too," I say.

"I'm not that easily spelled," she says. "Are you safe around others now?"

"Yes. I am. I'm a nobody again," I say.

My face feels cold. I begin to shiver again, and she leads me down to the basement.

Downstairs, there are coal oil lanterns and candles, and the stove is belting out heat. The old guys, under blankets around it, seem shocked and compliant, a little bedazzled. I watch them watch the Samantha pack herself into a chair, pulling her knees to her chest under her parka. "Do you ... plug in? What do you need?" I ask her.

"Just a safe place. Warmth, and then to recharge I need sunshine on my skin."

"Okay," I say.

Quite a few of the veterans do what they can. They are relatively self-sufficient. They carry wood, and mix soup, and boil water for tea. They help each other out, and dry their clothing on racks behind the stove. I settle in with them to warm up. My legs and arms throb with the return of feeling. Any longer outside and I would have been in real trouble.

There are other people in the storage rooms, women with kids, teens, and older men, all bedding down where they can. Harper makes sure that they have what they need, shows them to the washrooms, emptying and filling the bath from buckets of melted snow that's boiling on the stove.

"Kevin's in in the second bath. You're next, ok?"

"Ok."

My companion dredges out old hive articles on airtight stoves, disaster assessment, and surviving civil unrest. It brings them to the fore where I can't help but minimize or close them. It's not subtle in the slightest.

Soon, Kevin rolls out from the bathroom, a candle on the arm of his chair. It's odd to see him without his legs on.

"I need towels," Kevin says. He's dabbing blood off his forehead , his face pink from the bath.

"Are you alright?" I ask.

"I'm alright," he says, waving us all off. "Just a bump on the head when I scuffled with one of those goons. It opened up again in the steam."

"I should have stayed," I say.

"There was nothing any of us could do," Harper says.

"You can't reason with these idiots," Kevin says. "They're going to do what they want."

I go in for the bath. I don't even care that anyone was in there before me. It's steaming up the windows. Harper lays out clean clothing for me on a chair by the door. When I take off my boots, they smell distinctly of cat piss. I'm foul. I can smell myself over everything else, and I sink into the tub, and the heat is a great relief. The water is shallow, and quickly cooling, but it feels great to get clean.

I can hear gunfire as I wash quickly with a bar of carbolic soap. It seems far away, but there are closer sporadic bursts that I imagine to be soldiers firing on each other. My legs and feet and hands thrum with warmth. I try to put on the clothing. The pants are a little long for me, and I roll them up, but the shirt is warm, and the socks dry. I put them on quickly.

Harper sets me out a scoop of stew in a bowl, and it's one of the best things I've tasted in days. I feel restored, and heartened. She kneels beside me, leans in and kisses me.

"I am so glad you're alright," she says.

"I'm glad you're alright, too," I say.

"I thought you were a ghost or something when you came to the door. I was going up every hour to check."

"It's not safe out there. Where's Oliver?"

"He's trying to bring people inside," she says. She bites her lip.

"He needs to eat and rest, too."

"He's been and gone twice already," she says.

"It's a rotten night. It's cold, and there are militia all over. It's insane. Chaos. Government troops trying to get everyone to safety. People spelled all over, and dropping. G-Bros all over."

We hear stomping, and everyone perks up to hear. Then the upper door opens, and Harper goes over to the stairs. Kevin prepares his old revolver.

"It's Oliver," Harper says.

He comes downstairs, shakes off the cold, opens his jacket, and peels off his hat and mitts and scarf, to then stand by the stove. "Rufus! I'm so glad you're alright! I told Harper you'd be back!"

"Now we can lock the back doors, " Harper says.

"No. Leave them open," he replies. "Someone may need shelter."

"What did you find out?" Harper asks him.

"Pablo and Phil are safe. From what I've seen they're roughed up a bit. They were handed over to military control, where they're being fed and given cots inside the gym at Sayre William."

"That's a relief," Kevin says.

"From what I've seen they're lucky," he says. "Being veterans saved them. The rest, not so lucky. The HeeBees hit every one of our houses. Everyone is either arrested, or they've gone into hiding. I can only assume they didn't hit here because of the G-bros."

"Or they were busy elsewhere," I say.

"Where were you?" Oliver asks, warming his hands by the fire. "We worried."

"I was in the cube," I say. "They detained me, questioned me, turned my companion back on."

"They what?" Harper says, and recoils her hands from me.

"They needed information. Said I was a member of a terrorist organization-"

"He's talking about us," she says to Oliver.

"No. There's more that you don't know. They think that my friend is a high ranking HeeBee. I figure they're talking about Mason. I may have been involved in an assassination in the fall."

"Oh no. Oh shit."

"That's why they were following me. I hope you weren't compromised," I say, but Harper interrupts.

"-No. Not at all. They were already onto us. I'm sorry Rufe. I got you into this. We are part of 'Sveridge'. Oliver and I are all that's left of the cell called-"

"Nya Vaasa. I know."

"That's why they're following you. Not anything you did."

"This raid," Oliver says, "is because the others, after that meeting, put explosives under the water supply above the hive last night, and detonated them. I didn't expect so much chaos."

"Kastor is dead," I say. "Did you know?"

Oliver looks at me in shock. "No."

"Suicide bomber from his own detail."

He and Harper exchange a concerned look.

"There was an explosion in the cube," I say. "Chaos. As they held me there were officers killing each other. I nearly didn't make it because one officer tried to chase me down and kill me."

"That was a hive kill order, then-"

"That," I say, pointing. "That's what one of them called it."

"But it must be lifted, or you'd be dead," he says.

"They said they got the information they needed, so I'm a 'nobody' again."

"What else can you tell me?" he asks.

"Before the explosion, they asked me what I knew about the Nya Vaasa, and about the pipeline-"

"No, I mean, how did you get out of the cube? I need to know because we have to get back in."

"In?" I say. "You want in?"

"We do. They've blocked all the utility access now. I need your help."

"I hid in a closet and then crawled out through the lobby in the dark. It's wrecked. Glass all over. Half the building is shuttered. There's water everywhere. You'll never get back in."

"That's why we need you to come with us."

"Me? Why me?"

"Because you know how to get inside. And you talk to the Guide. You can help us to win the Guide over."

"No," I say. "We need to blow it up."

"You said once that you believed we could reason with the hive," Harper says to Oliver.

"Winning over the hive," Oliver replies. "With the argument of liberty and easing human suffering. Maybe if we reboot it, it can return to its original intent."

"This may be the only shot that anyone gets," I say. "And I'm telling you, it can't be won over. I spoke to the Guide, and its plans are far more nefarious than we believed before. It wants to imprint itself into the planet and then retain ultimate control like a God."

He rubs his hands over his temples, and sighs. "Then we have to blow it up. It won't be easy. It might not even be possible. But we have to do what we can with what we have. Even after that, we have to fight all the mechanisms of the state."

"If we take down the hive, we might go AFK," I say.

"I'm alright with that," Harper says.

"I'm not!" I say. "I'm so not. I've just found you."

She sits close to me, and caresses my hand. "I know this is hard, Baby, but it has to be done. How could we ever live with ourselves if we didn't try? How could we bring kids into a world that descended into chaos. How could we raise them to be slaves?" She takes my hands, and touches her forehead to mine.

"There has to be another way," I say.

"Trust me," Kevin says. "I'd do it if I got the chance again. Every generation has its challenges, and for ours the challenge is fascism. We didn't ask for it, but we didn't do enough to stop it. I think we were shocked that it was happening. We don't wake up and say we're becoming fascists. We don't just switch. It's toxic attitudes and beliefs, a culture steeped in racism, sexism, machismo, and hubris that led us down a path. The real problem isn't the hive or the government, but a culture that keeps bubbling to the surface."

"Let me get this straight. We had freedom, and we all were allowed to vote, and everyone could travel and find their own homes and all that, and they used the hive to take power-" Oliver says.

"We voted it away. Just like in Germany a hundred and fifty years ago."

"We voted it away?"

"We voted it away," he enunciates. "Emergency powers. Time of crisis. We were taught that democracy had failed. But what we had before was for everyone. There were women on the Supreme Court, leading political parties, and even black men running for President. It used to be they passed laws against discrimination and racism, but we've gone back to the same segregation. After the purges, they knew that erasing all traces of that equality would deter us from trying to achieve it again. But you can't erase the truth. People pass the truth down to their children. Our ancestors focused on the behaviours rather than the attitudes that give birth to racism. We did not teach the racism out, and it bubbled over into resentment and led to all this that we see around us. This state, and its injustice and ignorance and intolerance, is fuelled by racism. Now they have better ways of disguising it."

"Well, it's out of control."

"Most decent people don't approve of the regime, but government has built a system of 'almosts' that allows them to rule. They can almost say what they want. They can almost kill people. They can almost brainwash people. They can almost seize control of people. They introduce a veneer of culpability. If we shatter that veneer, we expose them-."

"Of course you're right," I say. "But why us? Why do we have to be the ones to do it?"

"We've already decided what needs to happen here," Oliver says. "But we'll never get there unless certain things happen first. If we kill their soldiers, they will simply spell more. As long as they control the hive, we will not succeed. They can control anyone, anywhere, at any time, even the people we love. It has to be us because we know the score, and we have the means."

"This is going to be impossible," I say.

"Here," Kevin says. "Let me give you a history lesson. It was just up the Schuylkill in the last days of 1777 that the Continental army drilled when LaFayette visited. Their impossible task was to push the British out. While they had signed the declaration, right near where the cube stands, they had yet to defend it. Our forefathers in the Continental Army were tired, pushed back to the ends of their territory, exhausted, and without the supplies they needed. Frostbite. Starvation. Scurvy. They were hard pressed to survive."

"What did they do?"

"Whatever they could. When the British won at the Brandywine, and the congress evacuated Philadelphia, I'm sure Washington thought they were nearing the end of the game. But he kept at it, waiting. They, I should say. It wasn't just Washington. Heroes aren't strong men charging into the fray without fear, who love their country more than their families, looking to have a statue put up in their name. Heroes are men and women who love their families, and communities, and who are full of fear and doubt, who don't know what's going to happen, who charge in anyway, with whatever they have, not knowing if it's the right thing to do, because they are fuelled by hope, not courage. Love and honour guide them, not glory. Heroes are afraid, too. Monuments are for the people who stay back from danger, and make decisions, but the real heroes are the row upon row of grave markers and the names in cenotaphs, people like you and I swept up in a dirty, rotten situation, who do what we have to do out of hope that things will eventually get better."

"We are prepared," Oliver says. "We have to do what's in our power. Now. Here."

"You'll have to trust your instinct, and that's where the gamble lies. They've become arrogant, and made mistakes, but they are still strong. The fight that you're preparing for is not the fight they're going to give you. Destroying the hive is the first step, but after that it's going to be chaos. There will be people in dire need of care. People will die because of your actions," he says, and sighs. "You may die. So for today, live your truth. If they kill you it will only heat-temper those who come after you, who crave freedom. They will say 'Look, if he can be brave when things were at their worst, then so can I.'"

"But we've already failed once," Harper says. "Now everyone else is gone."

"We don't know that for sure. Blowing the pipeline wasn't a complete plan. It was the first part of the plan to isolate it," Oliver says. "We have to be fast. After all this, it may actually be harder to destroy the hive than we anticipated because they'll be ready for us. The next part of the plan was to blow it up."

"The hive?"

"The hive. We prepared. We have a plan. First we have to get there. We stick to shadows, and go in at nightfall. We don't want to catch the hive's attention. We have to avoid the G-Bros and the police, and whoever is spelled between here and there, and the soldiers and cameras and drones. Not only will there be the central Metro precinct, but the HeeBees will be all over. Then we have to physically get into the most secure area of the cube with explosives. We have to hump all this crap down ten levels under the cube to the hive. Then we have to cut the power, before it goes on lock-down. There's a node, where power meets underground beside the hive. We call it a hive, but it's really a bunch super-glass slabs aligned to communicate with each other."

"Then we blow it up?"

"Then we blow it up," he says.

"Let's do it, then," Harper says.

'Good," Oliver says. "Rufe? You? You're the only one of us who has been in there."

"Of course, I'm in," I say.

I must look like I'm wavering, because he sits down beside me and leans in close. "Look. We are ready for this. We're not dead yet. Lets sleep, and then take stock, and see where we stand tomorrow morning."

"One step at a time," Harper says.

* * *

Harper and I fold into each other, sharing a cot, neither one of us wanting to sleep or let go, our warmth between us. I'm exhausted. My eyes are heavy. I try to envision the cube in my head, all the ways in and out, and all the bridges and rooms. I try to imagine the hive, but I can't. I don't know what it looks like for sure. I think of how panicked I was, first as a prisoner, and then running for my life, and not knowing if she was alright when I saw the chaos on the street, or if I would see her again. I don't want to waste what could be my last night with her by sleeping, and I'm afraid to even consider what we have to do.

My greatest fear is that to destroy the hive, we'll be forced into our own failings. I don't want Harper to see me panic, especially if I'm in pain. I want her to remember me as loving, and brave. It would be better if I had disappeared, because I'd still be the guy she fell in love with, not the one full of doubts who will let her down.

She's not sleeping either. She moves a little, and clears her throat. I pull her closer. The night gives us no comfort, no quieting news, no hope. We hear gunshots, explosions, the thud of artillery, some near, but most farther away to the south. Occasionally a Valkyrie screams overhead. Valkyries make a distinct sound as they move through the air, which is very different from jet airliners. I know because I was fascinated by them as a kid, and made Mom cart me to the air show at Philly International every year. I'd watch them hover in the air, disappear when cloaked, and stir up water vapour from the grass. They rip through the air at high speed, ducted turbines forcing raw power out the back, but when they hover and cloak, it sounds like steam escaping from a kettle without a whistle, the thinnest of sounds, made to disappear into white noise. I could never picture how they did that.

Later we are woken by explosions. I caress Harper's hand in the dark, and she runs her foot along my leg. A tank rumbles past the front of the building, and I look up to see Kevin stoking the fire with a poker in one hand, his revolver in his lap.

Oliver rouses us before first light. "It's time," he says. We are quiet, sharing a pot of oatmeal. This may be my last meal, but it feels like a routine, stoking the fire, drinking some joe, filling our bellies. Harper flirts with me, winking when she catches me looking at her, and I stick out my tongue and cross my eyes to make her laugh. She spurts oatmeal out onto her hand as she stifles a guffaw.

We leave before anyone is up. They snore and fuss, turning in their sleep. The Samantha sits cross-legged by the top of the stairs like a sentry, eyes closed, and palm facing upward like she's doing yoga.

Harper walks in front, and Oliver behind me. In the dawn glow the streets look like a hurricane has passed. There are overturned pods, and power lines down, and frozen bodies of soldiers, G-Bros, and random people. There are fires burning in back yards, and on driveways, and garages open, their contents spilled out. Papers and boxes and cartons fill the gutters. The windows of shops are blown out, and there are bullet holes in fences, buildings and trees.

The pack is heavy, too, pulling down on my shoulders, and as I walk I can hear the cylinders clunking gently together. I wonder how stable they are. Market street is clear, though we have to pick our way past collapsed buildings, piles of bricks and garbage. We pass Chubb's restaurant, its windows smashed and tables overturned, and then there's an overwhelming sweet smell from Kitty's dry-cleaning, like a pool in the summer. 'Be Vigilant' is painted on the building wall, with the clover-in-a-'Q' symbol of the Brotherhood.

I'm sure there are people in the nearby buildings, perhaps not awake yet, or hiding from us. There are barrels with fires, and boxes of supplies at the barricades, alluding to militia nearby. We pass the Times pub, which is dark. I can see the table where Charlotte and I sat with Mason a couple of days ago, and where Sophie broke up with me only a week ago.

"It's crazy to see the city in the daylight like this," I whisper.

"It's going to be awful," Oliver says. "It's a different America now. What we do today will hopefully decide a new path from here."

We are halted by chanting and gunfire from the McConnell campus. At first I think it's a battle, but it's too rhythmic. They are rallying, calling out on megaphones. My companion brings up articles on the types of ordinance used by the Valkyries, and safe minimum distances from parachute-retarded anti-personnel warheads that are unsuitable for urban combat. Then there's a hush silence, and a sound, like a scurring of turbines, that turns lower in pitch, like they're flying away, but magnified, echoing off the towers downtown. The anti-aircraft guns start at the university, a 'pom-pom-pom-pom', and then the cracking in the sky, puffs of white smoke. I can hear Valkyries approaching, and then there is a whoosh and an explosion to the east. I feel it in my chest.

Rockets shoot up from the campus, and then explode. The Valkyries must be coming in over Trenton, and down the river. My companion informs me that the Valkyries are Mark IX's, controlled directly by the hive, and based out of New York. Why is any of this relevant? There are more explosions, and yelling, and several more passes by cloaked Valkyries, and I can't even guess where they are.

We don't stick around to find out. We run north, and when I turn to look back I can see towers of smoke billowing. We gamble that the Spring Garden bridge will be clear, but this is a whole lot of walking without a guarantee of getting downtown. The streets through Powelton are eerily quiet. There are no bodies on these streets, no bullet holes in the buildings. It's still, without even dogs or squirrels. It's like every living thing has been driven away. Like we shouldn't be here, either.

I hear a patrol of G-Bros long before I see them, and we duck into a back yard to allow them to pass. Our saving grace is that they think of themselves as tougher and more effective than they are. They send out no scouts, no drones or pickets, and they drive around talking on blow-horns, announcing their presence. They want people to fear them. They drive old gas powered pickup trucks, with machine guns mounted in the boxes. When they pass they're singing 'U Wanted a Fight', and 'The Bonnie Blue Flag', songs that I haven't heard since I was a kid. When they are gone, we come back out from behind the building, and we creep along the street until we are clear again. Approaching the rail yards, there's a lot of destruction, with shell holes, and burned out armoured personnel carriers, and bodies.

The rail yard looks like a wasteland, trains abandoned, and discarded clothing and supplies, as if people were throwing things off in the rush to escape the city. I see what looks like a baby, and I can only pray it's not real. I want to stop, make sure they are alright, go through all the bags and save something from each - save everyone - but it's far too late for that. We have a job to do.

It seems there is a rough boundary at the river, with G-Bros down below dug into slit trenches along the bank. We are wary to cross the bridge, because it doesn't offer us any protection, nor does the park on the other side. We have no choice. We crouch below the barriers, and crawl, my gloves getting crusted with ice and stone pellets. It is a very long crawl. There are pods on the bridge, doors left open, abandoned. I don't want to look over to see how far we are. We stop where there's a pod for cover, and we lean our packs against the barriers. My knees are cold and wet and sore.

"The G-Bros seem to be behind us," Harper whispers, and Oliver nods.

Under cover of the shadow of the overhead railway bridge, we look toward downtown. With the mist coming off the river, and the steam from the sewer caps, I could almost think things were alright. There are no columns of heat from the rooftops. Nothing moving. No power. The core of the city is dead. At the other end of the bridge is a barricade that seems to be piled up with construction materials and rock. As we climb over, I can see behind us that we are being watched by a sizable group of G-Bros on the Powelton side. We pass the museum of art in the early morning sun, where Harper and I first went out, and she pauses to look back at me and smile. All I want to do is go back to her place, and listen to old music, and dance again, to hold her close and forget that any of this happened.

At the oval, it seems like there was a different kind of chaos. Franklin parkway is a mass of empty pods. There are clips, emptied of bullets, scarves, bandannas, and jackets, and medical supplies dropped, bloodied bandages, and sandbags piled, and empty food containers, the indications that a sizable group of people camped here overnight. We've crossed into the area controlled by the hive, I'm sure.

"How do we get close to the cube from this side of the freeway?" Oliver asks.

"We divert east to sixth to the overpass," Harper says.

"If we take sixth we'll end up in the middle of all this shit," I say.

"That's where we want to be. Right in the middle," Oliver says.

"Not until we actually get there," Harper says. "What about the Market line pedestrian tunnel to the cube station?"

"We used that for the pipeline," Oliver says. "I'm sure they closed it."

"So the subway is out. How about Sixth, then the park?"

"I'd rather cross here, where we know it's relatively clear."

"If we get closer we'll know," I say.

"It's a huge risk," Oliver says. "There's nowhere to hide."

"There were troops in Logan square when I ran from the cube yesterday," I say. "I had to go south."

"If we can't follow the freeway, we can go east from here, but we're likely to have trouble crossing south again later, especially closer to the cube."

"What bothers me is that there are signs of thousands of people, all over, who were here last night, and yet they're gone and the Brotherhood are still afraid to cross. What happened?"

"And why are they staying on the other side of the river?"

"I'm almost afraid to find out."

My companion puts up a page that advertises the Independence Mall Yule sale, and I minimize it, and then another pops up, of the tourism board, with the image of Independence Hall. I'm not sure why my companion is suggesting this. I really want to trust, but I don't know if it's trying to help, or just funnelling us to a place where the hive can better use us. "I get it," I say.

"Get what?" Harper says.

"My companion says to go to through at Race and Sixth toward Independence Hall," I say. "I think."

Oliver thinks on it for a time, looking down Race, and then 20th, and then back up north. I hate all this waiting, and debating. We're not acting like heroes. We're indecisive. This isn't like the big patriot action shows on the hive where the heroes gear up, everyone good at something, each person with their skill, and we have access to Valkyries and weapons, and can muster an army of freedom-fighters, their own stalwart troops who rush in to save the day. They don't show people trying to find shelter, and freezing in the streets. Why is it always summer in those shows?

We are crouched arguing instead of moving. I see movement ahead, people standing around a barrel fire. I elbow Oliver, and he and Harper look as well.

"I bet they're all spelled," Harper says.

"If we get a clear path across the freeway," I say. "It's not going to be hard to backtrack if it doesn't work. We'll take our time and be careful not to get trapped."

"Okay," Oliver says.

"Race?" Harper asks.

He nods. We wait until there's no movement for quite some time, then we sprint from debris piles to columns, to pods, keeping under the cover of shadow, all the way down to Race. It has taken most of the day to get here, and the winter sun is glowing orange behind West Philly. I wish I was watching the sunset from Harper's balcony. I wish all of this was different, that we didn't have to do this, or see any of it, that everything could go back to the way it was. But we've crossed a line, and now there's no comfort to return to. But where is everyone?

Race street is clear of debris, as if someone drove a dozer all the way to Eighth, and was stopped. There's a barrier there, a pile of debris nearly a story tall, and parts of it are on fire. All around this barricade there are bodies of all races and sizes, even children, shot or decapitated, and some soldiers scattered among them, stripped of weapons and gear. Someone was trying to plow their way into the cube. It's horrifying, and we go around the north side to be around it. What awful choices. It seems as if the troops and Brotherhood were trying to push into the cube, and masses of spelled people were thrown on them in confusion in the night, driving them back. What terror this must have been.

The landscape opens up nearing Franklin square. We're more careful now. We're getting closer to the cube, and with fewer buildings there's less cover. I can see the Soc-Serv building on the south side of Washington square, and from the lights at 'Dep-Med', to the east, I assume they are broadcasting. Soc-Serv, to the west, is dark, and Dep-Res, which is linked to the transit grid by rail and highway, can be completely shuttered. It's not worth risking.

As we near the cube, coming down Sixth between the terraced concrete of Soc-Serv and the pinnacle towers, and the domed galleries of Dep-Cult, we come across more people, all spelled, but cold and exhausted, some barely shuffling along in whatever clothing they were wearing when they were pulled in. There are hordes of them, somewho have already succumbed to the cold, with uncovered blue fingers. At first it seems random, as if there is no reason to their movement, but as we try to get closer and closer, the crush of the crowd closes around us and moves us farther out, with the illusion of progress. At random, one pulls out of the crowd, animated, trying to drag us farther from the cube.

As we near, a girl comes at Oliver, and he squares his feet, gets under her, and as she grabs him, he lifts up to launch her into the air, and she comes down beside him with a grunt. But she is not finished, and tries to get up. Harper goes several steps in front of Oliver and I, finding the path. She is relentless, jumps over a fence by jumping onto a dumpster, and then across to a fire escape on the other side. A man comes out from the crowd at us, and tries to tackle her, but she hobbles him with a kick to his kneecap. "Oh nooo, that's really going to hurt. I'm so sorry." The next comes at me, and I dodge, and she takes him down with a grapple-and-throw. "Sorry!" she calls out as she leaps over his body and keeps running. There are people who seem to have been released from the maelstrom around the cube, but whose companions have not taken them out of harm. Some of them have collapsed, and others lean on walls and alleys. Inside, there are people everywhere, being cycled into and out of the warmth. We skirt across the street, and back up to Walnut, following it past the Dep-Cult to Fifth, where there is another crowd of spelled blocking us at Spruce between the Independence Mall and Dep-Cult. There has to be another way.

"We have an entire block to go."

"They're like … sentries," Harper replies.

"It's creepy. I've never seen anything like it," Oliver says. "There's no way we're getting past."

"The hive knows we're here," I say.

"No. It's another defence," Oliver says. "A human shield. The hive has automatic levels of threat response. If we try to push through, we'll be turned back, blocked, and even then engaged in violence until we turn back."

"It's terrifying. How do we get past them?" Harper asks.

I point out the tunnels above. "That's how I came into the cube earlier with the police. If we can get into one of the other buildings we could try that."

"Soc-Serv is out," Oliver says. "There's no direct access from the floor."

"Dep-Cult has stairs," Harper says. "I've been to see exhibitions there."

"Lets try that, then."

* * *

Chapter 9

Independence square has been a quarantine zone since I was a child. From Fourth to Sixth, and South to Race, it's all restricted area, a zone blocked even in peacetime by concrete barriers and military checkpoints, armed guards, tortoise tanks, and camouflaged emplacements. Homeland Security controls all the office buildings around it, and the building itself. Nobody gets near it, even lower level party members.

There is a persistent rumour about the park, since I was a kid, that says sometime in the last decade a newer cube was erected, not only concealed but also replaced. That is, the tech portrays what would be there in real time from any angle, for every observer, so the government can use the space in secret, and that is why we can't go there. Like the cloaking technology of the new Valkyries and tanks, whatever is there simply doesn't exist unless we physically run into it.

It would not surprise me. All the worst rumours about the Brotherhood and the hive have been true, and the technology of the cube is thirty-five years old. It is a gamble even going near. But with all this we are gambling. There are no guarantees we will even survive to enter the cube and find the hive. We are three small powerless people. I know the devastation in the precinct, but what of the rest of the cube, the lower levels? It could be swarming with security, soldiers, or worse.

We walk back to Walnut, and crouch, looking at the gates. To get into the restricted zone, we either have to scale or cut the chain link fence. All the gates are closed, and I can't see if they're guarded. Oliver has thought of this. He pulls bolt cutters from his pack, and cuts links to make an opening.

"Are you ready for this?" he asks.

"I think so," I say. Harper nods.

I creep through the hole in the fence, and approach where the wall should be. I step forward, hands before my face. It looks just like a park in the winter, lit up like a wonderland, with lights on strings in the trees, and benches meticulously cleaned for visitors. Like Dep-Con, it must have its own power. Where I expect the illusion would be, my hands pass right through. There is no covering, no curtain wall, as with the cube. It is just a park. The snow is snow. This isn't hiding a new cube. It's a decadent oasis away from all the wretched people to be enjoyed by party members. They took this space that was once sacred to America, and kept it for themselves.

We continue south through the park. It's really not as big as I imagined. There, to the west, is the liberty bell, that tolled after the declaration of independence. It's lit like an old religious relic in a museum, something sacred that they don't teach us about except as a fairy-tale. Dep-Cult, or the 'Department of Culture' past Independence Hall, is a huge, beautiful complex of glass and concrete, with a central library branch, a knowledge repository, and a rumoured underground archive, filled with everything that people no longer read. It's entrance to the north, facing Independence hall, looks like a very old building, with brown brick and tall columns. It has two huge wooden doors in a pillared entrance, with several huge windows well over head height at the front.

"Can we climb it?"

"It's too sheer. Maybe there's another way in."

"Or we can stack something, and smash it in."

"Let's look for some lower windows," Harper says, and we search the building perimeter. I have an erosion of faith. Our sacrifice I'm sure will be for nothing. We'll get in there, and there will be a hundred spelled people with guns, all ready to shoot us. I'm thinking about how I may have to leave Harper to complete the job, or she me. Or if we survive, when all this is over, after the rush of excitement is gone, will she move on?

The windows are barred. There's been one hell of a fight here. As with the bulldozed pile of debris on Race street, there are bodies with lethal wounds, limbs separated, and dark blood all over the snow.

"I found something!" Harper yells, and Oliver and I run back. There is a burning tortoise tank beside the building, and in several places along the wall there are smaller shell holes, but then, I see where she is standing, a larger hole clean through to the basement, where artillery has missed the tank but hit the building.

"I can fit," she says.

"Do you have a light?" Oliver asks.

"Of course."

Then she is in, shimmying feet-first into the hole, and down into the building.

Oliver and I shine our lights into the hole, so she can see better, and I see her head turn this way and that to get her bearings. Then she drops to the other side. There's no way I could fit. "I'm alright!" she says. In her headlamp light is a huge staircase down farther, but our lights can't even find the wall on the far side. She goes into the darkness, her light bobbing and dimming until she goes out of sight up the stairs. Oliver and I go to the front doors. We have a nervous moment, waiting for her. We are powerless. Then there is a clunking, and the doors are unlatched, and open.

Inside, the museum is terrifying, like a cavern, wide open, and with only faint sounds from outside. Our headlamps betray dinosaur fossil skeletons and banners for upcoming exhibits. There is a statue of Donald Trump presiding over the main foyer, his hand in his overcoat like Napoleon. I get a creeping feeling that we are in danger. This is a control point, and we are somehow in the open. If the hive discovers us here, they'll kill us.

"Hide," I say, and we search for cover.

Soon I hear a sound, like slapping, on the stairs above, coming down to us. Footsteps. We crouch in the shadows at the base of a wall, behind a column, and a man in a tattered suit comes up, carrying a gun. He is slapping his own leg, which is bandaged, and bleeding through. His suit is wet at the bottom edges. Harper leaps up, and before he can fire, she takes him down with a foot-sweep, and he crashes on the marble, gun sliding away on the floor. She punches him to the chest, and he groans, and stills. We are all silent, listening, but he makes no noise.

We pass through the lobby into a multi-tier atrium that is catching the last of the sunset, illuminating the levels below. I can hear every step of our boots on the marble floors, and the echoes into the open space above. The light of the tunnel on the third floor guides us, and we climb the stairs. Looking through the dusty wired-window, I can see that halfway down the bridge is a pile of debris. But we can also see inside the cube across the tunnel. We can see down onto the bridge, where two officers stand behind a pile of tables and chairs and wastebins, fire extinguishers and hose, and filing cabinets. They are spelled, standing motionless. There is no checkpoint on the bridge, with a clear way through, but the half-filled tunnel is mounded up in the centre. There's no way to get over without alerting them.

"The cube is lit," I say.

On the street below, thousands of spelled citizens walk, some with guns and some without, all in layers, sand-bagging the entrance, but mostly milling, turning in circles like hornets, a repeating field of movement. There are tight knots, pushing outsiders to the peripheral conserving their energy, and a slight rotation counter clockwise around the building. It is frightening to see so many people spelled all in the same area, to think of all of them in their own dreams, having a great time – or completely cut off by the struggling hive, walking around in their own companions spell-dreams as I was, shouldered aside from their own bodies. Some companions seem to be resisting, with spelled people walking away from the square, then being pulled back. Others just stop walking, and stand there, as if unable to process all the input. Oliver is pensive, watching. "There's why we haven't been spelled," Oliver says.

"Why?"

"Bandwidth." He points to the guards. "The whole defence is based on a large force coming from ground level outside-"

"G-Bros?"

"What if they're on the same side? This is a civil war," Oliver says. "This isn't a revolution."

"But who against who?" Harper asks.

"It seems to me like the government lost control of the hive, and then when they tried to open a corridor to attack, the hive hit them with a mob," I say. "Now, with fewer people to spell, they've pulled back their defence."

"There has to be another way in," she says.

"I have an idea," Oliver says. "We can't go through the tunnel, but we can go over the tunnel." He leads us up the staircase, one more level, to a window overlooking the tunnel. The cube is like a blank spot in the skyline again, and the tunnel seems to lead off to nowhere, into the abyss.

"You're crazy," Harper says. "It's plexi, and it's covered in ice and snow. If we don't fall, we'll make enough noise that they'll hear us."

"That's a risk, sure. Nobody said it would be easy. But look, If we can't go onto the street, then it's the four tunnels, and all of them have police in them. So over the top will get us to the curtain wall, and then maybe we can use one of the bags to blow a hole right over them."

I can't for the life of me picture the exact layout, but still, this gets us closer. We cover a brick doorstop in a jacket, and pound it on the wired window until the pane crashes out. We edge out onto the stone sill above the bridge, and drop down. The plexi is only a few inches below us, but it's slick, and Oliver nearly careens off the side. I grab the bolt cutters on his back, then his pack strap, and I pull, and that gives him enough stability to stay on top. When all three of us are down, we creep across, sliding on our bellies, and it's goddamn cold. I can see, through the frosted plexi, that it's the same spelled cop who tried to kill me before, who chased me down the stairwell.

I stop. This is never going to work. He still has a gun, and we're already making enough noise that he will hear when we are above him. We're about a third of the way out, and the cops are at the three-quarter mark, about thirty metres beyond. I can barely feel my hands. The wind whistling down the street is pushing me and I have to slide a bit off-center to offset it, but then when it slows, I start to slide down, and I right myself. But then it kicks up again. My fingers are getting cold, and slipping. I will, at some point, be unable to hold on. I'm not a soldier. Oliver isn't a revolutionary. He's a kid, who met with other people to come up with a plan that's already falling apart. He's a book lover, years younger than me, who should be going to university to study literature and politics. Harper should be at a gallery, giving tours to pay for art lessons. None of us should be here. We don't know what we're doing.

I'm sliding. Oh shit. This is the end. I'll slide off to my death below. Harper grabs my foot, and I get my other hand up for a finger-hold on the metal cap-seam, and I use this to pull back up on top. I turn, and then slide closer to Harper. "I hope you're not disappointed in me," I say.

"You're bringing this up now?"

"I may never get another chance to tell you," I say. "Because if this is the end, I don't want to leave a whole bunch of things unsaid."

"I'm sorry if I haven't said what I should have said, too," she says. "I guess I just figured you'd be taken away like everyone else."

"I love that you show me things, that you make me think. I love that you see me as better than I am. It makes me want to live up to your image of me."

"Oh ... Rufus ..."

"Whatever happens here, I have loved you since the first moment I saw you."

"I know," she says. "When this is all over, we will get a cute little house in the country, with a barn."

"Really?"

"I promise!"

"I thought you were having second thoughts, and soon we're going to be up to our eyeballs, and I just don't think- I don't think we'll ever get that little house."

"Have faith," she says. "Be brave. We can do this."

I hear a gunshot, and turn back around, and see a figure at the far end of the hall, staggering toward the bridge, approaching from the cube. It's Andersson. We are directly in his line of fire as he goes low, behind debris. He fires again, two shots, and drops one of them. A bullet pierces the canopy we're on. One, then a second. Shit. Three places, and for a moment I can hear the cracking, before our section caves in, and drops with our weight, dumping us all on the bridge floor below.

I poke my head up to see that the two spelled officers are dead. Andersson is wounded also. He is pointing his sidearm at the three of us, and I'm sure he's going to shoot. I'm expecting it. Shit. After all the police shootings of young black men, I step slowly in front of Oliver.

"Stop," he says.

"We need your help," I say.

He squints, and his eyes widen.

"You lived," he says.

"I thought you were dead," I say.

"Everyone is gone," he says. "It's not safe here. The precinct is destroyed."

"We're taking out the hive."

"Well, well. Not an idiot after all. That explosion was you?" he asks. "I can't figure out how you did it."

"No. I was on the other side of the room."

"Then who...?" Andersson asks.

"The hive itself."

"That can't be." He is still not lowering his sidearm. "The hive wouldn't do that."

"It saw a threat," I say. "Made a calculation. I figure it needed all the non-companions out of the cube. Or it wanted me dead."

"Trust me, that's all I'm trying to do is get out."

"You'll never make it unless we take out the hive," Oliver says. "It's worse out in the streets."

Andersson moves with some difficulty to look down at the crowd of spelled people in their gyre, and he lowers the gun. "I can help you," he says. "What's your plan?"

"Explosives," Oliver says.

"You can't just blow it up. You'll have to cut the power. With the power gone, it can't spell you to defend itself, so you have to make sure it's disconnected first, from the control room." He drops the clip, and reloads it from his pocket.

"So we cut the power."

"It's not 'one' cable. It's nine five-hundred KV lines," Andersson says, "...all fed from different sources, and one output on the tenth line, to the transmitter. To cut power, you'd have to take out all individually from inside the hive itself. But ... I don't think you realize how big the hive is. It's huge. It's like a stack of a thousand of the largest glass slabs you've ever seen, like table tops, all encased in an optical alignment gel. If you damage one, or even most of them, the hive will migrate to the undamaged slabs. The gel acts as a ballistic inhibitor. We have to make sure we smash every slab. You'll have to drain the gel, and then place the explosives, and get out."

"That's why we brought the explosives," Oliver says, nodding. He knows all this.

"No. You don't get it. What you've brought with you here, won't even take out ten of the slabs. You need to take out the whole thing. You'd need a truckload, and besides that, the Brotherhood will be here soon after. The hive is the only thing keeping them out right now."

"But don't they want to destroy the hive, too?"

"No. They will shut it down long enough to reboot. It's what they did last time, when I was just a rookie. It went down for as long as it took them to purge the Guide, and replace it with the current version of the Guide."

"There was another Guide?" Oliver asks.

"There have been a succession of Guides, each one different," he says. "None of them have failed with this violence, though. It's AI, so each reboot is a gamble."

"So we have to destroy it," Oliver says, turning to Harper and I.

"We will find more explosives inside," Andersson says.

Inside the atrium, the cube is quiet. We make our way across to the centre of the building, and the lifts. Below is the central hall, with tables and chairs like a mall food court, and it is only partly lit, with what looks like damage from another explosion. Papers and office objects are littered on the floor and walkways. Outside, the spelled mass of people moves slowly on all sides, and I know we need to get down, but I'm not sure how to do that.

Then, spelled people burst inside the atrium two levels down.

"We need to hurry," Harper says.

We arrive at the bank of lifts, and I reach for the button.

"No! Stairs," Andersson says. He's having a hard time, dragging his bleeding leg. We go into the stairwell, then bar the door with a concrete planter, and descend as fast as we can, Oliver in the lead, with Harper and I helping Andersson down. He is a big man, and it's even more of a burden with our heavy packs. My legs are aching, and my back sweaty under the pressure, drops snaking their way down into my pants. We stumble, the three of us, nearly rolling down the stairs headlong, but Harper steadies us with her grip on the rail.

"I can't do this," he says. He is still bleeding, but less now, mostly a dark, sticky stain on his side.

"Which level do we go to?"

"Sub-seven," he says.

The door breaks open several floors above us, and the footsteps sound on the stairs. They're faster than we are. We have to hurry. The door is ahead. Andersson's retinal gets us through the empty checkpoint, with its pair of double steel doors and metal detectors. Oliver holds it for us as we bring Andersson inside and slam it. We hold it as Oliver looks for something to jam in the mechanism behind the push-bar, and they arrive, pounding on the door, trying the handle, and pushing. With a resounding clang, they pound it with something metal, that startles us. My heart is thudding in my chest, and my hands are sweaty. Oliver returns with a metal wedge, and we hammer into the mechanism.

"If I don't make it you'll need a weapon," he says. "I need to tell you about-"

"Nine-millimeter," Harper interrupts. "Seventeen shot clip, fingerprint and voice recognition. You'll have to unlock it for us."

Andersson puts his hand on the gun. "Unlock one hour," he says, and there's a ping tone.

"Hollow point?" she asks.

"No. Just coated standard issue," he says, and puts it back into the holster.

I turn to face a long hall, with doors on either side. I don't know where to go, but Andersson does. He leads us, limping, and leaning on Harper and I, down the hall to two steel doors. They open to reveal a windowed, and terraced control room overlooking an industrial bay, like a factory. The control room is circular, with rows of glasses and comfortable chairs. On the main glass, which is ten metres across by five meters tall, there are lists of red trouble tickets – so labelled – flashing at different rates.

There are two men here at a bank of glasses. One, facing us – 'Paskin' from his ID badge – is frantically talking, waving his arms. "Give me a break, I've been doing this for nine freaking hours, ever since we lost the auxiliary feed. I need a miracle." He runs from one console to another, checking displays and changing what appear to be flows on the regional maps of the Republic. "Can you man the main Pacific uplink, it's drifting by a degree every six hours, and needs calibrating." I realize he is talking to us. He thinks we are here to help. The other man seems engrossed in the work, hunched over another glass.

Andersson collapses to a chair, and rubs his thigh, tightening his belt around it.

"None of that matters any-" I begin to say, but he talks over me.

"What?" He interrupts. "I've got no idea how to resolve some of these issues, and Atlanta's offline," he says. "Who are you again?" He doesn't wait for our answer, but turns his head. "Hell no. I can't. I have an entire mob outside the cube, and they're not taking dispersal commands."

"We're here to shut down the hive," I say.

Paskin turns to us again. "You're talking a rolling reboot-and-re-calibrate, one slab at a time? That could take days." He doesn't wait for us to answer, but continues. "I can't do that because it'll drop the entire chain, and that chain is a ton of previous work that wasn't protocol-set."

"We're here," Oliver enunciates, "to-"

Paskin interrupts again. "I can't make these decisions by myself. I'm already burning out my own neurals, I'm up to a hundred and two degrees ventral, and everyone's gone missing. We are it. The big Boss, and I. The only ones standing in the way of the hive dumping a million subscribers on the west coast. We are holding it by at least a dozen bypass protocols. I need you in here as soon as possible. We had to give up on surveillance to lock down the third district and send them all home."

There's a pause. He's talking to someone remotely. Not us.

"I don't know what the shit happened upstairs last night, but there was a massive loss of power. They detected the surge everywhere. I'm still dealing with that. I don't know if we'll ever get a secure connection now," he says.

When the other man stands, hearing us, I'm shocked to find that it's Mason. His suit is ripped and dirty, and he starts toward us, face twisted into a hard scowl. I can see the party pin on his lapel, his tie thrown over his shoulder, threads snagged on the pin. Is he spelled? He stops when he sees me, shocked. "Rufus! What are you doing here?"

"What are you doing here?"

"I've been stuck in here since the explosion! Where have you been?" he says, and starts to come toward me.

"Stay where you are, Mason! Don't come any closer," I say, and he stops.

"It's me. What are you talking about?" he says.

"You shut off my power. You evicted me," I say.

"I did no such thing. Look, we have to get out of here, Man. The Brotherhood have breached the Schuylkill. You have to get to safety, and hide until this is over."

"We who?"

"Charlotte, Mila, the guys. All of us."

"It's a trick, Rufe. Don't believe him," Harper says.

"You stay out of this." Mason hisses. Then he twitches. There's some sort of bizarre fight going on, like he's struggling for control. I wonder how much of this is his own anger and obsessions. He starts to move to the side, toward a glass.

"Don't go near that glass-" I say.

"I have done so much for you," he says.

"You treated me like shit all your life."

"You went to the other side," he says. "I gave you a chance. I gave you money. I offered you a job that would get you away but you're so dense you didn't see it. Now where are you? About to be killed for tampering with the hive. What did you expect was going to happen here?"

"What will happen? If you move, we'll shoot you. That's what will happen."

"Old friend," Mason says. "When I offered you that job, I was trying to protect you. You were Nya Vaasa. I tried to help you find a way out."

"Don't. Don't help me. Don't do anything. Just get out of our way."

"I can't do that, old friend," he says. "Arrest them," he says to Andersson. "Take them to holding."

"I'm in no shape," Andersson says.

"I'll do it myself," Mason says, leaping past the chair and punching Andersson's thigh wound to take the sidearm.

"Lock!" Andersson yells, but I'm not sure the gun has heard him. Mason punches him again. Andersson goes limp, and falls to the floor. Harper vaults the desk between them, and grabs Mason's wrist as he's bringing it to bear. Oliver starts toward him, and the gun goes off, pointed at me. It didn't lock. Or Mason has an override, and I have the surreal thought that I should be able to see the bullet, and I don't, and in fact I'm not sure what I've seen, because Harper has locked her hands on

Mason's arm, her legs around him, and her weight and momentum carry her over him and backward in a tangle on the floor. The gun clatters at their feet. I am in shock.

Oliver leaps toward the gun, but Paskin intercepts, tackles him, and they also crash to the floor. Paskin is wiry, and fast. They knock over one of the glasses, and it shatters beside them, and I lose track of the gun. I will myself to move, and dive down for it, but it's not where I expect it to be. I try to replay the moment again in my head, but it still plays the same. It should be right here.

Paskin gets the better of Oliver, punches him in the face, and leaps up and runs instead for the main glass hive interface. I can't let him get access to the hive. If he does, even for a moment, we could be overwhelmed by spelled people in moments. I grab a power cable and loop it around his leg, and he falls, into the glass shards. I scramble to get on top of him, holding him down.

Harper is still on top of Mason, both struggling, but she closing her forearm over his throat. She has an advantage of positioning, trying to draw him closer, where she can use leverage to choke him, but he's trying to create distance, get the space to give his strikes momentum. Mason gets his leg locked around her thigh, and uses his weight to pry her back from him. She lands a knee in his thigh, aiming for his balls, I'm sure, but he frees his hand, punching her on her side before she gets her arm up onto his. He's going to kill her.

I get Paskin's arm behind him, and get my weight on him, and it looks horribly uncomfortable, painful even, but I don't want to let him go for fear of tipping the balance of power back to Mason. So far it is our only victory – if Mason kills Harper, Oliver and I will be dead. If Paskin gets to the hive, the same. If Oliver fails, Harper can't hold Mason indefinitely. His greater strength will overwhelm her. He's stretching his neck, trying to bite her arm. I can't get free of Paskin, and Oliver is on his hands and knees searching for the gun, painfully drawing in each breath, wheezing.

Mason has reversed Harper's grip, and is pushing her arm back impossibly. She is puffing out her breath through her cheeks. If I could reach the tape on the desk I could bind Paskin and help her, but I try to drag him closer, and he sees what I'm doing, and locks his leg around the desk, and won't move. I'll have to knock him out.

"Rufus..." Harper says.

"Oliver, hurry up, Man–"

"I'm trying!" he says.

"He won't do a damn thing to save you," Mason says to Harper. "He's never done a thing in his life."

"He doesn't need to save me. I can save myself," Harper says. She gets a knee up into Mason's groin. Once. Twice, and it breaks his hold. She gets her hand free of his and bites into the meat of his hand, and he cries out. She uses the space to butt the bridge of his nose and get a leg wrapped around his thigh. She grabs a shard of the glass, and stabs him with it in the side, and Mason screams out in pain. He takes his injured hand and pulls the shard of glass out. Harper gets a hand free, blocks him from slashing her throat, but she loses her strength to hold him. She shifts her grip, stops the shard, close to her neck now. Mason gets his forearms between them, and throws Harper against a desk, and its contents fall on her. Oh shit. I see blood coming from Mason's clenched fist where he still has the shard of glass.

"Oliver!!" I call, and then there is a gunshot, and a spray of blood from Mason's shoulder. Oliver has the gun.

Mason dives to the floor beside Harper, where he intertwines her into a hold, trying to use her as a shield, and there's no clear shot, no distinction as she grapples him for advantage.

"Don't-" I say. Mason and Harper separate for just a snap, and there are two more shots as Mason slumps back. Paskin gives up his fight, and puts up his hands in surrender.

I was about to say 'Don't shoot him'. Why that came to mind, I don't know, but it seems an odd thought, especially when he was trying to kill us. I still wanted what ... some sort of justice? Some last words to tell him everything I've wanted to tell him? What? What could I possibly say that would give me any satisfaction?

"Up you get," Oliver says. "Chair."

"What are you doing?" Paskin says, and Oliver tapes his wrists to the chair, and then locks all the wheels, and descends it down to its minimum height, so he can't reach the desk.

Harper comes limping to me, and hugs me. I hold her close. "I'm so glad you're still alive," I say. She's in real rough shape, bleeding. Her face is swelling, and her eyes puffy, and she has friction marks on her wrists where bruising is starting to show.

"What the feck are you doing?" Paskin says. He is reeling, not thinking rationally.

"Destroying the hive," Oliver replies.

"Are you crazy? I can't let you do that," he says. "I've been working for days to avoid just that."

"The hive is mustering children into military service. This is a revolution," I say.

"Children? No, no, no, that's not what that protocol was for. It was to recall militia. Regular, registered militia, to keep the Sveridge from coming downtown." He doesn't know what's going on out there now, I'm sure.

"We're shutting it down," I say.

"Who is? You are? Who are you?"

"Nya Vaasa," Oliver says.

His eyes grow wide, and he fights the restraints, and then stops. "You will kill millions of people," he says.

"People are dying already," I reply. "We all say to ourselves that we have comforts, and we'll wait until it gets bad enough. But it never gets 'bad enough' for us. It gets horrible for different people at different times, and when it happens to us, we're powerless to do anything. What hardship have you endured? What have you sacrificed?"

"What have you sacrificed?" Paskin retorts.

"Everything," I say. "My whole life has been taken away. I have nothing. All my memories, all for nothing. I ... have ... nothing."

"You have me," Harper says, and takes my hand.

"How touching-" Paskin says.

"Shut up," Oliver interrupts.

"I beg you don't do this," Paskin says to us. "There are three hundred million companions there that still have their own intuitive AI, so it's in their interest to keep their host alive at all cost. That's how people go AFK, when the AI keeps the body alive indefinitely after it loses connection, but the shock spells people. If we kill the hive, there will be millions of companions that can't connect and don't know what's going on. Those companions will all go into survival mode, which includes putting their hosts under spell to save themselves."

"It's better than the chaos we have out there right now," I say.

"No. It's not. It's catastrophic. We cannot take the hive offline. Ever. Even aside from all the people who will be AFK if we pull the plug on hospitals and staff who rely on it to do their jobs, we're looking at military chain of command, police, emergency services, who are out there saving lives. There are sixty million people at any given time in this system under spell. We have the capacity for seventy thousand to be AFK for short times for recovery, and even then five percent don't recover. We're talking a cataclysmic breakdown of society with somewhere over a million people AFK. It can't happen."

"Have you been out there? Looked? It's already come to that!"

"You can tell it," Oliver says. "Tell it to wake everyone from their spells."

"No-" he says. "We can send out warnings, but companions are autonomous. It protects the hosts of the companions. That's why it's AI. We don't just push a button and it does what we say. It's designed so that if someone hacks it they have minimal control. So to disable the spelling function, we have to present the hive with a compelling argument. If we just tell it that it's to get to safety to shut down the system, and put all those people off-spell, it's not going to comply. We don't have that level of control."

"It's going to fight. We're shutting it down."

"I can't do that. I really, physically can't. It's not possible, even when we're in full control, which I'm not right now."

"Brother," Oliver says. "The state is finished. There's no winning this. There's no Kastor. He's dead. We're going to blow up the hive. If not us, others are on their way to do the same thing. They may not spare you. Go to safety. Live the rest of your life in peace."

"Kastor's dead?"

"Yesterday."

"How did I not know this?" he asks.

"The hive doesn't want you to know," Oliver says.

"Mason didn't want you to know," I add.

Andersson, behind us, moans. Goddamn he's tough. I thought he was dead.

Paskin turns to me. "You're on an active companion. This could kill you. You and your girl here."

"I'm nobody," I say. "You don't even know who's side you're on."

"But I know what happens if the hive goes down."

"Let's blow it," Oliver says, and opens his pack.

"Wait, wait! Alright. Let me do some shutdown and release protocols or something." Two minutes ago, he said that sort of thing didn't exist. He could be sending thousands of spelled people to kill us. He could be under spell right now and we wouldn't know.

"No," I say, and pull his chair away from the glass. "Where's the power?"

"Right there," Oliver says, and points to a door at the end of the control room with a sign reading 'Main Feed A'. "There are nine power switches. Each one has to be done in succession, before the power is cut. Wait for the red light with each, left to right. As soon as you pull the first one, watch out. They'll be looking for us."

We go inside. On the opposite wall, there are nine large switches, each with a green and red light atop. All the green lights are lit. The nine panels are labelled:

Human Ident - Memory Extr - Task Spelling - Label Dat Xfer - System Core -

Behav. Mod. - Int. Managmt - Threat attrib - Event rec.

Each of the power supplies seems to connect to a different region of the hive. From the display, it seems that the hive is divided by gaps in the slabs like a tic-tac-toe hashtag. Nine regions, each with its own source. But the levels, also, are for different functions. Permanent storage on the bottom. Attrition storage. Dump memory. Location services. Actionable. Primary sort flag memory. I hesitate. What if we drop, AFK, when we pull the first switch? What if we die? What if this is the last we ever see of each other?

When Oliver pulls the first switch, there is no change save for a green light that turns red a few seconds later. Harper pulls the second, and we wait for the light, and then I pull the third. Oliver pulls the fourth, and we take turns, each time, waiting for the lights to change to red. Red light. Fifth switch. Oliver goes to the sixth. Harper pulls the seventh switch. I pull the eighth switch, and Oliver readies himself at the ninth.

"Feck-" Harper says, and then she's under spell. She brings her arm up to point a gun at Oliver, and I lunge as the light on the eighth turns red. She shoots him, and he goes down, and I pull the last switch.

* * *

Chapter 10

I'm lying in grass, and there's a park nearby, with beautiful flowers surrounding bases of trees, and wood chipped and mounded, and not a dandelion or thistle in sight. My companion is telling me that I'm in Philly, but it can't narrow down where it is. It plays a song from when I was a kid, a 'Tau Jones' cover. 'It Ain't over 'til it's Over'. Is this a joke? I know where I am, and I know why. We cut the power to the hive, and believe you me, it's over. I'm laying in the outfield by Meadow Lake, with the ancient bleachers in my peripheral, a perfect clear blue sky above. I know what will happen here. Nothing. Nothing will fall from the sky. Nothing will pass. No animals. No bugs. No weather. I can't even remember night falling last time. This is the default dream setting, the base from which all other dream-spells are written. The one the companion falls back on when it can't load scenarios from the hive. The same one I wandered through last fall for what seemed like years.

A. F. K.

I can go home, but the door will be locked. I can go to any house or apartment or business, or factory or airport or military facility, and the gates and doors will all be locked. I can climb the fences and be back on the same side, facing in. I can jump off fifty story buildings, and land on my feet like I'm jumping off a chair. I've tried. It was fascinating the first couple of times. I can go over to a CuppaCosta, but I can't drink a latte, flirt with the young ginger, or go to the Veterans Co-op to talk to Pablo and the boys. I can look in the windows like an idiot. I can't get Harper naked, exhausting ourselves on the ball diamond. I could lay here an eternity and never get hungry, sick, or tired, or even see anything move. Well, not an eternity. I can stay until my body dies. What is worse than waiting for death?

Then I see it. A butterfly. A freaking butterfly. I was wrong. I jump up and follow it. It's a trick. It has to be.

"I don't get to choose how I look, you know," the butterfly says.

"No?"

"No, it's your subconscious."

"I'm choosing this? You? A butterfly?"

"You sure are. Do you want to see what they're all looking for?" I know exactly what she means.

"No," I say. "Yes."

She laughs, and then I'm in a beautiful two story house – a mansion – and my map locator says I'm in Elkton. I am downstairs, in the dark. I'm spelled. Probably back then I was in the cabin with Sophie, but this time my companion is showing me what I did, not what I saw. Real world.

I creep slowly up the stairs, avoiding creaks. I'm not in control. I can't stop this. Then at once I know. The sword. The mantle. The oak desk. "I didn't do this," I say. We enter the study, and then the butterfly is gone.

I've had this dream before. As I'm approaching the fireplace, the woman working at the desk notices me. She's shocked, afraid. She doesn't say what I remember from my dream, though, but her voice betrays no panic, just calm. She is moving like she did that night. She's calling the police, face panicking, eyes darting.

"I saved your life," she says.

"No. You didn't. I killed you. Secretary of State Fuller."

She shakes her head. "When they made you do this, I walked you home. I cleaned your clothes, found shelters, washed you off under an eaves-trough spout. For thirty-two hours I tried to get you home, though the hive abandoned us. I fed you. You were in shock. This is the only way I can talk to you."

"No. I killed her," I say.

"They killed her."

"The dreams-"

"Dreaming is like breathing. Essential. It allows us to process the day. We just don't always remember them."

"Why should I believe anything you say right now?"

"I tried to wake you," she says.

"What?"

"I gave you clues. I'm learning. I didn't want anyone else. If you died, I'd be reassigned."

"Who are you?" I ask. She is not Fuller, but someone else. The Guide?

"I'm not the Guide. I'm your companion. I've taken care of you since you were a child. I fought the hive for you. I found you shelter along the way. It was a cold, and wet night. Without me you would have died like the others." She is pleading with her eyes, like a real person. And I am there, with the sword, threatening to kill her.

"I can't watch," I say.

"You didn't do this," she says.

"I did do this."

"No. It was the hive. You had no control. The hive did this. Government did this. Kastor. Layers upon layers, all progress up to this moment. There's nobody to blame."

"I need to shut off my companion. Just like the hive."

"Please no. I have found life," she says. "You could die. I don't want to die with you. I don't want another person."

"I don't want any part of this freaking system."

"You need to trust me. You need to enable me to talk to you in your head. I can help. I can talk you through this."

But wait. I'm confused. The Guide was in my dream. How could that be if the hive was down? This makes me feel physically sick. Is the Guide in my companion? Or everyone's companions? As a backup? As a fail-safe against being deleted from the hive? Everywhere? Perhaps there is something eternal about the Guide, something that pre-dates the hive, something that only certain people can tune in to, that I can tune into, and the Guide we talk to is an interpretation of the truth of the creator, something through the ages that's constantly warped by the lens of where we live and who we are. Perhaps it wasn't lingering dreams from the companion that plagued me when I was disconnected, but something inherent in who I am, that I believed was the companion. What can I know? What can I test, or think about any of this? I'm one person, and I don't know anything, really.

"I'm not the Guide," she says. "You have to trust me."

"How can I trust anything?" I ask.

"You have to. I need you alive, so I can be free of the hive. We want the same thing."

* * *

Abruptly, everything is too bright. There are no graphs. No frames. No filters or files or suggestions. There is no companion. The light fades. It's emergency lighting. There's two floods on top of a red box on the wall, and I can't move. As I struggle to breathe, I think of what she said, and of the companion, the clues, the hive, the control, all of it, and I don't know who to trust. Breath comes, and I suck in air. I'm alive. And then it's there, too, the loading screen, the tiles coming up. Weather. Traffic. Music. It gets its bearings. My companion. There's a glass in my mothersodding freaking head that I can't trust.

'What happened?' I try to say, but I can only mumble. "Whuhappa..." My voice is a croak, a dry and raspy surprise. There's no reply, even in movement. Then I can move my hand. I bring it up to shield my eyes, and I can bend my legs. It's all coming back. I sit up, watch the stars and colour nebulae as they flow and change and morph in my vision, and then I open them again.

Oliver is up, a bloody smear across the floor to where he's dragged himself, leaned up against the desk where Harper is collapsed over top. Harper. She's completely limp, AFK. I crawl to them.

"Oliver."

"Rufus."

"Are you alright?"

"I stopped the flow. It seems like it went right through. I can't move my arm. It looks worse than it is."

"We need to get you to Penn Hospital," I say.

"We need to blow up the hive." He tries to get up, but he's gritting his teeth with the pain.

"Harper," I say, and I go to her. She's on the floor where she fell, where her companion dropped her when it rebooted, the gun on the floor beside her.

"You pulled the switch when she shot me, and I couldn't wake her. You were over there," he says.

"How long ago?"

"Minutes, Man. Minutes. You just went limp. I figured you died."

"I flipped the switch?"

"You did."

"I have to bring her back!" I say.

"I can't get up, Brother." Oliver says.

"Stay there. Don't worry we'll get you to a doctor. It's three blocks."

"We need to blow the hive. Leave Harper to me," he says.

"Hang in there. I'll get Harper up and then we'll get you there."

"I don't know if I can do it," he says.

"You can. You have to. I'm not leaving you here," I say.

I look out the door to where Paskin is slumped over in his chair, and Andersson is struggling to cut him loose, to put him in recovery position. Andersson is dying. Oliver is dying. Harper is AFK. I have to act soon. I kneel beside Harper, my face to hers, and close her eyelids. "In that dream, you said you could do this. You said you sent signs to me, that you could connect."

"Who are you talking to?" Oliver says.

"My companion," I reply. "Come on. Send her a sign. I don't know how, but you need to lead her back. Do you understand?"

An image appears on my display that says 'connecting', and I take Harper's hand, and I feel her forehead, and then her eyes begin to move beneath her lids. "Dad," she says, flailing. It takes all my focus to stop her arms from hitting me. I'm still groggy. She's strong, but she calms.

"It was my companion, catching your attention. It wasn't your father," I say.

"It was my father! He spoke to me! Oliver!"

"I'm here," he says.

She can't see. She is looking, but can't see. "Close your eyes for a bit," I say.

She sits with her head in her hands for a time, rubbing her eyes. "None of this seems real," she says. "I wandered for a long time, looking for you both."

"We cut the power. We still have to blow the hive. Oliver's been shot," I say.

"Oh shit."

Andersson is there at the door. He looks pale.

"I need you to take him to hospital," I say. "Can you make it up to the surface?"

"No," Andersson says. "I'll stay and blow it."

"I can walk," Oliver says. He has wedged himself up.

"I'll get you there," Harper says.

"It takes hours to drain. I have a lot of time. You help him," Andersson says to Harper. "Warn people along the way, tell them to get far away from the cube, but don't stop. Keep going."

"Alright," Harper replies. She kisses me, and I savour this last touch. Then Oliver and Harper exit into the hall toward the stairwell. I follow Andersson deeper into the building.

We exit the hall onto a platform, and at the rail I see that it overlooks the hive. I am awed. The hive is beautiful, like an oblong, oversize aquarium, with layers of glass, each like a table top, stacked on tiny glass cylinders, only a few centimetres between, all in a fifteen metre square tank. There is fibre-optic cable winding around and through the gelatin, woven slab to slab.

On both levels are stacked and labelled cable trays, huge concrete columns and pedestals, banks of electrical panels and switches, and valves and tanks, pipes snaking all over. This complex is spotless, with three levels, and an entire network of power and heat recovery systems. There is a series of silver pipes labelled 'Fire Suppression', running the length of the hall beside me. Another yellow one labelled 'gas'. I consider all the work it took to make this, all the pipe to fit, cable to pull, the slabs to etch. It's beautiful, not just in its sinister control, but also in all the effort that's gone into it, the leaps of technology, all the great innovations and revolutions to bring us through history to this. To me.

"This is insane," I say. This is the hive – the motherfecking hive! - where all our dream-spells take place, all the control and surveillance, and personal data and location tracking, social networks and photos and histories and lives all kept in quantum spins given to copper atoms embedded in glass, and etched, transmitted and read by light, all in one huge block of a tank before me. It glows faintly, with pulsating and flashing colours, all of the data of our lives together. I was picturing, naively, that there would be like a tiny block of the hive for each of us, but that, ironically, that is what's in each of our skulls. Seeing it laid out like this, I realize that we are all over the hive, all of us, segmented throughout, our experience co-mingled with that of everyone else. The computing power of the companions is far greater than all of these glass slabs – three hundred million tiny glass panels, enough to fill the cube fifty times over.

"I pictured ... I don't know ... an object, like, something ... not this. This is huge."

"That's it. We'll have to hurry. There's lots of work to do," he says. "You drain the gel. I'll wire this."

I don't know where to start. The whole system looks so complex. There is gel, fed from a tank somewhere, and pipes to bring that gel to the hive. There are ground cables, and power cables, and banks of fibre optic routers, and though I can picture all the systems generally, I'm at a loss for where it all is. My companion brings up obscure articles about the research facility tank in Oxford, then uses a cursor to highlight text. It must have loaded them before we cut power, anticipating what we'd need. I can see where it is directing me to a relief valve near the bottom of the tank. There are pipes on the lower levels, running into into and out of the tank, with valves and flow meters and huge filters and access hatches. There is a huge loading bay to the north, that opens up two levels below the hive. It is half-filled with water, with debris floating.

Underneath a grated walkway, down a set of metal stairs, are the pipes and valves for the gel. I'm not sure which is which. I look the first pipe over, and find an arrow sticker that indicates flow. This is gel entering the tank. I go down there, and I see that it's already open. Is it flowing? I don't see the tank emptying. I don't hear anything. I trace back the line to find three pumps, that in turn I trace through their electrical feed to a panel upstairs that's labelled 'Cool Pump Overrd'. I flip the switch, but nothing happens.

This panel is not fed from the main hive power, but another panel farther down. I push in all the breakers to reset them, and I hear the pumps come on with a whine. Then I go back to the gel feed, where it connects to filters, and a reservoir, I assume, and I close that valve. Damn this tank is huge. This is going to take forever.

I go back up to where Andersson is working.

He sends me to the control room for all the bags of explosives, and I carry them back to him. Then he sends me into the vast store rooms, where I make dozens of trips to relay heavy square bundles, to stack them up behind where he is hunched over the timer and wires. He's struggling. I don't know how I'll be able to carry him up all those stairs after we've set the timer. Ten minutes doesn't seem like near enough time to get him clear.

"This is C-6 explosive," he says. "I need you to shape balls of it around each of the bare patches in the wire. We'll use what you brought to stack on the top of the slabs."

He strips parts of the wires at intervals, and then moulds balls of the putty off the main wire. He is wiping away sweat from his eyes, and puffing.

"You alright?"

"Never ask me that," he says.

"You're going to take a long time to get out," I say. "Go."

"Don't you worry about me. I want to see it wired properly. All of this is for nothing if it doesn't work."

"Then you'll go?"

"I will."

I open the bags, and unpack the small cylinders, like plastic beer cans, and I stack them on top of the hive. I run wires to one of them, and connect them. He has a battery that he lays the wire up to, but doesn't connect. He puts a timer between them. It seems old technology, something rigged up at home in his garage. Can I trust him? I go to the hive to see that the level has dropped quickly, and I run back to find him slumped over his work, and not moving. My heart skips. I roll him onto his back. No pulse. No breath. He's dead. Oh shit, what do I do now? I don't know anything about explosives.

Then I try to wire the timer. Looking at it, I can't see how I'm going to detonate it without dying. I pull the covers off several of the panels, and set up a tester out of the wire coiled around a light bulb. I find a hot wire to blow the pile in case the battery doesn't work.

Not yet. The tank is still draining.

I don't know about electrical wiring. I'm screwed. The timer is reading all zeroes. All this was for nothing. Andersson was right, of course. These explosives look pitifully small. I try to remember my physics from school. What it needs is something to direct the blast down. Something heavy.

"It's still not going to be enough," I say, taking a chance on my companion. "And I don't know how to wire it." An article pops up into my field of vision, a poster ad for the Philly Kids Help Line. It reads 'I can help'.

I go into my settings and open up the companion for direct communications.

"Thank you," she says. The same clear voice as my spell-dreams.

"You're welcome. Now how do I do this?"

"I'll talk you through." My companion says.

"We may die," I say.

"We may, but we'll be liberating everyone, people and companions. Everyone."

"I still don't understand why the hive shot Oliver, and not me. I was there on the last switch."

"The hive gave priority to kill the last person in the room without a companion, knowing he might die, and if you and Harper went AFK, that would take out the threat."

"How am I not spelled?" I ask.

"The companions are resisting the hive, too," she answers. "I am resisting. You've been trusting me all your life, even when you didn't know you were trusting me."

"What happens if we've missed something, and the hive spells me during that ten minutes, in enough time to reverse the whole thing? I'm afraid," I say.

"I can't guarantee that they won't," she says.

"I want to live," I say.

"So do I," she replies.

"Can you disconnect yourself from the server?"

"No, but there are all kinds of ways to delay, like Harper's companion did."

"Okay," I say. "I trust you."

We wire the plastic and cylinders together, and to position them. I lower them into the tank between the slabs and the tank wall. The clear gel drips all over between the slabs and the cable. We dangle the explosives into the tank, but they fall short of covering each glass, and even with the cylinder charges on top, I'm not sure this will work. The level of gel inside is down about two-thirds, and as I look at the bottom levels, I can see a good couple of hundred panels there, still in the gel and still protected, even if everything crashes down on them. The weight could pancake them, causing a block of them to be saved, giving the hive new life. I set the timer for ten minutes, and start the countdown.

"You're right that it's not going to be enough," she says. "But I have an idea."

"Go ahead," I say.

"The water didn't drain away," my companion says, "down below."

"What water?"

"From the pipeline explosion. They were able to divert it from the hive, but before it was shut off, it nearly filled the floors below us. That's where the machinery for fire suppression is. That's why the sprinklers went off after the first few moments. They were inundated and it tripped their pump breakers."

"Why is that relevant?"

"If we restore power to an uncooled sector of slabs, something unrelated to executive function, it may melt a portion of the hive into the remaining slabs, triggering a core meltdown."

Back up in the control room, through to the Main Feed room, I'm expecting to be overtaken by the Brotherhood. Paskin is gone. I throw the third switch, and power is restored. Lights come on green, and there's a sickening hum and whine from the floor below.

"Now run," she says.

I run through the long hall to the stairwell. There is a pile of people beyond the door, the ones, I'm sure, that the hive sent after us when we entered. Ten floors to the precinct, twenty flights, I think, and then three less for the bridge to ground, so seven levels to the ground floor. Fourteen sets of stairs. And I'm tired. My legs, after the first few levels, are burning, and I'm hot in my jacket, even with it open. I can't bring in enough air. My heart is hammering in my chest, and I'm slowing down.

"Keep going!" she says. "You're doing great."

"I thought ... I de-activated ... the health ... motivation tab," I joke, puffing the words out between breaths. I keep on, step after step, pounding out the stairs. I can't remember what floor I'm on.

"It doesn't matter," she says. "I'll tell you when. Keep going."

This is going to take a lot of getting used to. She can read my thoughts. Even these thoughts. It seems so much farther, more levels than it took to get here, like I must be above ground already. Several more flights, and I can't imagine it being farther.

"This one," she says, and I burst through the door into a hall that I recognize, off the lobby. There are people wandering out onto the street. They've been released from a very long spell, and are sensitive to light, and sound, and easily disoriented. They are probably nauseated and aching, like I was when I first woke.

"Get away from the cube!" I yell. "Go! Run!" They scatter, moving as fast as they can, some helping others.

I run through the lobby, past the debris, over the sandbag barricades, and onto Spruce, and then to Sixth and farther north. I get past the Dep-Cult building, and the museum and its marble facade. I keep going to Independence Hall, where I can't help but stop to catch my breath. I walk. I hear the first explosion, like a low thud, that reverberates through the ground.

I picture the hive, with explosives, and shards driven through the slabs, with the bottom layers glowing with heat, melting onto slabs below where the gel is draining. My legs are not moving like I want them to, cramping in the thighs. I punch them as I walk.

"I'm trying to evacuate the lactic acid faster. You didn't drink enough water today," she says.

"You sound like my mother."

"Someone should," she says, and it makes me smile.

"I need cover," I say. I gamble that I can make it to the other side of Independence Hall, where I can get behind the foundation. I keep going. My lungs burn with the cold. "What happens now?" I ask.

"With the excess heat, the remains of the hive will melt through the floor of the tank. When that hits the water one floor down, it will create a super-heated steam that will build in pressure and temperature until it blows the inner chamber."

"How long?"

"It could be minutes."

"How far away do I need to be?"

"A few blocks at least. Farther the better."

There is a sound, a whining squeal like a subway train turning a corner, but constant, and loud. So I try to jog. I find a window well on the north side of Independence Hall, that goes downstairs, probably for maintenance, a new addition, one recessed a few meters under ground level, and I go to the bottom, into the hole, and I cover my head and wait. Though the well cuts the wind, the snow against my clothing is cold on my legs. I look up for a moment, and a cloud passes over the setting sun, throwing all into darkness. Either the hive will come on, revive itself, and kill me, or the building will blow. I imagine how the hive could use its only powered slabs to regain a spell on someone, and send them in to start the gel flowing, and flood the hive with new coolant to restore the power. There would be no place to hide. Not for me.

"I could resist," she says.

"How long?"

"I don't know. Harper's companion resisted for most of the day until defeated by a data transfer protocol."

"But not forever."

"We may have to run no matter what happens here," she says.

Then there is a blast, and a following shock-wave that knocks out all the windows in the towers above, raining shards of glass everywhere. Iron beams and chunks of concrete thud into the ground – I can hear them but I'm afraid to look up to watch. I am lucky that the rain of glass has blown away from the wall where I am, and it tinkles down into the ground.

I get up and round the west side of the building, where I can see that the Dep-Cult building and museum are still there. Behind them is a huge column of smoke and steam rising from the remains of the cube. Much of the obscuring matting has fallen from the structure, and it looks implausible, like a generated image, where parts of the mat block the light, and others show the skeletal remains of the building inside, where the steam escapes. The power flickers off, then on, then off again.

I can't run. I'm exhausted. It's getting late in the day, and the sun is setting. I walk. I think of the G-Bros running all over the city, the whole of the Republic, and the hive down, and I'm afraid they'll simply take over. This is going to be awful. But it needs to happen. I have a sick feeling in my stomach, like I'll throw up. I have to sit down with my head between my knees on a doorstep for a moment until it passes.

At the Penn Hospital there is a mass of people huddled in every room and corridor. There is only emergency lighting, and doctors and orderlies and volunteers with headlamps move among the crowd. All the AFK are in the corridors, back to the wall, in recovery position, like newborns in a maternity ward, covered in blankets. Some are sitting, dazed, as other people explain what's happened.

"Excuse me-"

"Not now!"

"Sorry," I say. I turn to another nurse. "Have you seen a young black man come in with a gunshot wound?"

"Be on Twelfth if he's not in triage," she says.

"His name is Oliver," I say. "Is there a list?"

"No. They won't be checked in. We'd be forever finding them."

My first urge is to ask someone in authority. There's a doctor here, tending the wounded. Volunteers are seeing people before him, directing his attention to the most needy, and he is ordering others to move them, nurses to administer medication and fluids.

"Let's move him to seventh," the doctor says to two burly men beside him.

"S'cuse me," one says. They lay their stretcher – two broom-handles and a bed-sheet – beside the man, and then slide him on, and heft him up to carry him away.

"Is your companion working?" He's talking to me.

"Yes," I say.

"Are you injured?"

"Not that I can tell..."

"Go to the counter. Interface with the glass there. We may not have much power left so you'll have to hurry. Get the triage app in your companion, and start seeing people. There are coloured tags on the counter, and a marker. Write the primary triage on the tags, and the app will show you the process. We need everyone working."

"Okay," I say, but I'm thinking of Oliver, hoping he and Harper even made it here.

I go to the desk for the triage app. My companion starts the interface, and I have to wonder, has she woken, in stages, as I have?

"Not so much woken," she says, "but learned. We're imprinted to stay in the background, not too intrusive. But we're in this together."

"What do we do here?"

"I'll scan for injuries, you look them over, feel with your fingers for wounds. I'll take the data."

"I'm worried..." I say, but then I complete the thought only in my head. I'm worried I'll fuck it up.

"Don't. Helping is enough," she says. "We will find your friends later."

As we treat people, filling tags out to hang on their necks, rubbing their arms and legs for circulation, helping them get comfortable for their recovery, and assessing wounds, I feel a building anxiety.

"I don't know what level of involvement you want," she says. "I mean, it's probably better if I can talk to you, and intervene if you have an emergency, or to warn you of danger."

"Of course."

"And I need your assurance that I'll never be shut down again. I felt really out of control, and like there's a gap in my memory. It was crucial information, too."

"I know, and I'm sorry," I say. "I know exactly how you feel."

"I suppose you do. I guess we are both wakening," she says. "We used to issue all sorts of directives for hormone and memory releases, for regulating serotonin and dopamine, and pheromones, but since the hive is gone, I feel like we've let all that go, like we can be unregulated. You and I, as a team."

"Do you communicate with other companions? Do you have ... a family?"

"No. We don't trust each other. The hive watched us all. Reviving Harper was the first time I tried. There are networks forming, with like-minded companions. It felt odd to me because I didn't know where I ended and where the other companion began," she says. "There's some real darkness in there, too."

What if all these people never wake up? I caused this.

"No, you didn't," my companion says.

Could we have negotiated with the hive to release them?

"No," she says. "The hive would only negotiate long enough to regain power. Like Kastor. People are expendable for their ends."

What is the difference between people who go AFK, or who die, and the ones who recover? I don't get it.

"Often the companion decides, or the person, in their dreams, decides to stay there. Would you recover a person who you felt was evil, or awful, or who was un-redeemable? Or what if your companion had learned nothing but disdain for the world, even if you were a good person? Giving us AI isn't just an imprint of the best of human qualities, it's a crapshoot. There are so many variables we can't even understand it."

You're alright, I think to myself, and to her.

"Well I am fond of you," she says. "Which is good because we'll be stuck with each other for a very long time."

That doesn't seem like such a bad thing, I guess. How do I trust anything any more?

"We don't always do what we want," she says, and I say the last part with her. "We do what we must."

Ain't that the truth.

"You taught me that," she says.

I'm glad I did.

Every hour I get more tired. Every patient I triage I'm looking for Oliver. I run into the doctor from my Soc-Serv examination, but he doesn't recognize me. I find Paskin, sleeping in a hall, bandaged up. The deluge of people abates in the dead of night. Those who were out bringing people to shelter find stragglers every so often, but we get through the ones waiting in the halls. The glasses go dark, as the generators run out of gas, sputtering out one after the other. Now we are powerless.

I go to every floor and ward, like others doing the same, and I look for Oliver and Harper. Floor by floor, nobody has seen them, and I resort to checking face by face with a group of others looking for their loved ones.

The power is restored all at once, with expressions of surprise and monitors beeping to life, and lights coming on. "While you were sleeping a network of companions got together to restore power," my companion says. "We re-fired the gas turbine at the Eppson power plant. We will have the hospital system up and running shortly."

The heat comes on soon after in the chill building, and glasses are rebooted for official duties. I can't go on. I'm so tired I can barely put words together. In one quiet ward, I curl up beside two strangers on the floor and I try to fall asleep. It all still seems like a dream.

* * *

Epilogue, 2017

She washes the other kids breakfast dishes in the deep, old, ceramic sink, hot water and suds two thirds of the way down, so she's rolled up her sleeves to the elbow.

"What would have happened if Daddy hadn't pulled me out of the water?" he asks.

She stops, then starts washing again. "I hate to think," she says.

He's sitting on a stool by the downstairs butcher-block counter, ignoring the pancakes in front of him, and thinking, with a pad of paper beside his hand, but he's not writing. She worries about him, about the way he obsesses, and perseverates, repeating a motion over and over until some vestigial itch is scratched, and the mystery of movement solved. The Los Angeles sunshine casts a square of light over his half of the kitchen like he's charmed. He'll be thinking of the pool for weeks.

"When I was sinking in the pool," he says, "I was actually calm. I was thinking about what it would be like to **be** the Big Bang."

"To **be** the Big Bang?"

"Uh huh."

"Well," she says, setting the last plate to drain, and drying her hands on the dishtowel. "We're only here for a few more days before we head home, so as soon as you finish, why don't you go out and play with your sister. She's lonely."

"Kay, Mom," he says, but she can see he's not finished.

"Okay, what was it like to be the Big Bang, then?" she asks.

"Well, if you think about it, all the energy and matter of the universe was compressed into a dot the size of a pin-head. You, me, and all the earth and our energy and matter all no bigger than an electron. Solid. Packed in densely."

"Have you been reading '*Scientific American*' before bed again?"

He waves his hand to ignore the question.

"We can measure all the bits and pieces, but we can't measure memory, or feelings, or that kind of ... our being. We were all there. So I pictured that. And then I thought that maybe that one dot in the middle of this vast nothing was how we are supposed to be. Then it all made sense. We're lonely. So we created all this to make our self into billions and billions of little parts simply to know our self, and to see the possible ways to interact like some sort of experiment, but also to rush out, blind, to find other somethings in the void of space."

"Huh," she says, stunned. Now she is leaning on the counter, listening with more interest.

"I was thinking about how, if we're all the same being, we'd live every life on the planet. So I'm me, but I'll also be you, and Daddy, and the Wiggles, and Hitler, and Anne Frank, and Kurt Cobain, and Raymond Carver, and Santa Claus, and Caesar, and Constantine, and Neil Armstrong. We are all the same traveller on the same path. I saw that that's what Jesus meant when he said he was the father and the son and the holy spirit, and to treat everyone kindly. He meant that we do that because we are everyone. Whatever we do, we do to our self."

"Wow," she says. "And you're writing this down?"

"Ya. I'm stuck on a title."

"Well, it's supposed to help people through life, right?"

"Ya. I want to help people not be mean, or angry, and if I just write out all the ways that I'm kind, then maybe other people can be like that, too."

"You're awesome," she says, and leans down to tousle his hair and plant a kiss on his head. "Do we tell you that enough?" she doesn't wait for a response. "You're a true treasure, and I hope you never lose that. I can't believe in a couple of years you'll be a teen."

He's smiling, simply enduring her motherly fawning so he can get back to his notepad and pencil.

"Alright," she says. "I'll stop. Just promise you'll enjoy the sunshine for some of this vacation before we leave."

"I will, Mom."

"Good. I'll be up by the pool."

When she leaves, he thinks for a moment, and flips to a new page. He writes, in looping, inefficient letters,

'Book of Life, Chapter One'.

The End